I0761069

Sheer

Also by Vanessa Lawrence

Ellipses

Sheer

A NOVEL

VANESSA LAWRENCE

DUTTON

DUTTON
An imprint of Penguin Random House LLC
1745 Broadway, New York, NY 10019
penguinrandomhouse.com

Book design by Laura K. Corless

LIBRARY OF CONGRESS CATALOGING-IN-PUBLICATION DATA
has been applied for.

ISBN 9780593854860 (hardcover)
ISBN 9780593854877 (ebook)

Printed in the United States of America
1st Printing

For Dana, who makes everything better

Sheer

PROLOGUE

At rush hour on a Wednesday, in the stifling purgatory between summer and fall, I do something completely crazy: I leave the office early. I've had a professional victory. Elizabeth, my brilliant publicist, has resolved a nagging issue at work and I can think of no better way to celebrate than vacating the premises.

My Uber carries me from the SoHo headquarters of my beauty company, Reveal, to my apartment building on Central Park West. Things that would normally irk me—the artificial cherry scent from the air freshener tree; the driver's choice of heavy metal, at an ear-splitting decibel level—glide over me, smoothly, like face oil. My body is airy, borderline levitative. I am not one of those New Age spiritualists, but I will venture to say the lightness in my bones is as much existential as it is corporeal. Something has shifted. After years of diminishment at the hands of so many men, of doubts from the Board and the public, I have returned to my signature pinnacle of achievement. Maxine Thomas the beauty visionary is back.

When the Uber drops me off at my building's awning, I pause before the doorman. I am not ready to settle on a sofa, glass of ice-cold vodka in hand. I don't want the day to end.

"I'm going for a walk," I tell my doorman. "A sunset walk," I add, as though that clarifies matters. "When do I ever get to do that?"

"Very good, Ms. Thomas," he says, closing the door. He smooths the placket of his black uniform. "Enjoy your walk."

The entrance to the park is across the avenue. A winding path beckons me toward the park's main drive and beyond that, to the reservoir with its sweeping view of the surrounding skyline and greenery. Every morning I rise at dawn to pound mile after mile into various dirt and asphalt trails; a leisurely end-of-day meander, though, with no purpose beyond visceral pleasure? That is the stuff of fairy tales.

Unfortunately, the dusty path circling the reservoir, no longer the keeper of the city's official drinking water, is crowded with pedestrians. There are the obvious tourists, with their long-lens digital cameras strung around their necks. The Upper East Side denizens in their clingy black yoga togs and quilted down vests, despite the balmy September breeze. The Upper West Side habitués in their slouchy track pants, unironic waist packs, and orthopedic footwear. A few extra-fit and misguided twenty-somethings have chosen the narrow trail as their running path. Shouts of "On your left!" and "Watch it!" puncture the urban idyll. Normally, the confluence of oblivious out-of-towners and ill-advised athletes would undo me. Not on this evening.

The sun is blood orange. Streaks of magenta and violet and coral zip across the sky. The pool of the reservoir is euphoric with color. I could dream up decades and decades of Reveal product shades from this beauty, though I prefer a more intimate source for my makeup inspiration: women. I am on the eastern portion of the reservoir path, parallel with the white curves of the Guggenheim Museum, when my phone vibrates.

The screen shows Elizabeth's name, so I accept the call.

"Elizabeth," I say. "You'll never believe it. I'm strolling around the reservoir at sunset, like some rich housewife with nothing better to do. It's fabulous. You should try it one day."

Elizabeth says nothing. I hear the tinkle of ice against glass. It doesn't seem like she is at the office.

"Elizabeth?" I ask. "Are you there?" I pause my walk and step to the side of the path.

"Max," says Elizabeth. She is the steadiest person I know and yet her voice shakes my phone. "We need to talk."

"So talk," I say. The sunset is peaking. The colors are so fiery I think my heart will burst.

Elizabeth talks. Suddenly, it isn't the sky but my world that is engulfed by flames.

DAY ONE

Morning

Bliss isn't a first-class ticket to Bora Bora. It isn't a prime-time table at the hottest restaurant in town. It isn't a lightning-fast metabolism that allows a young woman to eat like an Olympic swimmer and still fit into her size twenty-five jeans. Grade-A Mongolian cashmere, custom-tailored shirts, jars of face cream boasting ingredients the FDA will never approve: Bliss is none of those things. It's the amnesia that coats your vision like Vaseline when you first open your eyes to the morning light before you remember the nightmare your life has become. Before you feel the weight of the world's disdain.

I wake at 5 a.m. like it is any other day. The bedroom is dark and cool. The sheets are silky against my skin. Habit propels me out of bed and into the bathroom to begin my morning toilette. It isn't until I am standing in the middle of that white marble room, one leg partially covered in the black spandex of my running leggings, that I realize I have nowhere to go. There are no meetings to attend, no company to oversee, and therefore no need to run before dawn breaks through the darkness outside. I have no reason to be.

Down go the leggings. On go my pajamas. Back to bed I trudge.

After years of 5 a.m. starts, my body refuses to rest. It is off to the kitchen, then, to brew some coffee. I sit with a searing mug, dark as a void, at my dining room table, soft light glinting off its polished surface, a blank document on my laptop screen. I am ready to type away. Stab away is more like it.

Before I disabled the search engine alert for my name, my phone hammered notifications at me like a firing squad. It is so interesting that *The New York Times* has no problem printing the word *bitch* but draws the line at *fuck*. That fifth letter makes all the difference.

This is the kind of thing that gets my blood burning. It's good no one's around because I'd scald them with my touch. Everyone on the internet thinks they know what happened. So does the Board. Only I know the truth. The Bible tells us that the truth shall set us free. If the Bible were written today that line would require serious revision.

I need to write my story, the one the Board will never hear and that the public will never know. Even my lawyer, Sandrine, will never grasp the full extent of it. Sandrine is my defense attorney, which suggests that I require defending. I guess I do in the most literal sense. But defensiveness implies wrongdoing and I am here because of someone else's wrongdoing. Two someone elses, in fact.

Ellen and Amanda. Two women who fucked me over. Thanks to them, I am hunkered down in my apartment, seething until the Board decides whether they will sever me from my beloved Reveal, the company I built from scratch.

Obviously, I can't say this to the Board. It would sound too angry, too aggressive. People like their women leaders unemotional. I can compartmentalize as well as any man, though when I do, I'm accused of being an ice queen or a power-hungry witch. No matter what, I am an outsider. My whole life, all forty years of it, has been one long battle to manifest my intrinsic worth in a world that has told me that I have none.

I have never considered my existence in its totality. Autobiographical exercises have always struck me as deeply self-indulgent. In this moment, I recognize that they don't stem from ego; they grow from necessity. Other people have painted me as a monster. I need to show who I really am. As always, transparency will be my savior.

I cannot scream my story from the rooftops—no one can stop me from writing it down.

Origins

It all started when I was six years old. That may sound young, but I was always precocious. My mother was out grocery shopping and didn't want to bring me, so she left me home alone in our white clapboard house. I understand this is something mothers are no longer permitted to do, that today they would be reprimanded and even arrested for such a misdeed; in 1980, this was a very common occurrence. My mother didn't have regular childcare. While my parents would splurge on a babysitter for the occasional date night at a restaurant or movie theater, there was no budget for a day-to-day nanny.

My mother wasn't negligent. She informed our next-door neighbor that she would be gone for forty minutes. Left to my own devices, I grew bored of the television set and wandered out of the living room, up the stairs, down the second-floor hallway. Nubby gray carpeting covered the warped floorboards. Into my parents' bedroom I went.

This room was usually off limits to me, explicitly so. My parents were adamant about their need for privacy. I was ordered never to enter their room without a preliminary knock, regardless of whether the door was closed or ajar. Even once they called, "Come in" or waved me forward, I never ventured farther into the room than a few steps beyond the doorway.

The spiritual dead bolt on my parents' bedroom only made it more appealing. My mother's absence was an opportunity of which I took full advantage. The oatmeal wall-to-wall carpeting in their room was more luxurious than the floor coverings in the rest of the house. I waded across it slowly; my feet sank into its plush pile. The floral sheets on the bed clung to the mattress like a second skin. Unlike in my room there was an en suite bathroom.

I tiptoed across the bathroom's cold blue tiles, as though my caution would negate any wrongdoing. In the corner, by a window that overlooked our small, well-maintained backyard, was a tufted stool on casters that fit tidily beneath the counter. When I knelt on the stool, I was barely high enough to see myself in the mirror. My downy, white-yellow head was nearly the same shade as my porcelain skin. Everything popped against that canvas, especially my molten-brown eyes, which complicated my angelic portrait with a flash of darkness.

There was a clear plastic bin on the counter, sectioned off like a cafeteria lunch tray. One of the compartments held a few short, wood-handled brushes. Another had a stack of closed metallic compacts. I tried to open the top one, but my recently clipped nails couldn't manage it. There was a collection of colored liquids, various pinks, reds, and oranges, in glass bottles. I had watched my mother apply these liquids to her toenails with the brushes built into the bottles' caps. She would choose a different one for each week of the month and then repeat the rotation.

A corner of the tray held six or seven shiny metal tubes that I had seen my mother use to color her lips. I reached for the nearest tube and after some fiddling managed to twist its cap off. Inside, there was a stub of hot pink that came to a rounded point. I didn't know how to push the hot-pink wax out of the tube, so I stuck my right index finger inside and rubbed it against the sloped top of the stub.

The substance was soft and slippery. It reminded me of fudge. I ran my right index finger across the underside of my left wrist, leaving a hot-pink streak in its wake.

I peered over my shoulder, out the bathroom doorway, across the expanse of my parents' bedroom. Then I went for it. I stuck my finger back inside the tube and mushed my finger against my lips. In the mirror, I considered my handiwork.

I had colored outside my natural lip lines. The messy slash of bubble gum made me look like I had taken a slug from a bottle of Pepto-Bismol. Why did grown women do this to themselves, I wondered, as I frowned at my reflection. My lips seemed alien, like they were no longer part of my face. They didn't look pretty or fun. They looked wrong.

Downstairs, the front door slammed. My parents' room was at the back of the house, so I hadn't heard my mother's car pull up the driveway. I quickly replaced the tube's cap and put the tube back in the bin. With a tissue from a box on the counter I wiped at my pink lips. It made the situation worse. I splashed water on my lips and rubbed them with my fingers. My mouth was still a furious pink. Then I had my first of many brilliant ideas.

I dashed for the stairs and tiptoed down. By some miracle, my mother had yet to call out my name or come looking for me. The front door was ajar and there were a few brown paper bags of groceries in the foyer. My mother was still emptying our car's trunk.

Her next destination was going to be our kitchen. That was where I was headed, too. I ran directly to the fridge and scanned the contents; nothing helpful presented itself. I opened the freezer door. Bingo.

The front door slammed again. I reached for a cherry Popsicle, ripped it out of its plastic sheath, stuck it in my mouth, and sucked on it. Hard.

"Maxine!" my mother exclaimed as she walked in on me, her arms full of brown paper bags. She set the bags on top of the kitchen table. "You know you're not allowed to have Popsicles without asking."

She snatched the frozen treat out of my hand and threw it in the garbage.

"Sorry, Mommy," I said, shrugging my shoulders and staring at the floor in what I hoped seemed like remorse.

"What were you thinking," my mother admonished, as she examined my face. "You're a mess. Go upstairs to your bathroom and wait for me. I'm going to scrub your face after I put these groceries away."

I hung my head and walked slowly out of the kitchen and up the stairs. A plastic footstool helped me see above the sink. I looked at myself in the medicine cabinet mirror and grinned at my cleverness. My mother hadn't spied any pinkness on my lips thanks to the Popsicle's red syrup. As I stared more closely, I noticed that my mouth had a ruby flush, different from when it was spackled in bubblegum beeswax. The cherry juice was completely sheer; it let my lips peek through. Why didn't women wear something that looked more like this, I wondered.

Well over a decade later, when I created Flush, a lip and cheek tint that was my first product for Reveal and that remains our bestseller to this day, it was in no small part because of this formative moment. At six years old, I had already uncorked the secret to professional success: never settle for anything that makes you feel like a stranger to yourself.

I'm sure this sounds hyperbolic as a founder's origin story. What kind of an egomaniac believes that she had already cracked the code to innovation while in kindergarten? At six years old, I couldn't foretell the vector of this discovery; now at forty, I know this was the beginning of my narrative.

In the suburbs of New Jersey during the mid-1970s and early '80s, the prevailing mind-set around female appearances was not one of self-acceptance. People today think the '70s were a hippie-dippie wonderland of natural beauty—the opposite was true. One of the most popular hairdos was an exuberantly feathered and fluffy concoction that required a blow-dryer, a curling iron, a round brush, and many cans of hairspray. On the other end of the trend spectrum was a straight, sleek, bottom-grazing style that was equally laborious to grow not to mention maintain. A major model of the era had a gap-toothed visage that suggested the appeal of imperfection. The reality is that she was a stunning woman who flashed the world an enormous middle finger, as if to say *I'm so beautiful, I can have a space between my teeth and still look better than you.* Hardly a rallying cry for the average woman.

No, the '70s were a lot of work for women if they hoped to fit in. As a kid, I believed that my mother's devotion to makeup and fashion was intrinsic to female existence, that it was normal to invest vast quantities of time into one's appearance. Not once in my childhood did I see my mother with a bare face. She had two looks. The first, for daytime, was lips- and cheeks-focused, a medley of peaches and salmons and creamy opaque textures. She loved a healthy swipe of pinkish-orange bronzer across and beneath her prominent cheekbones.

The second approach came out at night. I always knew when my mother had evening plans. Around 4:45 p.m., she would head upstairs to her bedroom. An hour later, she would reemerge in a new outfit. Her hazel eyes would be circled in dense turquoise or winged with black strokes or accessorized with an extra-long, double-thick tassel of lashes. I wondered how she could see through all that makeup.

My mother was blond in the way that I am currently blond, with a lot of help from Chemistry class. Every six weeks or so, she would touch up her roots with packages of hair dye from our local drugstore that she mixed in a Tupperware container. Her hair was naturally wavy, so she blew it into obedience and teased it with a fine-toothed comb to achieve the full, bouncy volume of a cosmetics campaign model.

The Lucite coffee table in our living room held a perennial stack of *Vogue* and *Harper's Bazaar* issues that my mother would riffle through. She would fold down the corners of pages and sometimes rip them out in her search for a look that would be noticeably attractive while also allowing her to blend in. She loved knee-length smock dresses over tailored blouses and mid-calf shirtdresses belted at the waist. Rarely did I see her in a pair of pants and certainly nothing close to bell-bottoms.

At night, my mother read to me before I went to bed. Her preferred literary material was fashion magazines. She found children's books to be overly juvenile, a view I never contested as very much the point of their existence. She would fetch an issue from the living room coffee table and then join me beneath my bed's quilt. I can still feel her smooth, freshly shaved legs against my bare feet as she prepared me for sleepy time with actress profiles and makeup tutorials.

"'If you scored a thirty-five or higher, you're a winter,'" she would intone, reading from a quiz about personal color palettes.

"'Vaseline is the most effective and economic eye cream.'"

"'Plaid skirts are in for fall, particularly midnight-blue patterns from Scotland.'"

"'Men like pink lipstick better than red lipstick because they find it less intimidating.'"

This was my version of a bedtime story. Recitations complete, my mother would kiss me in the center of my forehead. After she was gone, the musk and jasmine and vanilla from her perfume would linger on my sheets, a second quilt of comfort.

One afternoon my mother deviated from her tried-and-true understated ensembles. She emerged from her bedroom wearing a top and matching maxi skirt, in a multicolored geometric print. She looked like she had been attacked by a classroom of kindergartners brandishing crayons.

"Your clothes are so pretty," I told her.

"Thank you, Maxine," my mother replied. She barely smiled when she said this. But I noticed an extra bounce in her step as she moved around the house. Then my father returned home in his rumpled tan suit. He walked into the living room and saw my mother standing there in her psychedelic outfit. Her face was radiant with pride.

"What in god's name are you wearing?" he asked as he took off his jacket and loosened his navy tie.

The glow of happiness drained from my mother's eyes.

"You look ridiculous," he told her. "Go upstairs and change. I won't leave the house with you looking like that."

My mother didn't protest. Her proud posture shrank and something inside me shriveled with it. This, I thought, is what it means to be a wife. You wear what your husband tells you to even if it mutes your joy. My mother left the living room. Upstairs, she changed into one of her solid-colored ensembles. I never saw her wear an exuberant print again.

Our house was in Paramus, known for Garden State Plaza, that gleaming mecca of American consumerism. My parents moved to Paramus in the late 1960s, before I was born, as part of the great development boom there. They were non-natives, so neither of them had a Northern New Jersey accent and I proved genetically allergic to developing one. My dad worked in the accounting department for R.H. Macy & Co., which was later acquired by Federated Department Stores, and the company owned Garden State Plaza until the mid-'80s. My childhood was funded by and predicated on the American pastime of shopping.

I spent many afternoons at the mall with my mother, wandering through the clothing aisles at Bamberger's department store, now Macy's, and the shoe department at Gimbel's. You could peruse these department stores for hours, running your hands through the knit polo shirts and sniffing baby powder–scented fragrances and maybe a spicy oriental perfume, as it was called back then, if you were feeling fancy. In those childhood days, the mall seemed like a religious institution. The rows and rows of cars in the parking lot spoke to its bounty of congregants. Garden State Plaza, GSP as we referred to it affectionately, was a mall designed to excite people to spend their hard-earned cash.

One December day, my mother picked me up from kindergarten and drove us straight to GSP. She had some holiday shopping to complete. I was her helpful little elf. We parked in the expansive lot, less cluttered with cars on a weekday afternoon.

I was ravenous for a snack. My six-year-old stomach growled, and my mother frowned at me.

"Hungry?" she asked.

"Yes," I said.

"I guess we can get something to eat," she said. "Quickly, we have errands to run."

My mother clasped my small hand in her silky adult one and led us in the direction of Friendly's. At a table there, I munched on a grilled cheese sandwich and fries, while across from me, my mother nibbled on a fruit plate and sipped her black coffee. Buttery crumbs from the grilled cheese clung to my tongue. The coarse salt from the fries lingered on my lips.

My mother stared at the fries on my plate. I had never seen her eat one before. Her diet was composed of vegetables, meat, and fish. When I was a toddler, she occasionally snagged a forkful of macaroni and cheese from my kid-sized bowl.

"Take one, Mommy," I urged her, pushing the plate in her direction.

"I shouldn't," my mother said.

"Why not?"

"Hunger isn't ladylike. I have to fit into my clothes and French fries will get in the way. You'll see when you get older."

I examined her dress with its tailored waist, then I looked down at the inch-long fries. "How could such a small French fry get in the way?" I asked.

My mother's face crinkled into a smile. "That's a good question. Okay, just one."

I handed her the longest, crispiest fry on the plate.

"It will be our little secret."

After my mother's lone French fry, she and I headed over to a garden store to scope out the Christmas tree offerings. We planned to return with my father to finalize our choice.

"I wish I could get that one," my mother informed the man in the overalls and plaid shirt who oversaw the Christmas tree selection. She pointed at a tall, full-bodied specimen. "But my husband will get angry. It's too expensive."

"I'm sure you can convince him it's not," the man said.

"You haven't met my husband," my mother replied. "He runs a tight ship."

In the earlier years of my childhood, GSP was still an open-air center, as opposed to what we now think of as a mall. Shopping was both an expression of leisure and an act of endurance. Things were on the chillier side that December day. Every change in degree and shift in the wind reverberated through the exposed mallgoers. I began to shiver and my mother draped a wool-clad arm around me, hugging me close.

"You're okay," she murmured.

Our walk back to the parking lot was a fantasia of clanging bells and twinkling lights. The air smelled of sap and crystallized salt. It started to snow. White flakes drifted slowly from the sky, leaving wet patches on my peacoat and my eyelashes shiny with their residual dew. My mother smiled at me so brightly, I thought I might explode from joy. I would have done anything to trap myself there, in that snow globe of happiness.

On the way home, we drove past an abstract mural on the facade of the Alexander's department store. Overlapping shapes of blue, red, yellow, aqua, and forest green danced across the wall. It was painted by a Polish artist who was a pilot during World War II and drew on this bird's-eye perspective in the composition. His creation acted as a Rorschach test for anyone who encountered it. Many people saw his intended vision of countries in those colored sections. Others spied the remains of a messy meal, a hot dog with ketchup and mustard and a side of blueberry pie, say, mauled across a clean, white napkin like the evidence of a crime scene.

My mother fell in with the latter crowd. She had zero tolerance for that mural. As we drove by it, she clucked her tongue and muttered, "Eyesore."

"What's an eyesore?" I asked.

"It's something that's so hideous it hurts your eyes."

I stared at the mural. It looked like the stripes of a rainbow, torn apart and scattered. "I don't hurt when I look at it," I said.

My reflection in the rearview mirror met my mother's hard stare.

"You're too young to see what a mess it is. Art is supposed to be beautiful."

From one angle, the mural's shapes reminded me of a church's stained-glass window. Those curved lines had a sense of motion, too, like you were on a swing ride at a carnival as the world around you dissolved into a spectacular blur. My mother wanted the mural to tell her what it was, clearly and explicitly. I wanted the mural to show me what it could be and in turn, what I could be, too.

If being like my mother meant I would lose these visions whenever I looked at this mural, then I no longer wished for that fate. Something broke inside me when I realized this, though I didn't process it until much later. There was a step-by-step plan laid out before me of how to become a woman like my mother, what clothes and makeup to wear, how to speak. But I didn't want a husband to control my wardrobe or the amount I spent on a Christmas tree. I didn't want to be a person incapable of finding beauty in the unconventional. There was no guidance beyond that path.

Not long after that Christmas shopping trip, R.H. Macy carried through on their plans to enclose GSP, endowing it with terra-cotta flooring, cavernous ceilings, skylights, and fountains. GSP was never quite the same after that. In its open-air iteration you could literally feel the wind on your skin as you strolled from shop to shop. It made your experience seem like it was part of a larger world.

Once GSP was enclosed, the act of shopping lost its earthy grit. A day at the mall became a clinical affair, full of recycled, temperature-controlled air and weird food smells. We weren't participating in a human endeavor toward self-betterment; we were ants in a pretty little farm, scurrying about, thinking life had meaning when any aerial view would confirm that we were indistinguishable from everyone else.

DAY ONE

Evening

I press Command-S and close my laptop screen. Tonight's dinner comes from a local restaurant. I don't cook and I'd prefer not to leave my apartment just yet. Normally, my consumption veers to the obsessively healthy. I am in the business of beauty, after all. If I want women to believe that I can help them look their best, I need to embody that ideal myself. Obviously, I benefit from this stricture. I may have demoted myself, years ago, from a string bikini to a one-piece bathing suit, but my weight hasn't fluctuated by more than a pound and a half in two decades.

There have been casualties, sure. What is life if not denials of current urges in the name of longevity? I don't eat bread, pasta, non-sweet potatoes, white rice, dairy, processed foods, white sugar, chicken, red meat, or gluten. Alcohol is my one indulgence: red wine, whiskey, and vodka, though no mixed drinks of any kind, save for the occasional martini. I allow myself a glass or two of champagne—Krug or vintage Dom Pérignon only—for a celebratory occurrence and I nearly always regret it the following morning when the sugar-fueled hangover kicks in. I swallow a handful of supplements, including reishi, ginkgo biloba, omega-3, calcium, vitamin D, and zinc, but I'm not one of those wellness freaks who chugs wheatgrass-turmeric-adaptogen smoothies like they've hacked their way into the fountain of youth. And intermittent fasting? Please. Where I come from, we call that an eating disorder and I prefer it that way.

This evening, I don't select a sashimi platter from my favorite Japanese place, or the tofu-vegetable stir-fry, light on the oil, from that Thai spot. No, I order from a burger joint. I overheard some junior women at the office chatting about this place in the elevator bank a few weeks ago, how this was where they went to splurge, calorically. I glanced at their fat-free physiques and thought, Just you wait, ladies. You have no idea what's coming down the pipeline.

When I was their age, I believed I was invincible. It's been over a decade since I've eaten a burger. And yet, tonight, I am ravenous in a way that only red meat can satiate. I pick up my phone and open my delivery app and the next thing I know, I am clicking submit on a cheeseburger and a side of crinkle-cut fries.

My dinner arrives in a brown paper bag, stapled at the top, its sides splattered with grease, in the hands of a delivery guy wearing a bike helmet and a reflective vest. He hands me the bag with a curt nod, though I sense judgment behind his eyes. I unpack the bag's contents in my kitchen, filled with the smell of fried fat and melted cheese and toasted bread, a scent so delicious, it makes me want to bottle it as a perfume. I place the cheeseburger on a porcelain plate and shake the crinkle-cut fries into a matching bowl. There's an individual packet of mayonnaise in the bag and I grab that, too, because at this point, who am I kidding.

I carry the plate and the bowl to my dining room table. I'm not sure why I bothered with it. People who come to my apartment rarely stick around long enough for meals. I sit in my dining room chair, a mid-century design with a caned back, cheaper versions of which are everywhere now. Cloth napkin in my lap, I stare at the hunk of meat in its toasted bun, melted Gruyère cheese and aioli oozing out the sides.

I think about my firm-for-forty-years-old ass and my flat stomach and my triceps, which hold their own in a tank top. Years of sacrifices, physical and mental, have gone into maintaining this silhouette. I have worked even harder to create Reveal. Now my position there is under attack because I had the audacity to believe that if I played by the rules of the game, I would come out a winner. That Board meeting announcement is imminent, I can feel it in my teeth. My job, my credibility, my power: they are all on the chopping block. I cannot allow rage to consume me like it has all those failed women leaders. Control is my best weapon.

These thoughts spin and spin and spin in my head—they make me dizzy. I stare at the cheeseburger, my mouth wet with desire. I just can't do it.

I take my plate and bowl back to the kitchen. With a final longing glance, I step on the pedal of my garbage bin and dump the juicy cheeseburger and salt-crusted fries into a pile of trash. My mother would be proud.

Natural Instincts

Consumerism and art continued their dual hold on my childhood as I aged into middle school. In the classroom, I was drawn to collage. I would tear sheets of construction paper and glue them atop each other in overlapping sequences, juvenile attempts at color studies. With felt-tip markers and crayons, I'd scrawl across these compositions to create texture. The markers left a wet, flat finish. The crayons made everything look waxy and thick.

A purple marker I was using began to run dry one afternoon while I still had an entire patch of construction paper to color. There was a bottle of clear glue nearby that I had used for the collaging. A secret force drew me to it, and I squeezed some atop the purple marker scrawls and patted it across them with my fingers.

The glue was sticky and milky with a sharp, chemical smell. As I blended the glue into the marker scrawls, it picked up some of the purple, turning a beautiful lavender. Once dried, the glue imparted a semiglossy sheen to the construction paper beneath it.

"What are you doing, Maxine?" said my fifth-grade teacher, Mrs. Simon. "You've made a mess! You're too old to be playing with glue like that."

My sixth-grade English teacher, Ms. Adams, was more encouraging of my artistic efforts. She noticed me doodling in my notebook, creating abstract gradients with an array of highlighters and pencils. When she asked me to stay back from class one afternoon, I assumed she was going to chastise me for ignoring her lessons. Instead, she handed me a book on Impressionist artists she had signed out from the library on my behalf.

"I thought you might enjoy this, Maxine," she said as she watched me flip through the pages of dazzling paintings. "You have a clear love of art."

I paused on two works of water lilies. The gestural brushstrokes and gauzy colors sent pricks of energy up my spine. I was lightheaded in the face of such beauty. I could have stared at the paintings on those pages for days and never have tired of them.

Ms. Adams smiled at my reaction. "I see I was correct," she said. "The Impressionists were obsessed with capturing the effects of light. They often painted outdoors. Their approach was less formal than what came before them and because of that, many people criticized their paintings at first."

"How could anyone criticize these?" I asked.

"It seems impossible today. But that's what happens when you're ahead of your time," said Ms. Adams. "It takes the world years, decades even, to catch up to you."

"It sounds lonely," I said.

"It can be," said Ms. Adams. "It's not easy being different. What's most important is that you're always yourself. Never forget that, Maxine. Authenticity is key to artistic success."

I wonder if Ms. Adams saw something in me, with her teacherly perspicacity, that I had yet to glean. If she knew that I was not like the other girls in my desires. I wouldn't put it past her. Like the very best educators, Ms. Adams taught me more than the subject at hand.

She showed me that the pursuit of beauty was a worthwhile endeavor, one that could evoke emotion in a viewer. Ms. Adams may not have had women's faces in mind when she offered me that Impressionists tome and the many other art books she recommended after that. Still, she handed me a critical tool for refining my eye: interrogation of the status quo. I wish I could thank her for that gift. Though I don't know that she would be pleased with how her former student turned out.

During the day, I experimented with color and texture at school and inhaled the famous works in Ms. Adams's reading list. At home, I flipped through my mother's fashion magazines. She had ceased her bedtime recitations as soon as I grew old enough to read on my own, so I took charge of my fashion and beauty education. It was the mid-to-late 1980s and contouring, bold lips, and in-your-face eye shadow filled the pages of *Vogue*, *Cosmopolitan*, and *ELLE*. Gone was the playfulness of the '70s. The '80s woman was ambitious, ferocious. She wanted to knock you out with her war paint.

To my early-teen eyes, that war paint seemed like a disguise. Those slashes of mauve and plum on women's cheeks looked like bruises. I would stare at a photo of towering supermodels, their faces a swirl of clashing colors. I could appreciate an abstract scattering of paint in the Alexander's mural; on a woman's face, it was less appealing. I longed to see what lay beneath all those cosmetics. What did their skin look like without stripes of sculpting powder? What rosiness hid under the thick applications of lipstick? I knew these women were beautiful. No amount of makeup could obscure that biological fact. Why, I wondered, would someone who looked like that choose to bury their natural glow?

I watched my mother react to their photos, how she would exclaim over the dress that one model wore or the jacket on another and wish, out loud, that she could own the same thing. These women and the way they looked were connected to my mother's lust for fashion and to her understanding of beauty and how she might possess it herself. I didn't get what my mother saw. These images didn't inspire me to rush out and buy a new outfit for school. They made me want to wash these women's faces, lather the soap and rinse them clean, so I could admire them in a pure state.

My mother's love of shopping and her quest for sophistication took us to New York on many a weekend. Reluctantly, my father would drive us all into the city. It's true he worked for Macy's, but like many men of his generation, he had zero patience for the pastime of shopping. As an accountant, he saw retail as purely business, something that should fuel his paycheck, not empty his bank account. Besides that, he had a modest employee discount at GSP. When my mother shopped elsewhere, it was an affront to his frugality and to this corporate benefit. The higher New York sales tax also enraged him.

"Do you really need a new dress? What's wrong with the ones you already have?" my father would grumble at my mother, as she emerged from a changing room in a Midtown boutique wearing a navy number with bulky shoulder pads and rows of gold buttons.

I'd watch my mother's face deflate and then expand with anger. As time went on, her resentment of my father's control of her wardrobe—and her makeup and extracurriculars—solidified until it coated her skin like baby powder and perfumed the air around her.

"You work for a retailer. Are you really going to argue over the appeal of new clothes?"

Seated in a chair near the exterior of the dressing area reserved for the husbands, my father stiffened.

"I hope other women spend all their husbands' hard-earned money on clothing so the company continues to profit. Not you. Who do you think is going to pay for that dress? Go get a job and then you can have your dress."

I stood nearby, refolding some sweaters tossed on a table display. The sweaters were in piles by color whose order I rearranged to create an ombré effect. A saleswoman paused beside me and admired my efforts.

"That looks so much better," she said. "Would you like a job here?" She winked and left to help a customer.

"See?" my father said. "Even Maxine understands the importance of work." My father's tense face softened in my direction. "Someone in this family will be self-sufficient."

His praise ballooned in my chest, then my mother's sharp eyes pricked a hole in it. Silent and red, she stared at herself in the mirror, at the dress she would never own, at the life she would never have because my father was the only one with a paycheck.

These outings usually ended in a mild compromise. My father would agree to buy the cheapest item in my mother's handful of selections. Over the years, I observed my mother choose an increasingly expensive range of options, pushing my father toward pricier purchases. It was one of the few victories she achieved in her marriage. Those shopping excursions taught me very little about fashion. However, I did extract some critical data. I vowed never to let a man determine my fate.

Not all my childhood ventures into the city revolved around clothing. Sometimes, my parents took me for an early dinner at the Automat. There was an Automat at GSP, but that location had table service; New York still had Automats whose entire walls were covered in glass lockers filled with individual salads and sandwiches and even steaks.

On a trip to the Automat when I was in sixth or seventh grade, the three of us were seated at a table beside two women. I was mid-bite of my hamburger. My father had already finished his meal and glared impatiently at my mother, who picked at her salad. The two women at a nearby table wore stonewashed jeans and leather jackets. They had short, almost boyish hair. The older of the two was a bleached blonde with dark roots. Instead of sitting across from each other, they were seated side by side. The bleached-blond woman said something to the younger woman and they both laughed. Sweet dimples appeared in the younger woman's cheeks and she reached for her dining partner's hand next to her on the table and squeezed it. The women gazed into each other's eyes with what looked like deep affection.

An unfamiliar sensation started in my stomach and spread across my torso. It tingled, like my whole body had fallen asleep and was now coming alive. The women continued to clasp hands. I'd never held anyone's hand like that. When my mother gripped my hand, it imparted safety. Nothing about these two women touching seemed safe. It looked electric and I wanted to know how that felt.

My mother's face curled into disgust. The two women saw my mother's expression and their hands jolted apart, as though repelled by some reverse magnetic force. Fear darkened their faces. They hastily loaded their plates onto their trays. Their chairs made a scraping sound as they pushed them back.

"Good riddance," said my mother to the empty air.

My father remained silent.

"Filth like that shouldn't be allowed in here," my mother continued. "It shouldn't be allowed anywhere. I should have known that's what they were from their hair. Only women like that have short hair." My mother looked at me. "Don't you ever cut your hair that short, you hear me?"

I nodded, more out of shock than acquiescence. My mother turned back to her salad.

Hot shame replaced the unfamiliar sensation that had seized me when the women held hands. I didn't understand why. I wasn't the one who had held another woman's hand. I wasn't the filth my mother had sent packing. On a cellular level, though, I knew the way all of us know and have always known well before our brains are willing or able to articulate it, that deep down I was the same as those women. Their attraction to each other, obvious even to a middle schooler, didn't seem dirty to me. It looked natural. Natural like clear glue atop purple marker. Natural like a woman's freshly washed face, free of heavy rouge and garish eye shadow. As natural as a grown woman wanting a new dress to make her feel special. In accepting their affection as natural, in refusing my mother's repulsion, I realized that to the greater world and certainly to my traditional Paramus family, I was the opposite of natural. I was disgusting. A thing to be cleared away like dirty plates.

"You've Got Talent"

It was a few years before I fully grasped the truth of those sensations from that Automat meal. In part, this was a product of the times. Anything sexual was laced with fear because of HIV and AIDS. Fear bred secrecy and there was no internet to supplement crucial, missing information. I imagine a twelve-year-old today would arrive at their sexuality with much more speed; they have been exposed to knowledge that helps them contextualize their feelings. They don't know how lucky they are.

Still, I wasn't a loner. By late junior high, I had crafted a good social circle. I was fair and blond and skinny. I made friends easily, not because I was "likable" or any of the other lame adjectives people insist are necessary to a girl's popularity but somehow never apply to boys. It was precisely because I didn't care too much what other people thought, particularly when it came to boys, that girls were attracted to me. Of course, I would later identify this nonchalance toward males for what it was: blatant disinterest.

My three best friends growing up were Christine, Stacy, and Karen. We all lived within walking distance of each other. We went to the same elementary school and the same Catholic church on

Sundays, though none of us were firm in our beliefs. It was the thing you did on the day of the week when GSP and all the other malls were closed because of blue laws. Of us four Stacy was probably the closest to devout, because her mother had grown up in Louisiana before she moved north to marry Stacy's dad. We all worried about hell and the existence of sins—well, I had many questions, but I pretended to worry. We just didn't think some light window shopping on a Sunday afternoon was cause for exile to the underworld.

Befitting her partially Southern roots, Stacy was the genteel one. She had corn-silk-blond hair and pale blue eyes that, unlike my dark ones, projected an aura of perennial innocence. Christine was the curviest of us. Well before puberty kicked in, her proportions seemed destined for conical bras and corsets. Karen was as straight as you could get, in every possible sense: a body that could be framed perfectly with a rectangle; lank hair the color of roasted almonds; eyebrows like ski tracks.

On a Sunday after church, we were kicking around Christine's bedroom, grazing on a stack of bologna sandwiches her mother had made us for lunch. We flipped through some issues of *Cosmopolitan*, *Seventeen*, and *YM*. Karen had *Cosmo* open to a picture of Brooke Shields, one of the most beautiful girls in the world and an Ivy League student to boot. Brooke's brown hair was teased and combed back from her face, her lips a slick of burnt cranberry, slashes of overripe peach running across her cheekbones.

Karen sighed. "I'll never look like that," she murmured.

I ignored the impulse to confirm Karen's suspicions—she would never look like that and neither would the rest of us. Instead, I glanced at the image of Brooke and then at the slim selection of powders, lipsticks, and blushers that crowded Christine's plastic bin on the floor by the window.

"I could make you look like that," I offered.

Karen rolled her eyes.

"Puh-lease," she said. "Unless you have a magic wand I don't know about, that will never happen."

"Not literally like that," I clarified. My chest ached a bit for the ease with which she dismissed her attractiveness. "I can give you the same effect."

Karen's interest was piqued.

"Okay, why not."

Christine had a proper vanity with a small stool in a corner of her room, near the window, so Karen sat there, her back to the mirror, and glanced up at me with skepticism. Through the window's panes, I could hear the delighted screams of younger children playing somewhere farther down the street. I looked at the magazine photo and began to pluck items from the plastic bin. Christine and Stacy gathered on Christine's bed to watch. The air in the room was charged with anticipation.

Christine's selection of cosmetics was limited, a mix of hand-me-downs from her mother and drugstore whims purchased with her allowance. There was no chance I would find the exact shades I needed to re-create the look.

Brooke's eyes were cloaked in a brown haze, so I pulled out some cases of dark powders. One of them was larger than the other and seemed like it was a bronzer; the smaller one had multiple rectangles of color in it. Christine had a tacky red lipstick that was altogether the wrong color for Karen—or anyone else, really—but I pulled that out, too, along with pencils in navy and black, another lipstick in an orangey peach, a tub of Vaseline, and two things that looked like blush in a mauve pink and a salmon.

I'm not sure what had possessed me to declare that I could replicate Brooke's effect on Karen. I wanted her to feel pretty, and even as a child I had a natural confidence that some might describe as cockiness. Looking at those random, mismatched cosmetics I'd pulled from the plastic bin, I was overtaken by a sense of having done this all before, though the opposite was true.

People always want clear explanations for artistry, like there's a step-by-step plan they can follow to achieve the same result. That's not how creativity works. There is an unknowable quotient that allows a visionary to make connections that others can't or won't see. The eye pencils and lipsticks were like markers and crayons. The eye shadow and Vaseline were construction paper and glue. Instinct filled in the gaps of my inexperience. Makeup was no different from art supplies.

I picked up the black pencil first and started to line Karen's eyes, then realized it was too harsh and opted for the navy one instead. I had propped up the *Cosmo* magazine photo against Christine's vanity so I could refer to it as I worked. Brooke's eyes had a browner, blurrier feel than what the navy pencil achieved, but I figured I could go over it with a brown powder to temper it. The brown eye shadow came with one of those small foam-tipped things, and I used it to blend the powder into a soft edge around Karen's eyes. The navy lines hidden beneath gave them depth.

The two blush colors were uniquely terrible and had accompanying stubby brushes better suited for nails, so I knew I'd have to improvise there, too. I started with the salmon one, to impart warmth, then layered the bronzer over it. Karen's face looked too orange, and the bronzer was shinier than I wanted, so I reached for the brown eye shadow.

"Are you using eye shadow on her cheeks?" Stacy asked, appalled.

"That's so weird, Max," said Christine.

Most of my friends and classmates referred to me as "Max," though my mother refused to comply. "If I had wanted you to have a boy's name, I would have had a boy," she would snap, as though such matters were within her control.

"Shut up, guys," I shot back. "I know what I'm doing. Besides, if you don't like it, you can wash it off."

The eye shadow lent Karen's cheeks the matte oomph I sought. Her lips were all I had left. With my finger I applied a base of the red lipstick—"Gross!" Stacy exclaimed, helpfully—to better control how much went on. That tacky red didn't look very good. I reached for the bronzer and patted that on, then daubed some Vaseline on top. Karen's thin, straight lips glimmered like fall foliage in afternoon light.

I stepped back for perspective on my handiwork. No amount of effort could transform Karen into Brooke Shields. Still, Karen looked different. Sultrier. Whereas before her face was a parody of flatness, her features like straight lines on a piece of notebook paper, now it was symphonic, a harmony of color and texture and liveliness.

"Well?" Karen said. "Is it good? I'm scared to look in the mirror."

I smiled in what I hoped was a semblance of modest triumph.

"Yes, you look great." I glanced over at Stacy and Christine. "What do you guys think?"

They scrambled off the bed and came to stand next to me, the better to examine Karen.

"Wow," Stacy said. "You could pass for eighteen."

"Smokin'," Christine agreed.

Karen shifted around on the stool and stared at herself in the vanity. She turned her head from side to side, taking in all the angles, her expression unreadable. Then she caught my eyes watching her in the mirror and her lips spread into a momentary grin before returning to their flat state of repose.

"Max," she said solemnly, as if uttering an irrevocable pronouncement. "You've got talent."

I flushed, shyness overtaking me for the first time in my life.

"Thanks."

"That wasn't a compliment," Karen chastised me. "It was a fact. You are really good at this."

It was one of the wisest things Karen ever said to me. She was, I can admit now, a real friend back then, someone who in childhood was unthreatened by my obvious talent. I have circled this planet enough times to understand how rare such unjealous candor is in another woman, let alone a teen girl.

Karen's distinction between paying me a compliment and stating an obvious fact didn't strike me as noteworthy in Christine's bedroom. After a stint at the top of my field, not to mention my recent, precipitous tumble, I see how insightful this was. Talent isn't a good or bad thing: it is a neutral entity. You either have talent or you don't and there's no way to change that. It's what you do with your talent, the work you put behind it, the many choices you make, that complicates the picture.

After that fateful afternoon in Christine's bedroom, I threw myself full throttle into my newly uncovered talent. Christine, Karen, and Stacy would rip out photos of models with eye-catching makeup from their magazines. At sleepovers I would practice on them using the increasingly expansive collection of cosmetics I purchased from the drugstore with my allowance. It was a win-win: they felt like glamorous models, and I got high on making them beautiful. I mastered the art of the smoky eye, the dramatic contour, the sculpted brow, the over-penciled lip. These trends were not my preferred aesthetic; they were the basis of my education. Like any artist, I needed to understand what came before me so I could break new ground in my own work.

I was never tempted to test out these iterations on myself. My own face remained makeup-free, which may seem counterintuitive or hypocritical. Think of how many fashion designers sport an all-black uniform or create their intricate masterpieces from their blank, white studios. That was me in that junior high and early high school phase. I kept myself pristine for the sake of my craft.

One day in ninth grade, Stacy asked if I would come to her house and do her makeup before school. There was this sophomore guy, Brad, a football player whom she had a huge crush on and wanted to impress. She thought a little zing to her daily look might have the desired effect. I hauled over to her house at 7 a.m. I remember the sky was cloudy that morning; it buffed the light that trickled in through her bedroom window and coated her skin in powdery softness.

The average late-1980s Paramus girl waltzed into class every day with a full-pancake look. I wanted Stacy to do the opposite. My goal was drama by way of restraint, makeup that was natural. None of the magazine images were subtle enough for what I sought, so I employed a freestyle approach.

I patted some moisturizer all over Stacy's face to act as a smoothing base. Her skin was clear to begin with, untarnished by the acne that had started to encroach on the greater adolescent population. It was on the dry side, though, and the lotion added some life. Using my ring finger, I dotted concealer under Stacy's eyes, down the center and the sides of her nose, in the middle of her forehead, and on the fleshiest point of her chin. I had recently purchased some disposable foam sponges and I used the blunter edge of one to gently blend the concealer in. A coppery eyeliner with reddish-orange undertones would make her blue eyes pop, so I went in close to her waterline at the bottoms of her eyes and then right next to the lash line on top. I softened those sharp edges with a cotton swab since this was a school day.

Powder blushes were all the rage back then, but ever since my glue-and-marker combo, I had become enamored of glossier textures. I saw them everywhere. In oily streaks on a slice of pizza. In puddles on the street a few hours after it rained. In the sweat that slicked the tops of my thighs on a sweltering summer day.

I hadn't found any alternatives to powder blush on my drugstore forays, so I'd taken to rubbing lipsticks into the girls' cheeks. That creamy consistency warmed up on the skin like melted candle wax and imparted the look of perpetual heat. Stacy's cheeks got a shimmery rose lipstick layered with a pale tangerine, to play off the orange glints in her eyeliner. The finishing touch was a light coating of dark brown mascara on her lashes and a few finger daubs of that shimmery rose on her lips, thinned out and glossed up with a dollop of Vaseline. A little extra Vaseline remained on my finger when I was done, so I rubbed it across her brows to make them shine.

Stacy followed along with my ministrations in her bathroom mirror. When I was finished, she stared contemplatively at her reflection and my stomach tightened with momentary concern. What if Stacy didn't like my handiwork? I knew what I had created was pretty, but that didn't mean she would agree.

"It's perfect, Max," she said, wrapping me in a quick hug. "Come on, let's go or we'll be late."

If Karen was my first test subject, then Stacy was client zero. Her words ended my brief bout of uncertainty. I had made Stacy feel beautiful. I could see it in the way she strode ahead of me and led us out of her bedroom, down the stairs, and into the car that would take us to school.

Stacy and I had American Literature first period, along with Christine and Karen. As I pulled my English books from my locker, I watched girl after girl, people we weren't even friends with, approach Stacy.

Jane, with her shiny mahogany head, sidled up to Stacy and examined her closely. "Did you get a haircut?" she asked.

Stacy shook her head no and smiled imperceptibly.

Becky, head of the cheerleading squad, a brash blonde who never acknowledged our existence, nearly sideswiped Stacy as she sauntered by because she was too busy staring at Stacy's face.

"Such a cute new dress," offered Amy, a senior who was dating Brad's football captain. Stacy wore a floral A-line number whose hem was practically frayed with love; no one could mistake it for a recent purchase. None of these girls cared. All they knew was that something about Stacy had changed. Therein lay my gift. Anyone could make up someone so that all you noticed was their purple eye shadow or their thick fringe of lashes; I knew how to apply cosmetics so that the first thing you saw was the woman's beauty. The makeup became one with the person, an extension of who she was—or better yet, who she dreamed of being.

By the end of that school day, Stacy had a date with Brad. I returned to my locker to stash my Chemistry textbook before heading home. I was tugging at a spiral notebook whose metal spine had become caught on the locker's interior holes when the hot breath of impatience tickled the back of my neck. I spun around and Nora, a junior, lingered at my side.

"Sorry for startling you," she said, then leaned against the locker beside mine. "I hear you're responsible for Stacy."

"Stacy is responsible for Stacy," I replied, out of loyalty to my friend.

Nora rolled her eyes like she could barely tolerate the presence of a freshman girl.

"I meant her makeup."

I closed my locker door and slung the weight of my backpack onto one shoulder.

"Oh. Yes."

"Think you could do the same thing for me?"

I peered more closely at Nora. Her skin bore the traces of mild acne and her brows required a formative encounter with a pair of tweezers. They say beggars can't be choosers. Well, I was never a beggar, but I was smart enough not to turn down a potential opportunity.

I smiled at Nora.

"Not the same thing, something similar. And I don't do handouts."

Nora's lips curled into an expression of superiority.

"And I don't do charity. I can pay. How about Friday night?"

I charged her ten dollars for the visit, the going hourly rate for a student babysitter. Nora mentioned our session to two of her soccer team pals and by dinner the following day, I had two more girls who wanted to procure my services. I agreed to go to their homes. They had to buy their own mascara because I didn't want to share that across "clients." I considered making them purchase their own concealer to avoid amassing multiple shades, but the range of potential skin tones I worked with was so narrow, there was no need. The fees I charged helped cover the cost of product restocking, with a little leftover on the side for me to save.

Word of mouth spread fast. Soon, I was making up four or five girls a week, usually on Friday or Saturday nights. Like a proto–Uber Pool app, I mapped them out and staggered them so that I could hit everyone in one night before they left for their respective outings. It was easy to cover my tracks from my parents by telling them I was at sleepovers or out at the movies with friends. My father might have been encouraging of my activities had he known, given his passion for hard work, but I suspected my mother would be jealous of any occupational pursuit, even one centered on beauty. I remembered how she had smarted when my dad had complimented my sweater folding in the New York boutique and figured my moonlighting should remain a secret.

Within a month, I created a viable business, unwittingly and long before entrepreneurship, particularly female entrepreneurship, was a buzzy talking point. It was thrilling to transform a talent into a legitimate enterprise with such ease. The need was there; I didn't create it. All I did was see it. To observe the desires of my clients was not the same thing as comprehending them, though. I couldn't understand why my classmates would go to so much trouble and spend all this money to secure the affections of boys.

I recognized, viscerally and painfully, that I was different. Even after that meal at the Automat with the two women, I'd managed to explain away any fluttering of errant desire as no more than an overbaked crush. In fourth grade, when I had changed out of my swimsuit in the oppressive dampness of a women's locker room and the sight of the lifeguard's pert ass had stirred something deep inside me, I had chalked it up to envy for her perfect curves. I had similarly shrugged away the transfixing sight of Susan's freckled neck one seat ahead of me in fifth-grade English class as merely artistic curiosity. However, a few years later, when Susan hired me to do her makeup before a date and I ran my gloss-soaked finger across her lips, I knew the electricity that prickled down my torso was not the standard bearer of straight teenage girlhood. I didn't want to be Susan or admire her fiery beauty. I wanted to screw her. In coming to this realization, I understood that I was screwed, too.

DAY TWO

Evening

If my teenage self could see me right now, she would be horrified. I appear far from the sophisticated woman she wished to become. When I'm not staring furiously at my laptop screen, I putter around my apartment like an old matron. I'm forty years old—forty-one in two months—and you'd think I was seventy or whatever age it is that people retire at. I have on the same baggy sweatpants I've worn for the past two days. They're navy cashmere, so I haven't hit total rock bottom. Here's the thing: Even cashmere sweatpants will stretch into blousy pockets at the knees after constant wear. No amount of luxurious material and fine craftsmanship can insulate you from human banality.

On her way home from the office, Elizabeth, my ever-loyal publicist, drops by my apartment for a drink and to make sure I am not hanging by a thin thread. I am not hanging by a thin thread. Cashmere is more resilient than that.

In addition to being Reveal's head publicist, Elizabeth is the closest I have to an adult best friend, which doesn't say much, as the empty pages of my proverbial Rolodex would attest. Elizabeth can't stay for very long. One quick round is all she can squeeze in—she has a cocktail event in Midtown to attend, to keep the flames of Reveal burning and such. She enters my apartment and for the first time in our years of friendship, *she* scans *me* from head to toe. This is a woman who wore stockings to her interview. I once spied a pair of rubber clogs in her hall closet when I was at her place for dinner. Elizabeth's idea of "style" is a dress with a discernible waistline.

"Those pants look . . . comfortable," she offers with a hesitant smile, her shoulder-length brown hair in a no-nonsense ponytail. "I don't think I've ever seen you so dressed down."

"Don't get used to it," I tell her as I pour her an inch and a half of Scotch.

"There's my girl." She winks.

For a few minutes, we sit in awkward silence, or as awkward as things can get between two people who have known each other intimately for over a decade. I hear the tires of passing cars on the avenue outside my windows. A siren wails into eternity many blocks away.

"Have you spoken to anyone?" Elizabeth asks. She crosses one long leg over the other. Tonight, she is in an inoffensive black sheath dress.

"Who would I speak to?" I ask her. She is seated on my tufted sofa. I used to have a low-slung Italian number, but I decided recently that my living room required structure. "Is that why you came by? To make sure I was keeping a lid on things?"

Elizabeth cringes in a way that suggests I might have hurt her. A sharp pang reverberates somewhere in my chest.

"Max, I care about you deeply. You know that."

"I'm sorry," I say. "I know. That was the stress talking."

There is an unsettling stillness. Elizabeth's mouth looks like it is struggling with the right words to release.

"Have you heard from her?"

"Which her—Ellen or Amanda?"

"Either."

The Scotch's mellow butterscotch turns bitter on my tongue.

"No and I don't expect to."

Elizabeth's heart-shaped face widens with something that looks like pity.

"Max . . ."

"I'm so angry."

"I get that," says Elizabeth. "But you understand why—"

"No, I don't. I really don't." Heat radiates across my chest. "Anyway," I pivot before Elizabeth can cut in with an expression of emotion, "I should probably leave the house at some point." I haven't left the apartment since that sunset walk.

Elizabeth frowns.

"I'm all for some fresh air on your own. You absolutely cannot be seen with anyone right now. Or risk having anyone come here."

"I would never." I attempt a wry smile and it doesn't land. "Are there men with cameras outside or something?"

"You don't need men with cameras; it's 2015, everyone has a camera." Elizabeth taps her phone on the sofa beside her. "It would be good to go outside, though. Alone."

It isn't so much that I fear running into someone I know—though the prospect of that is not appealing—but that I am so filled with rage, I worry I might explode on an innocent pedestrian, a doorman, a child, anyone who looks at me for a second too long. The unfairness of it all makes my skin burn.

"I'll think about it," I say. "What event are you attending tonight?"

"Cocktails for the Women Mentorship in Business nonprofit."

"You're kidding."

Elizabeth flashes me a knowing smile. "I wish I were. The guest of honor is that young multimillionaire who wrote that bestselling memoir last year and then stepped down as CEO of her company a month later."

"I don't know who you mean," I say. "That's an interesting choice for damage control."

"For the former CEO or for Reveal?"

"Both."

"Oh, speaking of books"—Elizabeth reaches into her leather tote bag on the floor by the sofa—"I almost forgot to give you this." She hands me some tome by a Silicon Valley executive about women getting ahead in the workplace. "I was at Barnes and Noble last night and thought of you when I saw this."

"Thanks," I say, wondering why Elizabeth thinks I'm in the mood to read.

"It could be a nice analog distraction from scrolling on your phone," she offers, answering my unspoken question.

"I'll consider it."

I swallow the rest of my Scotch. Elizabeth does the same with hers. She stands up from her chair and I walk her to the front door, where she folds me into a careful hug. A pocket of pent-up air in my lungs releases into her embrace.

"I'll call you tomorrow."

Then she is gone and I am alone.

That book sits awkwardly on the edge of my sofa. I pick it up and barely glance at the cover, with its catchy title and smiling female leader, before I toss it into a junk drawer. The only type of distraction I enjoy is a warm body; barring that, I return to my computer and continue to type.

Cosmetic Awakenings

I've never been interested in porn. It's not just because porn typically caters to straight male desire, without female pleasure in mind, or worse, with female debasement as the goal. I also take issue with the idea that someone else is permitted creative control over my sexual imaginings, which are far more exciting than anything those "film" directors could dream up. Why would anyone relinquish authority over their fantasies? Porn is a mediocre shortcut, it's lazy, and I prefer to be in charge.

I didn't have sex with anyone in high school. Once I became cognizant of my feelings for other girls, I experienced the various stages of processing that occur when people realize they belong to what is now called a "marginalized group." First, there was fear. I could imagine my Catholic parents disowning me, dropping me off at some wayward girls' orphanage with a half-empty suitcase and a pair of expressions that said *Never call home*. Then there was confusion because I didn't know anyone like me and therefore had no model for how my life would play out. This was followed by anger since I knew this was a secret that I would need to keep on the path that I was slowly building.

One stage I didn't encounter was guilt. I wasn't a very good Catholic for many reasons. I can't explain why guilt never rushed over me in the same way that it has swallowed many other gay people. I've always had an unshakable conviction that this is who I am supposed to be. I knew it when I smeared that Popsicle juice across my lips and when I patted that makeup on Karen's face. Ms. Adams's kindness reaffirmed this for me. I was aware that my sexuality was something I needed to hide, yet it was never something I wished to change.

There are girls who, upon recognizing their gayness, would avert their eyes in gym locker rooms and avoid sleepovers because they worried another girl's body might incite impure thoughts. I was not one of them. The way I saw it, I had purchased myself a golden ticket to a theme park of girl-on-girl fantasies by way of my maquillage business. Sally needed flushed cheeks for her pre-necking milkshake with William. No problem. I'd rub shimmery peach lipstick into her apples—my signature move—and a couple of hours later, I'd rub myself off as I imagined that I was the one sucking on her olive neck. Angela wanted a wide-eyed gaze for a sunset picnic with Jack. I'd fluff her eyelashes like down pillows in a five-star hotel, stare into their gray-green depths, memorize every glint and shadow, the better to imagine them scanning my naked body with unadulterated lust as I came for the third time later that night. And so on and so forth.

My town's Catholicism was the perfect double-edged sword. It was part of the reason for my secrecy, yes, but it also provided me an ever-believable cover for not pursuing a boyfriend like the male-crazy teens in my high school. I was a good Catholic girl, who abided by the tenets of my shaky faith and didn't gallivant with boys. No parent or teacher questioned my lack of heterosexual desire; they saw it as a symptom of my piety.

There were three girls who never entered my fantasy realm: Stacy, Christine, and Karen. Not because they were unappealing, but because they were my friends. It would have been the equivalent of sexual attraction to a cousin or a sibling.

We had this gym teacher in high school. Yes, I'm aware this is a cliché. No, it doesn't make what I'm about to say untrue. We had this gym teacher in high school, Coach Parker. She went by Coach, not Ms. or Mrs. the way non–physical education teachers did. Coach Parker was a large woman. She was over six feet tall. Her shoulders were very broad, to the extent that I wondered where she purchased her jackets and sweaters. Her hair was cut in a choppy bob, not quite as short as the hair of those Automat women, but short enough to arouse suspicion in early-1990s Paramus. Then there was Coach Parker's walk: clunky steps, each one heavier and more awkward than the last, her hips wide and tight. Coach Parker walked like she was trying to crush humanity beneath her size-eleven shoes.

Behind her back, the girls in my class did not call her Coach Parker. They called her Coach Pecker. As in, "Coach Pecker wants to stick it to Lisa's mom" or "Coach Pecker has a hard-on for Mrs. Lewis," etc., etc. Every time a girl would say this, my stomach would clench. I knew I looked nothing like Coach Parker. I walked like a ballerina by comparison. My hair was long. I wasn't the same as her. Except that I was.

It was softball season—again, a cliché; again, not untrue here—and our gym class was divided into teams. This was probably sophomore year. I was on Christine's team. Stacy and Karen were in the field. Christine was up to bat, and I sat on the bench. By this point, Christine's curves were so luscious, even mothers and grandmothers eyed her when she walked down the street. She was not so well endowed athletically, though. She swung and fully missed two easy pitches.

Coach Parker came up behind her to help Christine out.

"You hold the bat like this," she instructed as she wrapped her arms around Christine and showed Christine where to place her hands on the bat. "Your stance is off." Coach Parker moved her hands from Christine's bat and down to Christine's hips, which she pivoted to the correct angle.

The titters started on the bench beside me. "Coach Pecker wants Christine." "Watch out, Christine—Coach Pecker has the hots for you." It was Karen who made the murmurs official. She marched over to the home plate from her spot at first base.

"Get your hands off her!" she snapped. "You dyke."

It was the first time I heard this slur. Not the last, of course. How did Karen know this word? Where had she learned it? I didn't need anyone to tell me its meaning. Part of me ached for the obvious intention behind Karen's word choice and for what it boded in our friendship. I was that word, too. If Karen ever found out, she'd call me the same thing. Another part of me wanted to distance myself from Coach Parker for the purposes of safety. If I stood too close to her, people might sense a hidden resemblance between us. A third part of me wanted to scream on Coach Parker's behalf. She hadn't done anything wrong. She was helping an athletically challenged student—she was doing her job. Male coaches patted their students on the back or chest or shoulders all the time and no one said a word.

These three parts, deep identification, self-preservation, and indignation, seemed in opposition to each other, still their result was the same: they reaffirmed that I needed to hide who I was. My desire, and the beautiful pleasure it gave me in the privacy of my bedroom, was never going to change nor did I want it to. This same desire—and beauty—was not something I could ever share publicly. It was not something I could share with my closest friends.

Coach Parker dropped her hands from Christine's hips and stepped back, away from Christine, whose face was bright red. Coach

Parker was trembling, with anger or shame, I wasn't sure. Karen stood there, hands on her own hips, and glared at Coach Parker.

"I think we should end class for today," said Coach Parker, with more grace than I would have managed in a similar situation. "You're dismissed."

Coach Parker strode away briskly in the direction of the school's parking lot. I stood up from the bench and joined Karen and Stacy, who gathered around Christine.

"Are you okay?" asked Karen.

"I'm fine," said Christine, whose face had returned to its normal shade.

"I can't believe she touched you like that. What a dyke," said Karen.

Stacy was silent, just as my father had been at the Automat. I followed her lead.

"She was adjusting my stance," said Christine. "I don't think she meant it that way. I wish you hadn't made a whole thing out of it."

"Oh, she definitely meant it that way. Just look at you," said Karen. "You can never be too careful. My mother says women like that are everywhere, in the places you'd least expect."

My makeup business continued to occupy me through the fall of junior year in high school. On a Saturday afternoon, I was walking to this girl Trisha's house, makeup Caboodle in hand. The leaves had started turning. A soft breeze rustled the trees' burnished plumage and made the hairs on the back of my neck stand at attention. I was distracted by an enormous puddle from the previous night's rain and was so focused on navigating around it without soaking through my sneakers that I failed to notice my mother, who rounded the corner of the street adjacent to the one I was crossing.

"Maxine!" she called. "What are you doing here?"

My head swiveled toward my mother. I had told her I was spending the afternoon at Christine's house, yet I was on the street where Trisha lived, completely in the opposite direction from Christine's place.

I halted once I crossed the street and my mother bustled toward me.

"Hi, Mom," I said.

"Aren't you supposed to be at Christine's?" she asked.

A sparrow chirped from a nearby tree. It fluttered down and landed on the sidewalk. Then it hopped into the sizable puddle around which I had detoured. The bird splashed with abandon before it took off into the air. I wished I could fly away with it.

"I am," I said, with no further explanation.

"So you lied to me? What are you doing here?"

My mother's gaze migrated from my flushed cheeks down to the pink Caboodle clutched in my right hand. Meanwhile, my eyes made a beeline for her clumpy mascara and overzealous bronzer. I desperately wanted to suggest that she employ a lighter touch when it came to her daily face and that I was exactly the person to help her do this.

"I didn't lie. I *was* at Christine's earlier. Then Trisha called Christine's house. She needed help with something."

"Trisha Daley? Are you even friends with her?"

My mother, who had to be dragged to a PTA meeting by the ends of her hair, really picked her moments to swan in with intimate knowledge of my social life.

"We have Trig together."

"So you decided to up and walk a mile to Trisha's house to help with her homework? You must think I was born yesterday."

After a few more rounds of verbal bobbing and weaving, I confessed everything to my mother regarding my business and the covert trips I had been making to various girls' homes. Initially, I thought the intrepid nature of my endeavor might win her over because she seemed, if not pleased, then less angry than I had feared. Her mouth, coated in a red that was far too warm for her pink-toned complexion, didn't curl into a smile, but it didn't settle into a reprimand either. I detected a tiny ember in her eyes. Was that pride cutting through her normally steely gaze? My mother and I had never been sympatico on creativity; ever since our disagreement over that Alexander's mural, I had steered clear of philosophical discussions. And I had kept my makeup enterprise a secret from her out of concern that she'd feel threatened by my earning power. Perhaps I'd underestimated her.

"You've been lying to us this whole time while you've had people paying you to do their makeup. You may as well be selling yourself," said my mother. "I have never been so disappointed in you, Maxine. This is not how I raised you to behave."

My mother had read *Cosmopolitan* when it first debuted. She had heard of female fiscal independence, though she didn't practice it herself. As suspected, my ambition really irked her. She was not pro–female entrepreneurship, certainly not for a teenage girl. A proper woman was obedient—she could make her own money, yes, but she did so within the preexisting structure that was available to her. She was savvy, not rebellious.

"I'll speak with your father about this," she chided.

That's how my first business went under. The pain seared me. It wasn't the unearned money that hurt, rather it was the end to the exhilarating high of creative autonomy. I couldn't be my true self like my friends. Through my entrepreneurship, I had expressed that self in the safe, accepted medium of makeup. Now that outlet was gone.

I wanted to take that goddamned Caboodle and hurl it at the ground, watch its contents shatter until there was nothing left but a mess of colored powder and cream, as useless to the world as my independent spirit.

I look back on that moment, with the benefit of age and time, as a crucial lesson for my future professional vector. Success requires perseverance and, above all, self-conviction. No one, not an investor or a colleague or a parent, will ever care about your artistic vision as much as you do. To manifest your ideas, you must exist in a continuous battle against naysayers, bolstered only by your personal faith.

At the time, such wisdom was not at my disposal. I was a teenager, with all the raging hormones that entails. How dare my mother, a woman who hadn't made so much as a dime since marrying my dad, question my desire to build a business. She was obviously jealous. My father chided her for her lack of profession, meanwhile her teenage daughter possessed more moxie than she ever would. She didn't want me to have something she herself couldn't grasp.

On that afternoon, I erected a wall against my mother, to insulate my still-forming identity from her hostile incursions. To this day, that barrier has never come down.

Vigorous Heterosexuality

The impenetrable wall between my mother's beliefs and mine was fortified by my father. As an adult, I wonder what drew these two people together in holy matrimony. I rarely saw them behave affectionately toward each other. They practiced nearly polar approaches to life: my father prioritized quantitative reasoning and discipline; my mother was, I can see now, both an unabashed sybarite and a conformist.

My teenage mind harbored zero interest in my parents' mutual attraction. Like most adolescents, I was only concerned with myself. After my mother informed him of my business, my dad called in a favor with a colleague in the cosmetics department at the GSP Macy's, which had taken over the old Bamberger's store. I heard my parents argue about this one night while I sat on the stairs and eavesdropped.

"Why does she need a job at all? She should be focused on her schoolwork," said my mother.

"It's good that Maxine was pursuing fiscal independence," said my father. "She was just too independent about it. A job will teach her responsibility."

"I don't want my daughter touching other women's faces. It's unclean. Who knows what kinds of women she'll meet there."

The way my mother said this, I question now if she had an inkling of my sexuality. Why did she think the Macy's makeup department would be a hotbed of woman-on-woman activity? Perhaps she had seen the term "lipstick lesbian" somewhere and taken it at face value.

"That's ridiculous. Maxine wants to work. She should do it in a supervised way." My father paused here. "At least one woman in this family is pursuing a career."

"If I didn't have a child to raise and a home to clean while you're at the office every day, maybe I'd have a career, too," said my mother.

My father snorted. "I highly doubt that."

"Hire a housekeeper, a cook, and a babysitter and then we'll find out," said my mother, knowing my father would never call her bluff.

Within the week, I had a part-time job behind the counter of a big-deal brand that shall remain nameless. Mom sat next to me as I called each of my "clients" to inform them that I would no longer be available for private makeup services. I had been demoted from managing my own schedule, rates, and aesthetic to being at a company's mercy. Gone was the sense that I was making other girls beautiful through my talents. I was now a cog in a large machine, shilling for products that I didn't respect in service to a corporation's bottom line.

I worked at Macy's on Tuesday and Thursday afternoons. The gig had a dress code, so on those days, I would rush from my last-period Biology class to the nearest girls' bathroom. In the grubby stall, the smell of bleach mixed with urine in the air, I would change out of my sweater and jeans into a collared black shirt and a black pencil skirt, both of which my mother had purchased for this job. I had a plastic name tag, too, rimmed in silver, that I would attach to the shirt's chest pocket with a safety pin. The store wanted us to look "neat and presentable," but still "warm and appealing," per the guidelines I received, which translated into combed and brushed hair, mascara, powder blush—gag—and an abhorrent cotton-candy lipstick that they insisted all the saleswomen wear for the sake of uniformity. I refused to walk even the few short steps through the bustling school hallway and out to my mother's waiting car with that pink on my lips. My coworker Linda had to hand-apply the lipstick to my mouth every time I showed up without it.

"Oh honey," she would cluck, as she swiped that disgusting stub across my lips. "Must we go through this every time?"

"This lipstick makes me wish I was color-blind," I'd retort, which always made Linda laugh.

The Macy's cosmetics department was a swirling hive of activity. The fluorescent ceiling lights emitted a heat that rivaled the burn of UV rays. All those metal, plastic, and glass stations conducted and refracted that warmth. They turned the entire floor into a blazing hellscape. Within minutes of my shift, I was sweating beneath my black button-down shirt. Droplets meandered across my back, collected in the cups of my bra; occasionally, an errant drip would make its way to my anklebone. Then there was the noise on that floor. Customers' voices and salespeople's coos of enticement had nowhere to land on those hard surfaces. Instead, they ricocheted endlessly from edge to edge. It was like we were trapped in a massive pinball arcade game, bright lighting, unexpected pings, and all. The prize wasn't a high score, though. It was the possibility of eventual escape.

Linda, witty and good-natured, was one of the best parts of that experience. While I'm sure she initially saw me as a spoiled brat whose Daddy handed her a cute job, in the end, she understood me better than most other people in my life. Linda was in her early thirties, a single mom who stitched together a series of part-time gigs, including waitressing and office temping, to work around her young son's schedule while earning enough to keep the lights on at home. Linda's ex-husband was a total loser, as she described him, a guy who had chased her assiduously throughout her twenties, only to leave as soon as he impregnated her a few months after their wedding. He hadn't stuck around long enough for Linda to divorce him. She had no idea where he was, and there were no alimony checks in her mailbox.

Before she was married, Linda had worked at a salon a couple of towns over, cutting and coloring hair and offering makeovers. She was the first person I had met who made a living from the one talent I possessed. That said, Linda and I had very different tastes. She was a child of the 1960s and harbored an abiding love for winged eyeliner and decadent eyelashes. Petite to my five-foot-eight stature, curvy where I was narrow and flat, raven-haired where I was flaxen, she was my visual foil, and my verbal one, too. I had a tendency toward dry rejoinders and my small-talk skills were nonexistent. Linda could chat a dog away from its food bowl. She would talk, talk, talk her way through a trail of customers during our shifts. By the end, she'd have racked up more than I managed to sell in an entire month.

Linda realized this from the outset and so she tasked me with inventory checks and general organization—putting bottles and vials back in their rightful places after customers had futzed with them, stacking the wipes and cotton pads we used when testing out products, for example. Still, she knew it was a disservice to shield me from front-of-house duties, not least of all because we earned a bonus based on our individual sales. Every so often, she would make me deal with a customer even if she was free.

"You have an eye," she told me one afternoon, as I applied a ring of taupe shadow to her lids in a particularly fallow hour. "It's your mouth that needs some work."

A couple of weeks before Christmas, Linda had stepped away in search of some burgundy nail polishes when a tall, chestnut-haired woman strolled over to our station. Instead of perusing the holiday lip glosses on display, she smiled expectantly.

"Could you help me?"

I glanced over my shoulder hoping to spy Linda. There was no sign of her, so I turned back to the woman in resignation.

"Sure," I said. "What are you looking for?"

The woman pulled a foundation bottle from the tan leather bag slung over her shoulder.

"I've been using this for years and I can't find it anywhere. Do you have it?"

I peered at the nearly empty bottle in the woman's hand. It was the brand's Moisturizing Longwear Base in Ecru, which had been discontinued three months ago, according to Linda, because the company wanted to push women to a matte skin finish, in keeping with the looks on recent fashion runways.

"Dry as the Sahara," Linda quipped, "that's what these people think is 'in' these days."

This customer's face was so full of hope as she waited for me to answer. And that face—it was pretty, in an unassuming way, but man was her makeup all wrong. Her black eyeliner was too harsh against her hazel eyes and brought out the dark circles beneath them. Her blush was a streaky salmon, and her mouth looked like it had gone mano a mano with a candy apple and lost. Buried beneath what I assumed was the bitter end of that Moisturizing Longwear Base in Ecru, her complexion was bouncy despite her middle age and only slightly feathered with fine lines. That Ecru shade was all wrong, though. Her skin had warm olive undertones; the Ecru was pinkish and a couple of shades too pale for this lady.

"The brand discontinued that line of foundation. Sorry," I said with sincere apology.

The woman's face wilted in defeat.

"Do you have anything that's similar?"

"No, not really."

She seemed poised to leave. I wanted to keep her there but didn't know how.

"Wait, why don't you try something else?"

"Like what?" Skepticism furrowed the woman's brows. "You just said you had nothing that was similar."

"Right." What would Linda do? She would build trust. "I don't think *similar* is the answer, but I have an idea for a solution. Give me a chance. Worst case, you hate it, I'll wash it off and I'll gift you some samples for your trouble."

The woman glanced at her watch and nodded her acquiescence. I led her over to a director-style chair near a vanity to the left of our station. I pulled a handful of products from behind the main counter and settled them on the vanity. There was a pile of cotton pads near a pump bottle of makeup remover. I moistened a few circles and swiped them gently across the woman's face.

"I'm Max," I said, trying to mimic the easy chitchat at which Linda exceled. "What's your name?"

"Pam."

"Pam, great. So Pam, as I mentioned, we don't have a foundation exactly like the one you've been using."

"You've made that pretty clear."

"Right. I have. This one here"—I indicated the bottle on the vanity—"has a matte finish, which makes your skin look bone-dry."

"Is that a good thing?"

It took all my strength not to snicker.

"I prefer the texture of what you were using before. Something even lighter would be better. I'm going to create that."

I pulled a generic bottle of moisturizer from the vanity and squeezed some into the palm of my hand. Then I added some drops from the matte foundation bottle and mixed them together.

Pam frowned.

"You have really good skin," I said. Linda had always told me, "When in doubt, compliment the customer. No one runs away from praise."

Pam's face relaxed.

"I don't want to cover it up as much as you're used to. This shade I'm using is called Sand. It's closer to your natural color."

With a damp foam sponge, I daubed the foundation-moisturizer mixture on Pam's forehead and cheeks and beneath her nose and gently tapped the sponge across her skin to buff away any distinct edges.

I stepped to the side so that I no longer blocked Pam from seeing herself in the vanity's mirror. Even in the tragic glare of the store's fluorescent lighting, Pam looked like she had returned from a recent vacation.

"Wow," she said turning her head from side to side. "I look . . . young!"

"You are young," I said. Pam rolled her eyes in reply. "If you buy this foundation, when you apply it at home, do what I did and mix it with your favorite moisturizer. Like, in a fifty-fifty ratio. If you want more coverage, add more foundation to the mix."

Pam nodded.

"I'll take a bottle."

"Great."

Pam glanced at the other products on the vanity.

"You were going to do more, right? Can you keep going?"

I smiled.

"It would be my pleasure."

By the time I was done, Pam had also agreed to purchase the cocoa liner I stroked across her upper and lower lash lines, the terra-cotta bronzer I patted atop her cheekbones and nose bridge—I instructed her to mix it with moisturizer, too, for a sheer finish—and the taupe eye shadow that I mixed with lip balm before daubing it across her lips. It was more than I had sold in the past few days total. As I rang Pam up, I noticed that Linda had returned and was studying me. Pam took her change, smiled one last thank-you, and glided away. Linda came to stand beside me.

"Nice job on that sale," she said.

"Thanks," I replied. "That was fun."

"It looked it. You know we have brushes here for applying makeup? So you don't have to use your fingers."

"I like using my fingers."

"It's more precise if you use brushes."

"I'm not aiming for precision. I want it to look natural. Fingers are more natural."

I thought of the Impressionists and their light, uncanny brushstrokes. This was my version of that.

Linda paused, weighing her words before she spoke. "Listen, the customer looked great, and she left happy. That's always a good thing. In the future, I would lay off the mixing and matching."

"I don't understand. I sold the products."

"Yeah, but when you use the products differently from how they're supposed to be applied, it can give the customer the wrong impression."

"What impression is that?"

Linda shook her head in frustration.

"That they're not good enough on their own."

I smiled. "They're not."

"That's not for you to decide. If the higher-ups get wind that you're sending people home with instructions for mixing their foundation with skin care and using eye shadow on their lips and applying blush with their fingers, they're going to fire you. I don't want that to happen."

I glanced down at the countertop. It was speckled with flecks of powder blush and drops of errant foundation. I rubbed at one of the foundation spots to see if it was still wet, then looked up at Linda's worried expression. I knew she was watching out for me, in her maternal way. It was moving that she cared what happened to me. But thanks to my vision, Pam had walked away gleaming. If Linda had helped her, Pam would have departed with a future of masklike skin. I hadn't just sold Pam a handful of products; I had given her the tools to a healthy self-image. If I were in charge, if this were my company, Pam wouldn't need to mix her makeup with moisturizer so it would sit right on her skin. The products would be so intuitive, she could use them out of the bottle.

I couldn't say any of this to Linda. She'd look at me like I was nuts. This was the first of many moments when I realized that being exceptional is a lonely business. So I shrugged my shoulders and drooped my features into an expression that I hoped read as meek.

"I get it. Thanks for having my back," I said, and walked to my vanity station to clean up.

For the rest of high school, I continued to work at the GSP Macy's. I refrained from giving my customers explicit advice on how to improve upon the brand's lackluster offerings, though I insisted on using my fingers. Every so often, I'd whisper a tip in a customer's ear when Linda wasn't around. My allegiance was to these women, not to the brand. Still, I needed to keep my job.

My school and work lives collided one afternoon of my senior year when Christine came by the counter. She was the only one of my friends ever to visit me at Macy's; Karen and Stacy were too busy with cheerleading practice and their boyfriends. Christine had a boyfriend, too, some doofus named Ted who was a captain of the basketball team. He was tall and gangly with mopey eyes and thick brown hair that fell across his face. Ted also had acne-free skin, and this genetic achievement made him the most sought-after adolescent boy in our high school. Christine brought him along to Macy's when she came to see me. Ted seemed bored senseless.

Christine used the brand's products and needed a new tube of lipstick. Her preferred shade was a dusty rose nude of which I approved. Christine had a full pout, framed by cool chocolate waves. The understated pink-brown emphasized her natural charms.

As I crinkled some tissue paper to stuff the bag holding Christine's purchase, I was surprised to notice Ted examining the lipstick display. In my time behind the counter, I had never waited on a male customer. No man ever ventured near makeup. Sometimes I spotted men perusing colognes or perfumes, presumably for their girlfriends and wives, in competitors' sections—the brand for which I toiled did not sell fragrance. There was one brand that had recently launched a line of skin care marketed at men, a development I found curious. I had never met a man who cared enough about his appearance to invest time or money into its maintenance, though admittedly, I didn't pay much heed to boys or men at all.

Ted plucked a garish fuchsia lipstick from the display. It looked miniature in his huge athletic hand when he brandished the tube at Christine.

"This would look so hot on you, babe," he intoned.

That "babe" taxed my gag reflex. Christine and Ted had been dating for about five months, which in high school parlance meant they were practically engaged. I knew she had slept with him. I was the only virgin in our group of friends, a fact I explained as a product of self-discipline combined with extreme selectivity. Even the supposedly pious Stacy had popped her cherry on a beach that past summer, with a fellow camp counselor who had told her he loved her and whom she would, of course, never hear from again.

"Really?" asked Christine. She took the tube from him. "I've never worn such a bright color." Christine glanced at me. "Max, what do you think?"

"Absolutely not," I told her as Ted frowned at me. "The one you bought is perfect. I don't know why we sell that color. It doesn't look good on anyone."

"Max has an amazing eye," Christine explained to Ted. "She's basically an artist."

"You should try this one, babe," encouraged Ted, as though I didn't exist.

"I don't know," said Christine.

Ted leaned in closer. He put a hand on Christine's hip and stroked it gently. "You'll look so hot in that lipstick and nothing else," he murmured. "I'm getting hard just thinking about it."

My gag reflex was in full revolt at this point. I expected Christine to laugh in Ted's face, to tell him that I knew more about lipstick than he ever could, and that she didn't take beauty advice from a guy who spent most of his life in a sweaty, perforated jersey. But Christine didn't laugh. Her ivory complexion flushed. She smiled shyly as she ran a hand up Ted's leg, high enough that I nearly asked them to leave before they got me in trouble with a security guard or a moralistic passerby.

"Okay," said Christine.

Ted pulled out his wallet. "I've got this," he said, like he was buying Christine her first home instead of a lipstick.

I couldn't ring up the purchase fast enough. Christine and Ted strolled away, hand in hand, surely headed straight to his twin bed with its sports-themed linens. I couldn't believe what I had seen: my otherwise intelligent, rational friend making a terrible choice about her appearance based on the opinion of a boy whose greatest concern was what color Gatorade he should chug after practice. Worse, she had dismissed my expertise in favor of his moronic preference. The Christine I knew had spent our childhood makeovers basking in the pleasure of collective female admiration. What I had witnessed, I realized, was the power of male sex on a straight woman. Ted didn't need to be right. He didn't need to have a working brain. The only thing that needed to function was his penis. The lipstick was beside the point. The whole thing was foreplay. Ted may have been a child, but he understood that if you flatter a woman's sexual ego, you'll have her licking your, well, I didn't want to think about that part.

I had no doubt that Ted's sexual fantasy of Christine, the very fantasy that had drawn him to that hideous fuchsia, was remedial. It probably involved a push-up bra and vanilla-flavored lubricant. My fantasies of women were more sophisticated. One of the many injustices of living in a straight world is that you are forced to watch an insipid lack of imagination win, repeatedly, over nuance. Of course, there was another crucial difference between Ted and me, beyond the extremely obvious: for me, the lipstick was never beside the point.

High school finally ended. I applied to NYU and was accepted. My parents were trepidatious about me living in the city full-time, so I promised them I would come home any weekend that they wanted, though I didn't intend to maintain this agreement. I would work part-time in the cosmetics department at the Macy's in Herald Square to keep out of trouble. The possibility of "trouble," however, was part of what drew me to New York.

When I applied to NYU, I told the school I hoped to study art history. My dad had other ideas. Since he was paying my tuition and room and board, I agreed to major in business and marketing. It was sleep-inducing with all those pie charts and graphs and numbers. Still, it got me out of Paramus and into New York, that was what mattered.

My dorm was in a brick prewar building off Washington Square. Jeannette, my roommate, was an effervescent brunette from Chicago. Our room was a tight ten-by-twenty-foot rectangle that was somehow supposed to accommodate two extra-narrow twin beds, our desks, and a pair of dressers. The walls were white and hadn't been repainted in many years. A water stain puckered and bubbled near the ceiling's one overhead light fixture. The windows were so thin, the drunken students' shouts crashed through from Washington Square. The week of my freshman move-in was steamy—there was a heaviness in the air that transformed the dorm into a human-sized bread box.

A couple of nights into orientation, Jeannette and I sat on our respective twin beds. Jeannette was painting her toenails a glossy cherry red, the chemical-sweet smell of polish drifting from her feet. I was flipping through her issue of *Cosmo.*

"We should take one of their sex quizzes," Jeannette said with a nod at the magazine. "See how we compare."

Straight girls and their bonding rituals.

"I'm good," I said.

Jeannette smiled.

"I'm a virgin, too, don't worry. Though I plan to take care of it quickly. There are some parties this weekend. We should hit them up."

"Sure," I said. "Sounds like fun."

"I saw this guy when I was moving in the other day. His name was Dean. So hot. He had on these denim cutoff shorts. I don't think he was wearing underwear."

"That doesn't seem very sanitary," I said.

"You're hilarious. I could see the outline of his package. I can't stop thinking about it." I must have grimaced because Jeannette quickly added, "Don't worry—I would never, like, take care of myself while you're here. Though I think we should work out a system."

"A system?"

"Yeah, you know, a ribbon on the doorknob or something to tell the other person not to enter. In case we're with someone or even if we're alone doing things. You know?"

The image of Dean's protruding package had eradicated any imminent hopes of my solo pleasure.

"Totally," I said. "That makes sense."

"Have you seen any guys you're into?" Jeannette asked.

"Not yet," I said. Jeannette's face drooped a little. "There's still time," I added.

"There totally is," Jeannette agreed. "I can be your wingwoman and vice versa."

Unsurprisingly, Jeannette and I did not become each other's wingwomen. By the end of the first semester, we were barely speaking. Not because of any hostility between us. She was confounded by me. True to her goals, she eradicated her virginity within the first two weeks of classes, then buried it beneath an increasingly large pile of interchangeable guys. I didn't judge her for this. But my disinterest in her pursuits or in male pursuits of my own created a gap between us that slowly grew. Vigorous heterosexuality was her only means of connection with other young women. It was a language I didn't speak and one I didn't care to learn. To Jeannette and to my other classmates, I was an indecipherable foreigner, unwilling to assimilate and therefore destined to be alone.

DAY THREE

Morning

Between typing sessions, I've been keeping up my daily skin-care regimen. Baggy cashmere sweatpants may have replaced my custom-tailored suits, but my face still gleams like a nominated actress's cheeks at the Oscars. First comes my cream face wash laced with glycolic acid to annihilate any signs of fine lines, sunspots, and uneven texture. Next is a toner with lactic acid, another exfoliant, to brighten my epidermis and prime it to receive the potent vitamin C serum that I pat on afterward. It's a little oily, that serum, and it smells horrific, like hot dog water, not that I've ever stuck my nose in the belly of a street vendor's cart. That vitamin C destroys free radicals, though, and I can't have those things damaging my complexion. Moisturizer comes after the vitamin C; I use a luscious cream infused with marine algae. Sunblock is the penultimate step, even when I don't leave the house. The final touch is a tightening eye potion, to give the appearance of eight hours of sleep, as I haven't enjoyed eight hours of consecutive sleep since high school.

I am tapping that potion beneath my eyes when I see it. Her toothbrush. It's hot pink with white ribbing and the blue line across its bristles is nearly worn down. It leans against the side of its plastic cup, staring at me, judging me. I don't know how I missed it until now. I guess I've been distracted—by the present or the past, I'm not sure.

Despite the faded blue line, the brush's bristles are perfect, like her face. Small and tidy and immaculately clean. I can remember when I gave her the toothbrush. This was about two years ago now, in 2013. I wrapped it for her, like it was a gift. It was a joke, of course. A toothbrush isn't a present, it's a necessity. And yet it gave me pleasure to offer her this object. It's the only thing of hers in this whole apartment, the lone physical sign that she was ever here.

I pluck her toothbrush out of the cup, hold it an inch from my lips, and try to breathe in her scent. Then I stick it in my mouth.

It tastes like minty paste, of course, and New York City tap water. I swear I taste her, too, as I run those bristles across my teeth. I imagine that the bristles' scratchy roughness is her tongue, that she is licking my mouth clean. At first, sweetness consumes me as I think of her powdery essence, her delicacy, the way she looked at me with her tapered brown eyes. Then I remember her darkness, how she cast me aside and punished me in the worst way possible. All that sweetness on my tongue pickles into something vinegary and sharp. I spit her toothbrush out. I nearly throw it in the trash, but I am not quite ready for that, so I place it back in its cup and rinse my mouth out with cold water.

The eye potion is dry. Its effect is difficult to discern. Bluish dark circles still hang beneath my eyes. Every morning, I tap this stuff on, with a mixture of determination and hope. Hours later, I undo that work with a night of insomnia. I lie in bed and stare at the ceiling as my mind churns and churns on Ellen and Amanda and the Board and the wreckage that my world has become. My life used to sparkle with possibility; now it is unrecognizable, so much so that I can't tell if I still exist. Maybe I don't want my dark circles to disappear. Maybe I need them to stick around. The truth is these dark circles are a symbol of time passing. They're like her toothbrush—a physical sign that I am here.

Caroline Part One

Ambition, not insomnia, was behind the dark circles of my college years. Early 1990s New York was a stark and welcome departure from Paramus. Cafés, bars, and vintage clothing stores were everywhere you looked, their colorful neon signage a beacon of promise. My fellow classmates clomped around in distressed jeans and chunky rubber-soled boots and cropped baby tees, their eyebrows pin thin, their lips clay brown. Minimalism was the skin ideal. Faces were astringent bare. Grunge made a play for attention: flannel tied around waists, layered hair unwashed for days, the edges of eyes dark and tightlined and smudged. You were supposed to be clean and scruffy, to appear like you didn't care, in a way that required considerable effort. Beauty and fashion embodied many contradictions.

Washington Square was a study in contrasts, too. It was a hub of caffeinated meetups and clandestine beer-sipping from brown paper bags that clashed with the verdancy of its vegetation, the gentle trickle of its central fountain. On any given walk, you could hear birds chirping and hungover teenagers groaning. Romance and seediness commingled in a way that I have never found in any other city.

To my underdeveloped brain, the strain of danger only amplified the city's illicit allure.

That first semester of college, I didn't have time to loll around Washington Square. I was too busy juggling boring Econ and the Art of Communication classes with my Macy's job. The store was an easy subway ride from NYU's campus. I would exit the station and emerge into Herald Square, a blunt triangle of urban real estate overwhelmed with pedestrians. Men and women in suits, some of them clutching briefcases, strode toward their office buildings. Unlike in Paramus, where everyone strolled with purposeful leisure, a sense that they didn't have anywhere else to be, in New York people sprinted, like metal balls shot out of a cannon. Within weeks of moving to New York, I, too, could sideswipe, tail, and cut off slower pedestrians like a veteran.

A billboard faced Macy's when I first started working there. It featured a blond, blue-eyed woman and an African American woman with short hair holding an Asian baby, the three of them seemingly naked and wrapped in a pink-and-green blanket. I would stare at this fashion brand's ad and wonder about the story behind this trio. The two women looked directly at the camera. Their gazes were unapologetic, almost challenging, as though daring passersby to question their arrangement.

The implied intimacy between these women gave me hope. Fashion campaigns are inherently aspirational, after all. The racial dynamics, though, confused me. A white woman and an African American woman with an Asian baby—how would that happen? Interracial couples were still not common, let alone a same-sex interracial couple with a baby of a third race. The people around me in New York were certainly more diverse than in Paramus, but this ad seemed to take things beyond the point of possibility.

One morning at work, I was washing some makeup brushes with

baby shampoo, caressing their wet, sudsy bristles before placing them, one at a time, on a towel I had laid out as a drying surface. Crystal, the ringleader of my coworkers, was at another station in our area talking a brassy redhead into purchasing a trio of eye shadows that would make her look possessed. As I glanced up from my makeshift drying situation, I locked eyes, momentarily, with a woman striding through the bustling aisles and directly toward my counter. She had thick, straight hair the color of mahogany and smooth, tan skin that gleamed with health. If you'd given me a pushpin and asked me to stick it on a globe to signify her place of origin, I likely would have dumped it somewhere in the Pacific Ocean and prayed it made landfall.

As she drew nearer, I ran my hands down the sides of my pencil skirt, flattening them instinctively. There was an involuntary tightening in my rib cage, like something was pushing to escape and I was forced to hold it in. This woman's face was unlined, but her bearing gestured at a maturity well beyond youth. She was directly in front of me now, the counter the only barrier between us. Her lips parted in a playful smile and her light brown eyes bore into me.

"Maxine, is it?" she said, glancing at my name tag, which was pinned mere inches from my right nipple.

"Yes," I practically stuttered.

She smiled again at my obvious nervousness. Her lips were pillowy. I could barely tear my eyes from them.

"I was hoping you could help me. I'm in desperate need of another one of these." She extended one of the brand's lipstick tubes in my direction.

I leaned closer to read the label.

"Satin Persuasion. That's one of our most popular ones."

"Is it? That's a shame. I thought I was too original to be popular."

The exchange between Ted and Christine from senior year flickered before me. Sexual innuendo, I had learned, was the best way to convince a customer of her beauty. I didn't have the freedom Ted did to be so blatant with women, not unless I was certain my words would be well received, and experience suggested they wouldn't be.

I offered this customer a tentative grin. "I'm sure you're very original."

"How kind of you to say."

The woman scanned my torso and hips and I warmed under her attention. Beads of sweat dotted my hairline.

"Let me get that lipstick for you, I'll be right back."

I crouched down to search through the cabinet. Lipstick was a reliable bestseller for every line. It was a staple for most women that defied economic downturns and flash-in-the-pan trends. One of the top brands in recent memory had started with only ten lipsticks; two years later it was everywhere. I hadn't been exaggerating Satin Persuasion's popularity. Its rust-brown color hit a sweet spot between neutral and smoldering, and it had been a nonstop hit since it was released a couple of years back. We were out, of course; we could barely keep it in stock. I stood up empty-handed.

"I'm really sorry," I said. "We don't have any left. If you want to give me your name and number, I'd be happy to call you when more come in."

"That would be great."

I handed her a pad and pen and watched her write her information. She held the pen delicately but firmly. I wondered what that same grip could do to my body.

"Here you go."

Caroline Walters. That didn't help my pushpin placement one bit.

"Thanks for your help, Maxine."

"Max," I said. "People call me Max."

"Do they? Well, Max, feel free to use that number to call me when you get it in—or even before then."

Had I heard her correctly? Sensing my confusion, she continued, "Since you couldn't take care of my initial request, not that it's your fault, perhaps you could make it up to me with a drink. On me."

A tickle began in the depths of my stomach and spread to the rest of my organs. My field of vision blurred at the edges. It was as if someone else had wrested control of my body's remote and was pressing random buttons with glee. Get ahold of yourself, Max, I thought. This woman wants to have a drink with you.

"That sounds nice," I said, intent on understatement.

"How about tomorrow?" Caroline asked. "Unless you have plans with someone else."

The next day was Friday. I usually spent those evenings sipping grain alcohol on the fringe of some dorm party. These forays always ended early, either with me in my twin bed beside Jeannette's empty one or worse, in the hallway, a pink ribbon tied around our doorknob. My only sexual experience was in the vivid onanistic fantasies that had begun in my teens. Here I had a real-live woman beyond my most hyperbolic imaginings asking me for a drink. I did not have plans with anyone.

"I'm free. Just let me know where and when."

"The bar at the Plaza Hotel, eight p.m."

"See you there."

Caroline flashed her full-lipped smile and strode away.

I wasn't sure if Caroline's overture had been a proper come-on or merely an act of politeness. Perhaps she had taken pity on my inadequate salesmanship. Luckily, Crystal cleared up any uncertainty. She sidled over, glanced pointedly in the direction in which Caroline had walked, then turned back to me.

"Daddy got you this job, right?"

"Excuse me?" I said.

"My boss told me we hired you because your dad called in a favor. What is he, some corner office dude?"

"He's an accountant," I said.

"An accountant." Crystal looked me dead in the eye. "Does Daddy the accountant know his darling girl is a dyke?"

Needles of cold pricked my skin.

"Don't worry, I won't tell," she continued, and smirked at my lack of reply. "So long as you don't give me a reason to."

Then she brushed past me, purposely butting my shoulder.

People in my adult life—straight people—have asked me, "Why aren't you out professionally? It's 2015. Who cares?" A lot of people still care, in fact. And they certainly cared back then. They cared enough to threaten you with discrimination or much, much worse. That fashion ad I walked by every morning wasn't aspirational—it was delusional. While I would never change my sexuality, I can't pretend that it hasn't been a liability and I refuse to make myself vulnerable to others. Crystal taught me that crucial lesson at a young age: if you don't want to get punched, don't lower your fists.

The way I saw it, Crystal's remark gave me two choices. I could stick around and be her sucker or I could quit. Later that day, I called my dad from the phone in my dorm room to tell him the news.

"Maxine, I pulled real strings to get you that job. I can't believe you quit. How does that make me look?"

I twirled the gray cord of the phone's handset around my left wrist so tightly, it started to cut off the circulation to my hand.

"I know, Dad. I'm really sorry."

"Are you at least going to tell me why?"

My left hand was getting paler and paler. It was starting to lose feeling. I wished I could tell him the truth, that my coworker had discovered my liability and threatened me with it. If I told him, her threat would lose its power.

I remembered that middle school meal at the Automat, how my mother's disgust had chased away those two women while my dad sat there silent. Had his wordlessness been a form of agreement with my mother? Or had it been an unspoken disapproval of her reaction?

"It wasn't the right fit," I said, employing a phrase I had once overheard my mother say to my father as explanation for ditching his coworker's wife's bridge club.

"You're nineteen. That's not for you to decide."

"I promise I'll find another job."

"Maxine, if you're serious about this whole beauty thing, then act like you're serious about it. I'm giving you a chance to see how it's done working for the best brand in the world."

The best brand in the world that couldn't make foundation look good on fifty percent of the women who walked into Macy's. Some experts they were.

"I know. I'm sorry."

A few more rounds of apology later, my dad and I said our good-byes. I unwound the cord from my wrist and watched as my flaccid hand turned pink with the rush of fresh blood.

The evening of my drinks with Caroline, I contemplated my reflection in the dorm room mirror. It was barely tall and wide enough to frame my entire body: long, pale legs; bony, narrow hips; a chest that couldn't fill out an A-cup bra. I didn't know much about New York's upper echelons back then, still I was wise enough to realize that wearing jeans to the Plaza Hotel was not a great idea. I had one black dress with me. My mother had purchased it over the summer and thrown it into my suitcase for school, so I had "something to wear on a date with a nice boy," as she had put it. Well, I was going to wear it on what appeared to be a date, so I guess I was meeting her halfway.

The dress was modest in length. It hit an inch above my kneecaps. The neckline swooped down beneath my clavicle and the arms had cap sleeves. It was nothing I ever would have chosen for myself, but it was the best I could do under the circumstances.

My hair had darkened in young adulthood to an ashy-blond shade that played off the depth of my brown eyes. I had added light drama with a thin line of chocolate next to my upper and lower lashes that I smudged with a cotton swab. I'd rubbed a peachy lipstick into my cheeks and had coated my lips with a clear balm before daubing a bit of the same lipstick on them. Then I'd blotted my lips lightly with a tissue to make the color appear like it had partially worn off.

One afternoon, I had caught some warm whiffs of a girl in my Econ class and had asked her what she was wearing. She had pointed me in the direction of a little shop in the Village that sold essential oils. I had purchased a vial of musk, a few drops of which I dotted behind my ears and on my neck. My skin tingled beneath the fragrant oil.

I rode the subway up from Washington Square and arrived at the Plaza Hotel ten minutes early. The bar's absurdly wealthy patrons were too intimidating, so I lurked outside near the entrance. A light November breeze raised the hairs on my arms, or maybe it was the prospect of seeing Caroline. It occurred to me then that she had no idea how old I was. Because of my height and the way I carried myself, I was often mistaken for someone in her mid-twenties. I didn't know what I would do if the bar's servers carded me.

Caroline materialized at exactly 8 p.m. If possible, she was even more stunning than she had been the previous afternoon. A black, satiny camisole with a lace inset at the bust clung to her torso. Slim black cigarette pants with sharp creases down the front were crisp on her legs. Her shiny hair was pulled back into a low ponytail.

"How polite of you to wait outside for me," she said.

"I wasn't sure where you'd want to sit," I tried.

With a wry smile, she pulled the door open.

"You look amazing, by the way," she whispered as she walked into the bar ahead of me. A lush, floral scent trailed in her wake.

Two rounds of double whiskeys later, we were at Caroline's sprawling Flatiron District loft and she was telling me, again, how amazing I looked as she unzipped me out of my black dress, kissed me deeply, and ran her hands up the insides of my thighs. By the time her hands reached their intended destination, my skin screamed with anticipation. She maneuvered me across her dark apartment, navigating around dining chairs and sofas, then pushed me onto her bed, removed my underwear, and took my virginity along with it.

Afterward, we lay sprawled on Caroline's bed. Her sheets were as powdery soft as the skin on the small of her back, whose mesmerizing curve I ran my fingers across, back and forth, back and forth like a pendulum. In the flickering light from the votive candles Caroline had lit, her skin had the rich glow of polished wood.

"What are you?" I asked.

Caroline lay on her stomach, her small head resting on a pillow facing me. At my question, she propped herself up on her forearms. Her lower back muscles clenched beneath my fingers and I withdrew my hand.

"What am I?" she parroted back at me.

"Yeah, where are you from?"

"I told you at drinks. I grew up in the Bay Area."

"That's not what I mean. Like, your parents. Where are they from?"

"They're also from California. Why do you want to know?"

"I've never seen anyone like you before. I was curious. I'm sorry."

The hard pinpricks of Caroline's eyes began to soften.

"Curiosity is fine. Asking someone what they are isn't."

"I get it."

"No, you don't. But you're young. There's still hope."

"How did you know to ask me out?"

"What do you mean?"

"How did you know I would be receptive?"

Caroline smiled. "Ah," she said. "It was instinct honed by many years of experience. You learn to see the signs."

"What signs?"

"They're in the ether. The way someone looks at you. The charge in the air when you speak to each other. You'll get a feel for it. It's something you figure out on your own," she said as she patted my arm. "What's your deal anyway? Besides working at Macy's."

The bar's server never checked my ID. Classy places were the easiest cons for underage drinkers because their staff were so drilled in hospitality, they wouldn't bother guests with unseemly questions. Caroline had no inkling that I was a student.

"I quit yesterday, after you left."

"Not the right fit?"

"Exactly."

Caroline sank back down into the pillow and turned onto her side. Her nipples were about three shades darker than mine.

"What's next?"

I shifted closer to her and flipped onto my side, too, so that our bodies faced each other, though mine was a few inches longer.

"I worked as a freelance makeup artist before I started at Macy's." I'd overheard a customer at Macy's refer to themselves as "freelance" in conversation. It seemed an appropriately vague and uncontestable term.

Caroline reached across the inches of sheets that separated us and began to stroke the side of my waist.

"Were you any good?"

I leaned my face into hers like I was going in for a kiss, then stopped an inch from her lips.

"I'm the best there is."

She glanced at my lips expectantly. When I failed to close the gap between us, she looked me straight in the eyes, like she had a day earlier across the blinding counters of the Macy's beauty department.

"Show me what you've got."

Caroline Part Two

Some of my career's biggest moments originated in bed. Take the morning after that first night with Caroline, when I did her makeup before work. Caroline hardly needed anything, she was that naturally stunning, more so after a night of hot sex. I seated her on an ottoman in her bathroom. A ring of bulbs surrounded the mirror above the sink; the heat radiating from them brought me back to the Macy's cosmetics floor.

I had already examined Caroline's face in detail when I woke beside her. Caroline's skin was unlined. Her undertones were practically solar. I had never made up anyone with skin like hers, in color or texture. For the first time, I was at a momentary loss to improve upon nature.

Caroline smirked at my hesitation.

"What's the matter—nerves?" She ran an elegant finger down the front of my torso. "If you're not planning to do anything, I can think of a better way to use this time . . ."

I gripped her hand and removed it from my torso. Though my insides twisted in response to her overture, I would not be deterred.

"You're stunning, you know that," I said. Caroline smiled. "But things can always be better."

Caroline's personal makeup stash was laid out on her bathroom counter. A collection of well-used brushes filled a plastic cup. I pushed the cup away. I hated the sharp lines and heavy application that brushes imparted. A face wasn't a literal canvas; I had evolved my thinking since middle school. Faces were attached to people. The makeup needed to sink into the skin, to blend into seamless oblivion, not unlike the melding of two bodies in a bed. Tools got in the way.

"You're not going to use those?" Caroline asked.

"I prefer my fingers," I replied.

"I bet you do," she said. "But we're talking about makeup. I don't want to look like a clown when you're done."

"Trust me," I told her. "I know what I'm doing."

I prepped her face with a light moisturizer. Then I swiped an extra dollop from the jar to mix with her concealer. There were no creases on her perfect face, but faint crescents of darkness hung beneath her eyes. I patted the concealer across them and underneath her nose and on the center of her forehead and chin. Blended with the moisturizer, it had the plush texture of a toasted marshmallow. I plucked two lipsticks, one a rose berry, the other a rich carnelian, and mixed them on the back of Caroline's hand to see their effect. Then I swiped their blunted ends across the apples of her cheeks and rubbed until they appeared feverish.

Highlighters hadn't become mainstream. Caroline had a pale iridescent eye shadow powder in her arsenal. I tapped it lightly across her brow bone and the tops of her cheeks. Her face was flushed and gleaming, like she had emerged from a lava hot spring.

Caroline was impressed.

"How did you get the concealer to disappear like that?" she said.

She gave me a long kiss and off to her real estate job she went. I lingered at Caroline's vanity, luxuriating in the success of the past twelve hours: I had lost my virginity to a beautiful woman, then I had enhanced her beauty. Days earlier, this happiness would have been unimaginable. It was a rare moment when reality transcended my most penetrating fantasies. I was as close to divinity as I ever managed. If only I had known how fleeting it would be.

Thanks to that morning-after maquillage, Caroline shared my name with a few of her fancy friends, who attended galas and other events for which they needed their makeup done. It was like my Paramus business all over again, except now I trekked to Park Avenue penthouses and Gramercy Park brownstones to caress the faces of millionaires' wives. There was Alexis, a thirty-something married to an M&A titan. She had an addiction to dark smoky eyes and Russian vodka. I met her halfway, tightlining her eyes with a gray pencil and finishing them with a matching powder that cloaked her gaze in a sexy smog. She paid me in cash and shots of Stoli straight from the freezer. Lauren was in her early fifties but appeared younger thanks to her dermatologist and off-label skin injections. She lived on lower Fifth Avenue, near my Washington Square dorm. Until she met me, her go-to evening move was a red lipstick that left her mouth like an open wound. I pulled her back from that ledge with a blackberry gloss that gave her face the ripeness of a late-summer day. I made Misty's and Dahlia's skin shine like polished silver, and I basted Tina's pout like it was a porterhouse steak.

I informed my parents that I would not replace the Macy's gig with another service-sector position. My dad took this with a mix of resignation and general sadness.

"Maxine," he sighed into the phone a few weeks after my fateful first date with Caroline. "How do you expect anyone to take you seriously when you're running around town doing makeup in people's apartments like it's a middle school slumber party?"

If only there were sleepovers involved.

"I'm making more money than I did at Macy's."

"It's not just about money."

"Says the accountant."

"There is no trajectory in what you're doing. It's a dead end. At Macy's, you get promoted to manager, then you move up to corporate . . . there's somewhere for you to go."

I was sitting on my twin bed, playing with the ragged corner of my woven comforter.

"Maybe I don't want to go anywhere. This is where I'm supposed to be."

My dad sighed deeply again.

"I want you to be secure in the long term. I can't afford to help you as an adult."

A piece of wool thread broke loose from the comforter's corner. I tugged at it repeatedly.

"I know, Dad. I want to be happy. Besides, some of these women are really wealthy. They could help me with a next step down the line."

Caroline's acquaintances were loaded. I'd walk into their five-bedroom apartments for families of three, and I wouldn't know where to look. They had living rooms, dining rooms, family rooms, and libraries, each chamber leading into the next to the point where you wondered if their homes had secret passageways to other countries. Their furniture was either very modern, all boxy angles and chilly materials, or comprised of antiques, scuffed but shiny, passed down through decades of family wealth. The art on their walls was by names that also filled the Museum of Modern Art and the Whitney Museum. There was one woman who had a famous Cubist work hanging casually in her entryway the way most people have coatracks in their foyers. *A souvenir from a trip to Paris*, she offered when she noticed me staring at the painting. *They ran out of mini Eiffel Tow-*

ers? I replied. That was the last time I made a joke about a client's wealth.

I learned other things, too, from these women. Alexis attended most of her events without her M&A husband. He was always at the office or traveling or doing god knows what. She had a retinue of strapping young men, most of whom I assumed were gay based on their availability and fashion sense. Alexis rotated between these men as dates. Straight women seemed much more comfortable with gay men than they did with gay women, I noted.

After the makeup was done, I often assisted my clients as they got dressed. Zipped them into their strapless gowns. Carried the trains of their dresses. Helped them into the cars waiting downstairs. Unlike Alexis's spouse, Lauren's husband acted as her date. I say "acted" because the role didn't seem to come naturally to him. He always slammed the door when he returned home, usually while I was mid-process. Lauren was charming, an easy conversationalist. She'd regale me with anecdotes from her latest charity board meetings or ladies' lunches. Whenever Lauren's husband slammed the door, her neck would stiffen and her posture would hunch over. Sometimes he'd stomp into the room, interrupt her, and demand to see what she was wearing.

"Not that one," he'd snap nearly every time. "Are you crazy? Important people will be there."

Lauren would flinch and offer other options until her husband gave his approval. He'd leave. I'd return to my work. Neither Lauren nor I would acknowledge what had transpired. All those big, beautiful rooms in her apartment were empty of affection or even mutual respect. I began to believe that the immense privilege of these women came at a heavy cost. It was a price I promised myself I would never pay.

Caroline didn't tell me how she explained our relationship to my new clients and I didn't ask. I assumed she told these women that she had met me through her job or while out one night. Obviously, I knew enough not to hint at anything more intimate than a superficial friendship between us. These women wouldn't have suspected a thing. Their minds weren't sophisticated enough to consider that a woman could look one way and swing in the other direction. Caroline was as feminine as they came; even in the pantsuits she occasionally wore, she exuded a doll-like prettiness. While my long, shapeless lines and angular features were far more androgynous, my blondness had always softened my tougher edges, like steamed milk atop a bitter, dark espresso.

I don't say this to boast. It's a fact. Appearances matter and mine, specifically, gave me a cover that many others don't have. I'm not proud of this, but I'm not going to shrink in shame over it either. A straight woman can enjoy her feminine beauty. I had to wear mine like hammered armor.

I continued to see Caroline multiple times a week for the rest of freshman year. During the summer break, I returned to Paramus and acquiesced to a part-time Macy's makeup job to appease my dad. Unfortunately, Linda was no longer there. She had moved to Pennsylvania with a new boyfriend, according to another woman. Caroline and I didn't speak much that summer. I told her that I was taking time off to be with my family; most of my clients traveled to Europe or to their country houses for the summer. I had a grandmother who wasn't doing well or something like that. Occasionally, I'd call her at the office from a GSP pay phone on a lunch break. We'd exchange some perfunctory words and she'd ask about my grandmother, but after the fourth stilted conversation, she told me to just call her when I was back in New York. Sophomore year started and we resumed our rendezvous.

I'm not sure if what we had could be termed a relationship. I only saw her after hours, at times and places she chose. Then we would head to her loft, where I would spend the night. She never asked about my apartment; I didn't offer up details of my own. It was like she knew, implicitly, that I was hiding something, beyond the same thing we were both hiding to the outside world, and she either didn't care or didn't want to know. I always left her apartment first thing in the morning, sometimes before she woke, to avoid any awkward run-ins with neighbors. We never went out with her friends and I didn't introduce her to anyone from NYU.

The second semester of my sophomore year, Caroline and I were at a dark, divey bar in the East Village on one of our nights out. When it came to the locales for our meetups, Caroline's taste ran the full gamut from posh elegance to gritty realism and she hardly ever repeated a place. She never told me why, but I figured it was out of discretion. We were careful never to act affectionately in public beyond the bare-minimum hugs and single-cheek kisses permitted to platonic women.

She and I sat in a back booth of this establishment. The benches and tables were all wood that had seen better days, and that past patrons had tattooed with their initials and witty observations: *Alex sucks!* for example. Caroline sipped a whiskey neat. I had a vodka and soda with lime. Caroline was in a weird mood. She kept making snippy comments about things I said. It was almost like we were an actual couple. She was in the middle of telling me about a ridiculous Tribeca loft she was trying to sell for millions of dollars—"The apartment is major, but who the hell wants to live in *Tribeca*?"—when Carl, this tall, scrawny dude from my Macro class wobbled up to our booth.

"Max? That you?"

It had been over a year since I'd started seeing Caroline. Initially, I had worried that any time we ventured within a twenty-block radius of NYU, we would run into people I knew. We never had and as a result, I had lowered my guard.

"Carl, hey."

Carl could barely stand still. He swayed gracelessly. His eyes were watery. College boys and their nonexistent tolerance levels. This worked to my advantage. I could discount anything incriminating he said based on his obvious inebriation.

"What are you doing here?" he groaned.

"Having a drink with a friend." I glanced at Caroline, whose face bore an expression of utter disdain. "Maybe you want to go home? I could help you get a cab." I needed to get him away from Caroline, stat.

"I'm fiiine," he sang. "Just wanted to see if it was you."

Carl turned and made like he was going to stumble back to the bar. Just when I thought I had skidded through this train wreck unscathed, he offered his parting words.

"Seeee you in class."

My spine went cold. No amount of intoxication could explain away that comment. My mind raced to concoct a justification for Carl. Perhaps I was taking a night class somewhere. Oh wait, that wouldn't work. Between Caroline and my makeup clients, my evenings were entirely booked, something Caroline knew. Besides, Carl, with his wiry limbs and juvenile face, practically screamed *I'm underage! Card me!*

Caroline stared hard at me, then looked off toward some future horizon only she could see as she took a long, deep sip of her whiskey. This only made things worse. Cold fear radiated from my spine to my arms, neck, and face. Finally, she turned her gaze back to me.

"How old are you?" she asked calmly.

Beneath the table, I gripped my thigh with my hand so tightly the crescent-shaped marks from my nails were still visible after I left the bar.

"Twenty."

"Fuck. You're in college?"

"NYU."

"So you're not a 'freelance makeup artist'?"

"I am now."

"And before—you lied?"

"I omitted some details."

Caroline glared at me pointedly.

"I *was* a makeup artist. Back in Paramus. I ran a business in high school."

"Doing what, children's parties?"

I sat up straighter at that.

"It was for girls who were going on dates. I had a full operation until I was forced to end it."

Elbows resting on the table, Caroline cupped her forehead in her hands.

"If those women find out you're only twenty, they'll kill me. You can't tell anyone."

"It's safe to say I know how to keep a secret," I noted.

Caroline took her head from her hands.

"This can't happen anymore," she said, lowering her voice. "It's bad enough sneaking around; now I have to worry people will think I'm a pedophile, too? No way."

Emptiness replaced that cold fear. Caroline was dumping me. I didn't raise my voice or cry. We were in public. I couldn't allow myself to feel the pain of this break, not now. I would grieve later when the time was right. When Caroline and her beautiful face weren't sitting across from me, lacquered in my betrayal.

"Fine," I said. "How about a proper farewell?"

Caroline complied. What can I say, even when they're furious at me, women can't turn me down. At five the next morning, I left Caroline's apartment for the last time. I never saw her again. I no longer needed her to pass my name around for makeup gigs. My clients did that for me. I had a wait list, thanks in part to my below-market prices. Caroline never breathed a word of her revelation to her acquaintances. It would have reflected poorly on her, sure, but I also like to believe that she did it out of respect for my talent.

As I trudged home to Washington Square, down the long, quiet stretch of lower Fifth Avenue, I was surprised by the hollowness of my stomach. I've never been one for waterworks, but I expected some repressed feelings of loss from the previous night to overwhelm me. Caroline was the closest I had ever had to a girlfriend. In many ways, she still is. I avoided the subway on my final walk of shame, anticipating the need for a private, teary-eyed moment. It was an unnecessary precaution: there was nothing except the empty reverberations in my lower abdomen.

I had never allowed Caroline close enough, emotionally, to leave a mark. She hadn't known how old I was or what I was studying in school, or that I went to school. She knew exactly where to put her fingers, how quickly to move them, and in what sequence of motions to make my insides explode. Even with a map of my brain in hand, she couldn't have pointed to the source of my deepest hopes and fears. I don't know that I would have been able to point there either. I had assumed that physical intimacy brought emotional connection with it, like a complimentary gift with purchase. It took me many years, far more than I care to admit, to understand that my natural capacity for compartmentalization was limitless.

Looking back on this moment, my reaction seems so obvious. Of course I did everything I could to mute the sadness of losing the first gay woman I had dated. If I had permitted myself to feel that sorrow, it would have annihilated me. A person like me—a woman like me—couldn't indulge in falling apart. Oversized emotional reactions are a luxury not afforded to those with secrets to keep and places to be.

I quickly filled the black hole of Caroline's absence with more bookings. There were a few women I saw on a biweekly basis, especially during the so-called season. I had thought "seasons" referred to changes in natural growth cycles, but among a certain echelon of New York, they were dictated by the whims of charity galas and their accompanying guest lists.

Ellen Atkins was a favorite regular client. She lived on Park Avenue in the upper Seventies. Ellen's apartment was on a high floor, a sign of the owner's rank in the residential pecking order, she informed me, with 180-degree views up and down Park Avenue's manicured lanes. Ellen had a scented-candle business, named ERA for her initials. This meant she rarely worked. She retained a studio-sized office somewhere in Midtown and a couple of times a month, when it was convenient—i.e., she was shopping at Henri Bendel and was "in the area"—she'd visit the poor underpaid assistant she kept locked up there "doing inventory" to see how things were progressing.

I didn't understand, at first, why Ellen bothered with this business; it wasn't like she was a criminal who required a front for her activities. For me, work had always been a necessity and a calling—I worked because I couldn't fathom doing anything else with my life. Ellen's husband, Donald, made a killing with a job in finance. They didn't need extra income, not that ERA candles did anything for their balance sheets.

Ellen and her husband spent a nice chunk of their considerable fortune on philanthropy. I was up at her apartment every other week, sometimes three times a week at the season's peak, to prep her for a night at a five-star hotel toasting ovarian cancer research or at a dilapidated bank-turned-events-space celebrating a boys-and-girls club for underprivileged children.

To go by the timelines of the anecdotes she shared with me Ellen was in her early fifties. Her skin was more olive than mine, thanks to some Mediterranean DNA from a few generations back. She exfoliated her skin into oblivion with prescription Retin-A, such that her face had the shiny appearance of a recently waxed floor. Her eyes were golden hazel. Her hair was in a dark brown bob, the front chunk of which had gone gray. Ahead of her time, Ellen refused to dye it; this silvery streak gave her otherwise traditional attractiveness an air of rebellion.

One evening, I was patting shimmery gray eye shadow into the creases of Ellen's eyes. We were in her boudoir, a room that extended off the master bedroom and was the size of many studio apartments. The walls were covered in a burgundy toile de Jouy and Ellen was seated on a striped velvet ottoman. The room smelled of the tuberose and pink peppercorn emanating from an ERA candle.

Donald entered the boudoir. He was tall and lanky with bushy eyebrows. His dark hair was trimmed in a crew cut, and he wore a tuxedo.

"Almost ready?" he asked.

"Nearly," said Ellen. "You look good."

"It smells nice in here. One of your candles?"

"Of course," said Ellen.

"Where were you when I tried you at two? I needed the name of that restaurant for a client. I hate when I get the answering machine."

"I was at the office. I forgot to check the messages when I was home."

This was a lie. Ellen had told me she spent the entire afternoon at the salon, chatting with friends between a trim and a blowout. Most of my clients went to the hair salon the afternoon of their events.

Donald's eyebrows rose on his forehead. "At the office—really? Aren't you industrious. Do I need to get you a home secretary or something?" He chuckled. Ellen's face tightened. "I'm surprised you found anything to do there."

"ERA is doing just fine."

"Since when do you settle for fine? Everything you do reflects on me."

"You mean us."

"I ran into Dave at the club. He was bragging that Bonnie's new jewelry collection is going to be in next month's *Vogue*. They might even do a story on their apartment next year. It's been a while since you were in *Vogue*."

"You know Bonnie. She probably bullied the editor into the placement. It isn't even real," said Ellen. She shook her head and my eye-shadow-covered finger swiped across her temple. I dabbed at her forehead with makeup remover and began to redo her eyes.

"Real is beside the point. It looks good," said Donald. "Dave was so smug. I wish I could have boasted about you to shut him up."

"You could have mentioned ERA."

"What would I have said?" Donald glanced at his watch. "We need to leave in ten minutes."

He exited the boudoir, never acknowledging my presence.

Ellen stared at me. "I do work on the candles," she said. "Just not today. Men don't understand how much effort goes into maintaining appearances. That reflects on him, too."

I nodded like I understood.

"ERA made a nice splash when I first started. I had a feature in *Vogue*. Bergdorf carried us for a time. Then our social lives became so busy. I joined those boards. There's always a party Donald needs me to attend to promote his image. The candles weren't a priority. You understand."

I nodded again.

"He really wants me to have 'a thing.' Bonnie has her jewelry. Ashley does custom sweaters. It isn't enough these days to run a household and a schedule and be a supportive wife."

The more time I spent in Ellen's world the more I realized that work for her and her cohorts was a matter of legitimacy. It made their lives appear substantive in a way that spending money you didn't earn never does. Women's empowerment hadn't positively impacted her daily duties or her long-term goals; it had burdened her with the expectation that she use her time for something other than party planning. Feminism had made her guilty. Hence the candles.

In my junior year of college, I began mixing my own makeup concoctions. At first I blended an assortment of cheaper drugstore products I purchased to maximize my profits, then packed them into plastic watercolor palettes from an art supply store and toted them around to my clients. I didn't want those high-end women knowing that I was rubbing a mélange of ninety-nine-cent lipsticks on the cheeks that they spent thousands of dollars annually moisturizing and brightening.

Soon my experimentation took me beyond the drugstore cosmetics aisle into the realm of natural foods. I became obsessed with re-creating my childhood cherry Popsicle look by mimicking artists who made watercolor paints from flowers and fruits. I purchased an illegal hot plate for my dorm—a single now, thank god—and spent hours boiling and straining concoctions of dried roses, violets, cranberries, and raspberries mixed with essential oils and water. Sure, they weren't professional, but I figured if they originated from edible plants, they wouldn't poison my clients.

By the second semester of my junior year, Ellen's desire for "a thing," however manufactured, had grown more potent. I was at her apartment ahead of a fundraiser in Central Park. She was on the organizing committee and, as such, she wanted a little extra oomph. For her starring role, Ellen had selected an emerald matte jersey gown. We had agreed on a striking, gold-flecked smoky eye and bronze tones on her cheeks and lips.

I pulled out one of my custom palettes and blended three different concealers to achieve the muted golden-green cast of Ellen's skin. Normally, she paid little attention to my ministrations. She was too busy chatting about her latest ERA candle scent or her friend's ghastly table manners. On this evening, Ellen wore a more observational air.

"What is that?" she asked, staring at my palette and then at my finger.

"My own mix. So it matches your skin better."

"You buy a bunch all from one brand and blend them?"

"They're from a few different companies, actually."

"Which ones?"

I held my index finger over my closed mouth to telegraph my refusal to answer.

Ellen chortled.

"Fine. Why a bunch of different ones?"

"To get the texture I want. Some are too heavy; some are too thin."

"I see." Ellen glanced at a series of small, clear bottles, holding an ombré of petal pinks and persimmons and burgundies, that I had lined up on her marble counter. "I thought we agreed on a neutral lip?"

"We did." My throat tightened at her seeming distrust. "Don't worry."

"I'm not worried, just curious. For some reason, I never noticed your whole tool kit until now."

Because you're usually too busy talking about yourself, I thought, but didn't say. I never minded her chitchat; it was entertaining to hear about a reality so far removed from my own.

I indicated one of the bottles with a liquid the color of watered-down cherry.

"I'm going to use that as a base underneath some beige and bronze lipsticks to bring some coolness."

"What is it?"

I picked up the bottle and shook it, then twisted the top off. Attached to the inside was a small brush. I had been repurposing empty nail polish bottles from girls at school as vessels for my dyes, cleaning them aggressively with nail polish remover, followed by hot water and soap, and then rinsing them with rubbing alcohol. I stroked the bristles across the underside of my left wrist. They left a transparent trail of cool cherry behind them.

"I'm using this on your cheeks, too," I said, flashing Ellen my under wrist.

Ellen gripped my wrist with her strong, bony fingers and rotated it to see the effect beneath the room's chandeliered light.

"You make this yourself? From scratch?"

"Yes."

"How clever. What gave you the idea?"

"A childhood love of Popsicles, if you can believe it."

A slow smile formed on her face.

"Have you thought about making more of it? Selling it?"

I screwed the cap back onto the bottle and returned it to the counter.

"Where would I get the money?"

"I could pitch it to Donald and be an investor. What do you think?"

My throat tightened again, this time with anticipation. "Where would I sell it?"

"You could start with all your clients. Let the word of mouth build. Get some press coverage. I know every top magazine editor. Maybe a department store might be interested."

A soft tickle brushed its way up my torso.

"You really think I could do that?"

Ellen arched her left brow. I had always envied her ability to do this.

"If you want it and you work hard enough, yes."

Hard work is my strong suit. Some might say it was a piece of my downfall. I am relentless once I identify a goal. It's not like I had an all-consuming social life, then or now, to distract from my tasks. I wanted this, oh yes, I wanted this. The prospect of my own beauty line turned me on even more than Caroline had when we were together. I lusted for what would become Reveal with a brightness that blinded me to everything else in my field of vision, including who Ellen really was.

"I want it," I said, with zero hesitation. "If you're serious about it."

Ellen held her hands out, palms open to the room's crown moldings.

"I'll speak with Donald. Now how about you finish my makeup."

DAY THREE

Evening

When I click out of the document and step away from my laptop I am in a weird mood. There is a strange, blunted edge to everything I do. When I stand up from my chair to get a glass of water from the kitchen, it is like half of me is gone. I seem to walk at an extra-slow pace, as though my movements are not my own. I am extremely tired, so tired I might fall asleep upright. My breaths are coming in so slowly, it is like my lungs can't be bothered to expand and contract.

I consider brewing a pot of very strong coffee. Shock the strangeness out of me. Then I think better of it. Why overstimulate when I can numb myself instead?

I pad over to my bar cart. It's a beauty, all shiny chrome and glass from the 1960s. I picked it up at a vintage store in Chicago a few years ago and had it shipped back to New York. My bar cart is well stocked with eighteen-year-old Scotch, top shelf gin, brandies aplenty. Tonight, I am not interested in something fancy. On the bottom ledge of the cart, a bottle of moonshine languishes. Someone gave it to me and I make it a practice not to toss out alcohol.

I grab the moonshine bottle by its stumpy neck and pour myself a shot. It burns like hell on the way down. And it has an effect. It pierces through the dullness, a bit. This is working, I think. I just needed a kick in the pants. I do another shot. The fruity sweetness coats my tongue and I am either going to vomit or be reborn.

I take a third shot, then amble back to my computer. Into the search engine's blank, expectant space I type: *Caroline Walters.*

It's not an unpopular name. There's a sixty-something poet who lives in Galveston. A twenty-two-year-old Icelandic chanteuse with 423,000 followers on Instagram. A Midwestern bank manager per LinkedIn. A flight attendant for Southwest Airlines, etc., etc. I scroll and scroll, occasionally pausing to walk to the bar cart and pound more liquid fire. Eventually, I find her. She is no longer Walters, goes by Anderson, lives in San Francisco. I guess she got homesick. Has a weekend place in Lake Tahoe, thanks to her venture capitalist husband. So her Instagram feed would suggest.

She has aged like nothing I've seen. Two decades have passed and she looks as lineless and bouncy as a teenage girl's ass. I find a photo from her wedding and zoom in, searching for a sign, some hint in her eye, that this is not what she really wants. That she's performing a role. The husband is okay looking, though with fifty million dollars in his bank account, does it matter? I go in real close on those mesmerizing eyes of hers and I find nothing, not one iota of proof that this is a sham marriage. She looks . . . happy. Maybe Caroline is a better actress than I am.

The prospect of her sincere joy sends me back to the bar cart. After another shot, I set up camp on the floor next to it. The carpet's originally plush wool fibers have worn down to nothing; they feel like stubble against my face. I don't remember what happens after that final shot.

Hours pass and I wake on the living room floor with an apocalyptic pain in my temples. I yearn for the black hole where my heart is supposed to be, the void that prevented me from crying the morning I left Caroline's apartment for good. Nihilism seems preferable to this self-destructive ache.

The path that Caroline followed, that could have been my life. I could have a husband, too, some sandy-haired beard to deflect unwanted attention from my predilection for beautiful women. Technically speaking, I could have a wife, with all the protections that straight people enjoy. Gay marriage became fully legal this past summer—at least until the powers that be rescind their benevolent gift. People act like this offering of a human right will suddenly eradicate the oppression that preceded it. What people don't understand is that if you've spent your whole life being told that you can't have what so many others take for granted, you actively avoid dreaming of that possibility. It's a question of self-preservation. Your palate has been so limited that when the possibility that you have been denied finally becomes a reality, you don't have the ability to savor it. A cherry Popsicle may as well be vinegar on your tongue.

I am attracted to women, and I am obsessed with women feeling attractive. How many other cosmetics entrepreneurs in this world can say that? All the gay men and straight women shilling for their versions of beauty: How many of those people even *like* women, let alone long for them? My sexuality and my artistic vision developed on parallel tracks; it is no coincidence that I started Reveal not long after my affair with Caroline.

The Board and my investors want the fruits of my desire, just not my desire itself. Forget being a consummate outsider: I am a Greek tragedy. Everyone knows how those stories end.

Lust in a Bottle

I miss when the end was too far off to contemplate and beginnings were my only focus. It didn't take long after that evening session at Ellen's to get the ball rolling on Flush, my first product for what would later become Reveal. Patience is not one of Ellen's strengths. She pitched the idea to Donald, "buttered up his ego," as she relayed it to me, about how correct he was that ERA had reached its natural conclusion. Told Donald she'd stumbled upon a great idea for a beauty business whose product would be a game changer. It would have a woman as its face, a female artist-mogul for the dawn of a new century.

Beauty was a big business. Makeup artist–driven brands, in particular, were garnering attention from customers and investors alike. One makeup artist had recently sold her company of neutral cosmetics to a major beauty conglomerate for over seventy million dollars. A different makeup artist had started a line whose cream-blush compacts and recycled-cardboard eye shadow palettes were selling out at cosmetics floors across the country. *Allure*, a magazine devoted exclusively to beauty, was five years old and a cash cow at Condé Nast. The money Donald had been feeding her to keep ERA alive could now go toward this new product. She and Donald would look modern, on trend. Donald would finally have something worth boasting about in his club's locker room.

Donald lapped it up. He praised his wife for her gumption and gave her a sum of initial investment money.

"It's the equivalent of spending the money on good PR," Ellen explained to me.

"Right," I said, unsure how I felt about my product innovation being compared to a public relations campaign for their marriage. But who was I to turn down this opportunity? Ellen had me sign an agreement, drafted by Donald and his lawyers—"to protect our interests"—that promised them a certain percentage of all profits. We were in business.

I skipped classes for a few weeks and pulled strings of all-nighters, mixing up batches of Flush from raw materials I purchased with funds from Ellen's investment. The plan was to do a small trial run of my own concoction before seeking out a formal laboratory. Whereas previously my remedial mixing had relied on boiled dried flowers and fruits for colors, now, I had the money and incentive to create something more potent. I researched other red-tinted cosmetics on the market and found that carmine, which is the cremated corpses of female tropical cochineal beetles, was the common ingredient that accounted for their bright, crimson tints. Carmine was expensive, but I convinced Ellen it would give Flush the necessary oomph to win over customers. A friend of a friend of Ellen's worked in the textile industry, which also uses carmine, and helped us procure a small quantity, enough for the trial run.

Look, I'm going to be frank: I was no chemist. These first batches of Flush were a bit amateur. Was the color exactly what I hoped to achieve? Close enough. Were the proportions identical for every sample I bottled? Unlikely. Was the stuff safe and chemically stable?

Who knows. The beauty industry is notoriously unregulated even when it comes to the biggest, most corporate brands. The FDA doesn't require that cosmetics companies do safety testing; there are no pre-approvals needed before you release a product. If something goes wrong, they have no power to issue a recall. I'm not complaining. This makes my job easier.

As a result, the history of personal care products and cosmetics is littered with ingredients that have caused allergies, illness, and even death in users. Flammable hair sprays. Lead-infused lipstick. Nail polish so toxic it proves cancerous. And don't assume those "clean" and "natural" products are any healthier: the FDA isn't regulating those distinguishers either. Beauty is a risky business for both sellers and customers. Anyway, no one got so much as a mild rash from those initial Flush batches, so I sleep just fine.

The early bottles of Flush needed some labels. I enlisted a girl in my dorm who had a background in graphic design to sketch out a dove-gray logo in a clean sans serif font that read *Flush by Maxine Thomas*. Then I took the template to a copy and printing store and had them produce stacks of labels. I filled a hundred empty nail polish bottles I'd purchased from a wholesale supplier with Flush, slapped on those labels, and distributed the finished product to my clients whenever I saw them for a private session. "A sample of something I'm working on," I told them with a wink. "I want you to be the first to try it. Let me know your thoughts."

They wore their Flush to chicken paillard lunches at French bistros and to rounds of lychee martinis downtown. They dabbed Flush on to drop their kids off at private schools and for doctor appointments on Park Avenue. Their cheeks and lips were lush like a pomegranate's swollen seeds as they had their hair cut and highlighted and blown out at the salon. Their faces shone as they downed double-shot, nonfat, low-foam lattes at their local cafés. Through all this, they fielded comments from friends and fellow parents. *Your skin looks* so *good. Did you get something done?* They smiled knowingly and reached into their designer handbags, pulled out my bottle of Flush, brandished it at the curious parties, and whispered my name and number. *Call Max. She'll hook you up.*

Today, Flush comes in ten different shades; back then, I only offered one version. Ellen encouraged me in that direction.

"Find a color that works on everyone," she implored after I showed her the array of options I had mixed, salmon and peach and tangerine and peony, glittering like rare jewels on her dressing room vanity. "It's easier and more effective to say 'Here is the only thing you need.' One-stop shopping."

"I want to introduce other products down the line," I said. "It's going to be a whole company: Reveal."

Before Flush, makeup was often viewed as armor, something women applied to ready themselves to face the world, to conquer boardrooms and bedrooms, without so much as a pore out of place. Even the so-called no-makeup makeup of the era necessitated a powdery canvas of matte skin that was blended and buffed and color corrected within an inch of its life. It was either that or the grunge aesthetic, whereby skin was bare to the point of nihilism. My products would reject both these options. They wouldn't cover up a woman's natural radiance. They would enhance it. I would create makeup that revealed who a woman really was—in her best light.

There was, for me, an added innuendo to this choice that functioned as a private joke. Revealing something denoted a kind of striptease and I knew exactly which layers to peel off, in the bedroom or otherwise, to achieve a desired effect.

Ellen arched that famous brow. "Reveal. I like it, it's clean, strong. Of course there will be a full line with other categories eventually.

But let's start with one simple message and product that everyone can wrap their heads around—until they beg for more."

There was a fact we overlooked, one that has become more apparent in recent years: that one person's version of "everyone" is too narrow. We are all products of our time. My clients in the late 1990s were predominantly white. Ellen's friends were all white, too. This shaped our perspectives. If I were ideating Flush today, I would likely release two or three shades at the outset.

The original Flush looked like blood. Our culture associates blood with violence—that is *bloodshed*, not blood itself. Blood is the life force rushing through our bodies. It is warmth and heart and, yes, beauty. Blood is desire and Flush was lust in a bottle. It made every woman look like she had a low-grade fever and a high-voltage orgasm.

Within a month, I had a wait list for Flush and I needed inventory—fast. I also had some urgent phone calls from the dean's office at NYU about my slumping grades. There were consequences to spending every waking hour stirring vats of Flush in my dorm's sink, and not just the dirty looks from the other students who shared my bathroom. Ever the magnanimous benefactor, Ellen proposed a solution to the inventory issue.

"It's time for us to enlist a lab and hire someone to mix this stuff up professionally," she told me.

"Sure," I said, "if you're paying."

"Investing, not paying. We should consider a trademark registration, too, for Flush. I'll call my lawyer."

Ellen saw to the minutiae. That was another of my mistakes, relinquishing decision-making to someone I barely knew. I was naive then. Ellen had everything I didn't: money, power, status. I didn't desire her specific circumstances—the husband, the socialite role, the pressure to be a supportive wife with a vanity job—but of course I wanted power. I believed that a woman who had so much while I had so little couldn't possibly harm me. My relationship with Caroline was over, I had no close friends; my vision was everything. Here was Ellen, excited to support my dreams in exchange for the sheen of ambition.

Ellen found a lab, with help from a marketing acquaintance, and I showed them my amateur version of Flush. The chemist warned me it would take time to achieve the result I desired, particularly since Reveal was a tiny upstart low on the food chain of their clients. I told my wait-list names that we were refining the formula and that it would be a while before their Flush arrived. They were vocal about their impatience. Why must they wait so long for their next bottle of Flush? Shouldn't a professional lab speed up the process, not slow it down? Even today, when we release a new product and tell the press that its development took eighteen months, people complain that we're exaggerating to create a more compelling sales narrative.

Well, first there's the months of research devoted to competitors' products, testing them to assess their strengths and weaknesses. Then there's the research of potential raw materials and the brief for the product, which you submit to a lab. There are the multiple initial formulas the lab sends you, all of which you and your employees—not that I had any at this stage—test. You provide feedback to the lab. They tinker. More testing. More feedback. This can go on for months. Even once you have final approved formulas you still have to assess costs, source suppliers of the raw materials, potentially change said raw materials to lower the aforementioned costs before you move to manufacturing. Despite the FDA's lack of regulations, most people will do stability and challenge testing to ensure the product's longevity. There's custom molds and packaging to consider. And there is marketing, PR, customer experience, and training, among other things, once you are up and running. At every step in this process something can and likely will go wrong.

This is all to say that developing Flush—on my own—consumed the rest of my junior and senior years. By the spring semester of senior year, my grades were in shambles, and I had a string of incompletes. A couple of months shy of graduation, I dropped out of college. I had missed too many classes. The only corrective would be to start my semester over in the fall. I had a hot new business on the verge of exploding and a devoted investor. I was ten steps ahead of my fellow students. A college degree was pointless.

I shared this news with my parents in person. They came into the city for dinner at a quiet, understated bistro a few blocks from Union Square, a restaurant Ellen had recommended to me once as the kind of "no-personality personality" downtown watering hole that attracted cultural sophisticates too proud to admit they cared about aesthetics. The only decor came from the framed black-and-white photos of famous intellectuals that hung on the walls. It was the perfect place at which to impress upon my parents the seriousness of my beauty endeavors.

We were seated in the middle of the restaurant's narrow tunnel, next to a column. Our placement meant that servers jostled us constantly. At least twice, I watched a bowl of French onion soup nearly topple off a tray as a passing server whooshed by.

The precarity of our table heightened the spiritual tension. My mother sat beside me, a plate of steamed fish and greens before her. She had convinced the chef that she had a deathly dairy allergy that could only be staved off with spartan food. My father was across from me; his entrée was steak frites, though his frites were nearly untouched in seeming solidarity with my mother. Then there was me: the newly minted college dropout devouring a juicy burger with undisguised glee.

"So what are your plans for the future?" asked my father. We had already exhausted the benign topics of weather and shopping over our mixed salads.

"Any prospects in the engagement department?" my mother added, helpfully. Her winged eyeliner was particularly dramatic that night. She was a few feathery strokes away from taking off into flight.

I daubed at the burger grease on my lip with a napkin and returned the stained linen to my lap.

"Actually, I do have some plans."

My parents' faces perked up, each hoping for their wish to come true.

"I'm starting a business. I've quit college."

I beamed. My mother swallowed her bite of fish. My father gripped the table so tightly, I thought he might break it in half.

"Maxine, dropping out of school is not an option. You need a degree so you can get a job, a *real* job, at a big company," said my father. "No one will hire you without a degree."

"I don't want a job at a big company. I want to focus on my business. Besides, I've missed too many classes; I don't have enough credits to graduate."

"Then you can redo this semester," said my father. He crumpled his napkin and tossed it onto the table. "I'll do anything I can to help you find a position somewhere, after that, if you insist on staying in beauty."

Heat prickled in my throat.

"I don't want to work for another company. My idea is brilliant. Why would I follow someone else when I have my own vision?"

"Maxine, honey," cut in my mother, "I thought we were done with this independent streak of yours. How will you ever attract a husband if you're running a business?"

"Assuming you manage to do that." My father snorted. "Do you know how many businesses fail? Working for a big company is the only way to have any security. You'll go into debt otherwise. How are you going to save for retirement? Have you thought about health insurance? My plan only covers you for three more years."

"You haven't even asked what my business is," I spat out. I grabbed a handful of fries from my father's plate and stuffed them indelicately into my mouth.

"What difference does it make?" my father asked. "Without a college degree, you won't have a safety net. If you can't afford to own a home or see a doctor or open a savings account, your choice of work is meaningless. It may as well be a hobby."

My mother pulled my father's plate out of my reach as she said, "You've had enough."

I wished in that moment to teleport back to my childhood bedtime, when my mother's soft perfume cloaked me in reassurance, not judgment.

"My idea is going to change the world," I announced.

"Every college senior thinks they're going to do great things," said my father. "Most of them won't. I'm trying to help you build a stable life."

"Screw stability. I want to be exceptional."

My parents stared at me in horror. All around us, the sounds of silverware clinking against ceramic and wine coursing into glasses echoed in merriment; at our table, chilled silence reigned.

"If that's how you really feel, fine," said my father. He pushed his chair back and crossed his arms. "Don't expect any financial help from me. You're on your own."

That dinner was the last time I saw my parents for the next few years; their dismissal of my ambition was a betrayal I have never been able to forgive. My career is inseparable from my personal value, and I cannot tolerate slights to either. During the rest of my twenties there would be occasional phone calls from my parents to make sure I was alive. Each time, my father would ask when I was going to come to my senses about work and my mother would inquire about my marital prospects. Eventually, I stopped answering or returning their calls and then the calls ceased altogether.

Later that night, I sat alone on the bed in my dorm room. The school would kick me out in a week. I had no money, no leads on where to go. I picked up the phone and dialed the only number that came to mind.

"Ellen? Sorry to call so late. I have a favor to ask."

I moved into Ellen's blue-and-white-toile guest room, and stayed there for the next three years. Donald put up an initial fight. I overheard them the first evening as I was unpacking clothes from a suitcase into a dresser.

"You can't be serious about letting this woman you barely know move in with us," Donald said sharply.

"This woman we barely know whose business you've invested in," Ellen pointed out.

"The investment is for raw materials, inventory, marketing. Not housing," said Donald.

"Think of it this way: we're saving on office space. Maybe you can deduct the guest room as a business expense."

"What are you—a tax attorney?" But Donald didn't push back.

To her credit, Ellen never dug around for the truth behind my need for immediate, free lodging. She accepted my explanation—an untenable roommate situation, massive credit card debt—at face value. Or rather, she accepted it for what it clearly was: a flimsy excuse.

"Here's a set of keys," Ellen said when she came into the guest room where I was folding clothes and tucking them into an antique wooden dresser. The brass set she handed me had more weight than I expected. "Not that you'll need them; the door's always open."

"Thanks, Ellen. Not just for these. For . . ."

My voice was stuck in my throat. Ellen's offer of room and board was an act of generosity to which I was unaccustomed.

Ellen wasn't one for sentiment, though. She stood there in her chic silk trousers, her streak of gray hair like a comet across her face, and nodded.

"Of course, Maxine."

Then she swept out of the room and I was alone, another decorative bauble in Ellen's glittering apartment.

Hot and Bothered

In the late 1990s, there was no Instagram. There was no Twitter. Online newsletters were not a thing. Google Maps didn't exist. If you were lost somewhere on the streets of New York, you had to stop a stranger to ask for directions. Cell phones didn't have cameras or the internet and many people didn't have cell phones at all. Your social network consisted quite literally of who you knew—and who those people knew. The most powerful tools for building awareness of your brand in this quaint, long-forgotten world were word of mouth and the press.

Ellen was the equivalent of a 2015 influencer in 1997. She knew all the right people, which is to say the richest people with the biggest mouths and the editors at the top magazines. Once the manufactured batches of Flush were ready in their custom bottles, I fulfilled the wait-list orders. We updated the logo to something more evocative. The labels read *Flush* in a gray scale of sans serif letters that transitioned from deep charcoal to the palest of pearlescent silvers. It wasn't long before Flush spread beyond my elite clients to their friends and relatives and lawyers and personal trainers and, in some cases, to their household staff. We had to produce two more rounds of bottles to fill the new orders. Six months after I moved into Ellen's guest room, she came to me with some exciting news.

"*Vogue* wants to do a story on you and Flush," she told me, her words breathless as she stood in the guest room doorway. Nothing gets a Park Avenue doyenne hot and bothered like the prospect of *Vogue* coverage.

"We should use this article to introduce the whole company," I said. "Time the launch of Reveal to this issue."

"Yes, let's do that. They want to take a portrait of you, too," Ellen added. "They're going to pull some looks."

"No dresses—please," I begged.

"It's *Vogue*," Ellen chastised me. "You'll put on whatever they tell you to wear."

That same year a Belgian fashion designer, Diane von Furstenberg, had relaunched her signature silk wrap dresses from the '70s to great acclaim. Everywhere I looked, at tables in downtown bars, on the subway, I saw her colorfully patterned, long-sleeve creations with their demure V necklines and thick knotted sashes. I had nothing against this style. It was far more elegant than the ragged flannel and platform shoes that had proliferated a few years back or the plaid kilts and knee-highs with which so many adult women relived their schoolgirl days. But it wasn't me. I could imagine a glossy magazine wanting to soften the power quotient of a female entrepreneur by wrapping her in an ultrafeminine dress.

On the topic of palatable femininity, one of the most iconic haircuts of the decade was a choppy blond shag on movie stars like Meg Ryan and Gwyneth Paltrow. Across America women were cropping their locks with abandon. It was all fine and well to have short, tousled hair as a woman these days, so long as you modeled yourself on an adorably straight rom-com actress.

The *Vogue* portrait session was at a studio in the far West Village, in a space that looked like a former garage, on a block dotted with turn-of-the-century town houses. The photographer was an up-and-coming guy who has since become famous. Fortunately, there wasn't a frilly dress or pink ensemble to be found on the rack of clothes the fashion editor had assembled. *Vogue* was obsessed with the minimalist, high-minded Austrian fashion designer Helmut Lang, who had recently moved to New York. The rack featured a lineup of his slouchy black tuxedo pants and sheer tulle sleeveless tops, some with slashed cutouts across the torso. The effect was soft-butch fairy queen. I loved it.

The magazine had a hairstylist on set, who slicked my blond hair back into a low ponytail with a deep side part. Using swipes from a tin of wax pomade, she patted down every baby hair until my strands were lined up in submission. Naturally, I took care of my makeup. I forwent foundation, true to my signature. At twenty-three, I had skin as perfect as it was ever going to be. I patted some oil-free moisturizer across my face to create a smooth, shine-free base to which my makeup application could adhere. With my ring finger, I dappled on a custom concealer shade I mixed for myself on my under-eye area, my chin, the bridge of my nose, and the slightly redder indentation beneath my nostrils. I tightlined my lower and upper lash lines with a cocoa pencil, then smudged some chocolate powder on top with a cotton bud so my dark eyes had some extra smolder. I added a delicate daub of champagne eye shadow in my eye corners for a subtle highlight. Flush gave my lips and cheeks a rosy glow, and I finished my mouth with a dainty pat of clear balm.

The hairstylist, Jessica, watched me in the studio's oversized mirror. She nodded her approval when I was done.

"You really know what you're doing," she said admiringly.

I met her gaze in the mirror. She had freckled pale skin and a halo of strawberry-blond hair that sat atop her head in a bun, strands poking out all over, on the verge of breaking free. She wore a simple black T-shirt and dark blue fitted jeans that highlighted her shapely thighs and butt.

"You bet I do," I replied, staring straight into her blue-green eyes. She didn't look away. Instead, a knowing smile teased at her lips.

Something had shifted after Caroline dumped me. I realized I was attractive to other women. Caroline had shown me this when she plucked me from behind the makeup counter. She had told me there were "signs" and that I would learn to sense them for myself. Jessica's unabashed gaze seemed exactly like a "sign."

I knew that love with another woman was an impossibility. The world kept reminding me of this fact. Harmonious love between men and women was barely achievable, and they had the luxury of legality. Sex, though, that had nothing to do with love or relationships. The sex part was great. So long as I separated the flirtation and the sex from its romantic complications—and kept that flirtation and sex on the down-low—I would be fine.

"What are you doing after this?" I asked.

"No plans," Jessica replied coyly. "What about you?"

"I have the interview," I said, nodding in the direction of the *Vogue* beauty writer who sat in a far corner of the studio, eyeing me impatiently. "After that, I'm free. I don't really know this neighborhood. Any suggestions?"

"I live a few blocks away, on Greenwich and Perry. Come have a drink after." Jessica pulled a piece of paper and a pen from her dopp kit and wrote down her address and phone number. She handed me the paper; I folded it in half and slipped it into my makeup bag.

"Thanks, I will."

"Better trot over there," she said, tilting her head in the direction of the photographer and beauty writer. "Jillian doesn't like to be kept waiting."

The photographer had me sit on an overturned crate; a gray drop cloth hung behind me. The next hour was a blur of flashes and clicks and "Yes! Gorgeous!" and Jessica touching up my hair, the lead singer of an Irish rock band crooning from a stereo. When the photographer was confident he had the shot, Jessica packed up and waved her farewell, with a sly wink in my direction. Jillian and I settled into a pair of black leather armchairs. She pulled a hulking tape recorder out of her handbag, placed it on the coffee table between us, and clicked it on.

"Tell me about the inspiration behind Flush," she began.

I gave her the origin story, including that cute anecdote of my childhood brush with a cherry Popsicle. Jillian's thin lips maintained their tight, unimpressed line. She wore a matte powdery foundation that didn't match her skin tone; there was a border of demarcation at the edge of her jaw, as though her neck had vacationed in São Paulo while her face sojourned in Iceland. That foundation had settled into the faint beginnings of creases at the corners of her eyes and across her forehead. It made her look older than I assumed she was, based on her junior editor status. Her lip and cheek colors were all wrong, too, like orange juice concentrate dumped on nonfat vanilla yogurt.

I finished my spiel. Jillian's lips seemed like they were trying to express a grievance or an unkind thought, it was hard to tell.

"So it's the equivalent of sugary syrup for a woman's face?" she asked.

"Well, that was the inspiration," I said. "But the effect is more postcoital than post-Popsicle."

"Postcoital?" she asked.

"Women look their happiest and most radiant after sex, from what I hear," I said. "Assuming there was an orgasm involved. Orgasms are nature's best beautifier."

"I see," she said. "What are you working on next? Are you starting a line?"

I love New York with all my heart. I've loved it since I first visited its teeming sidewalks as a suburban kid. That said, New York is not a place that ever permits complacency. Just when you think you've accomplished something noteworthy, when you've sold your first painting or published your debut novel, along come the curious onlookers begging you to tell them what's next. I hadn't even sold Flush to a department store and already this *Vogue* editor wanted to know my five-year plan. I guess I should have been flattered by her faith that I would last long enough to have a next thing.

"I am starting a line called Reveal early next year. We're giving you the scoop," I told Jillian, flashing her a disarming grin. "Trust me, this is only the beginning."

There were no formal plans for Reveal beyond Flush. I was a twenty-three-year-old playing at adulthood and flirting with beauty stardom. After the interview ended, I practically sprinted those few blocks over to Jessica's apartment. Nothing turns me on more than the prospect of my own success.

By the time that *Vogue* story came out ten weeks later, it was 1998 and Jessica and her fantastic ass were small objects in my rearview mirror. I was on to my next stop, one of the most pivotal of my career.

DAY FOUR

Morning

In my chilly, dark bedroom, I open my eyes, reach for my phone, and glance at its illuminated screen to see a notification from Elizabeth. It is "the email." The subject line reads, *URGENT: Board Sets Meeting Date*, punctuated with one of those tiny red flags, as though the word *urgent* in all caps isn't alarming on its own.

The timing of this email couldn't be more ironic. Just as I finish reliving the launch of Reveal I am faced with the possibility of its demise. Well, not Reveal's demise, but mine. The Board members of Reveal have set a date for the meeting, five days from today, during which they will decide my future at the company. What this means is that those six Board members, Ellen chief among them, will consider both sides of things, mine and Amanda's, and arrive at a conclusion. As if there are only ever two sides and no one is aware that triangles or squares or pentagons exist.

Elizabeth's email is from her Reveal account, so it features the bland language of corporate responsibility avoidance. She knows that I will understand this as a necessary evil rather than a slight. Just in case, she has followed up with a text message from her personal cell.

I'm sorry. Wish I had more info to share. Call if you need ANYTHING.

Elizabeth should not be concerned. Sure, I had a partial breakdown last night. A release, really. And now, I have recovered. That's what women like me do. We bounce back—fast—because we can't afford to dwell on regrets or worst-case scenarios. This isn't therapy, it's leadership. You reap what you project. I am confident in my rightness. I am the founder of Reveal, a woman whose beauty vision earned her a profile in *Vogue* at age twenty-three, too important a figure for a Board to risk losing. This email is really cause for celebration. It marks the road to my impending freedom.

I text Elizabeth back some banal drivel in keeping with her tone.

All okay. Doing just fine.

Boosted by thoughts of my eventual win at the Board's hands, I stride to the kitchen where I scoop some pre-ground coffee into my machine's gold filter and press the brew button. I notice a slight tremor in my hands. Must be low blood sugar.

My kitchen is as pristine as the rest of my apartment. The most I've ever sprung for in the help department is a housekeeper who cleans my already immaculate place a couple of times a week. It's the easiest gig she'll ever score. The coffee table is unblemished by the dreaded tchotchkes and decorative glossy books that are all the rage in design magazine pages. My tidiness is a symptom of my adult candor: what you see is what you get.

That self-sufficiency extends to my professional life, too. But Ellen convinced me, when Reveal's shining success first exploded, to hire an assistant. Her argument was that my brain could be put to better use than filling an appointment book and answering my own phone; let some cute Ivy League grad do those things so I could focus on product development. How nicely that has turned out: Amanda was my fifth assistant and the first one whose name I learned.

I trusted Amanda with the maintenance of my life. When the moment suited her, she snatched my confidence and thrust it back in my face. Her motive was upward mobility, I assume. She probably struck a deal with Ellen or the whole Board. One "difficult" founder served straight up in exchange for Amanda's own career ascension at Reveal.

Did she send them text messages? Emails from an anonymous account? Do Ellen and the Board possess details of my alleged malfeasance? The possibility is sour in my mouth. It leaves a bilious film on my teeth and tongue, the kind that no amount of high-end coffee can wash away.

Image Is Everything

After Reveal officially launched as a company in 1998 with Flush rebranded under its umbrella, nearly two years after I first mixed those amateur versions, I hurtled forward at a sonic pace. That early stage of Reveal was a sleepless blur of constant iterating and steep learning curves. All my energy went into the proliferation of Flush, while my makeup clients became side work. In some ways this was the toughest period of my career, from the sheer demands on my time. Through another lens it was the freest. There were no employees to manage, a Board was years away, and my sole investor was Ellen. We had nowhere to go but up.

The *Vogue* story on Flush and Reveal dropped. Ellen was not pleased with the profile's pull quote: "Orgasms are nature's best beautifier."

"Have you lost your mind, Maxine?" Ellen asked me, the *Vogue* issue trembling in her hand. "You are clearing all talking points with me going forward."

"It's a great quote," I said. "And an accurate one."

"We didn't discuss marketing Flush around sex. I would never have agreed to that," said Ellen. "It's tasteless, unseemly."

"All makeup is about sex," I fired back. "I just made the point more explicitly. Anyway, Flush is really about seduction, not in-your-face sex."

"You described it as an orgasm, that sounds like sex. Women don't want to talk about that *explicitly*," said Ellen.

"Yes, they do. Everyone is obsessed with Tom Ford's collections for Gucci—the models look like they came straight from bed. All the women you know go to that salon on Fifty-Seventh Street to get Brazilian waxes," I argued. "Women today love talking about sex."

The hottest models in fashion magazines were tan and bubble-butted and hailed from Brazil. Vibrators were petal pink, with rabbit ears to tickle your clit. Women's pubic regions—and anuses—were now hairless, save for sliver-thin landing strips that evoked a dictator's mustache or a Caribbean airport. *Sex and the City* premiered on HBO a few months after Reveal launched. Ellen came around to my sales pitch once I was flooded with phone calls from interested parties, women who wanted me to take them on as clients, retailers who wanted to sell Flush.

We bought ads for Reveal in some of the major glossies—*Bazaar*, *Allure*, and *ELLE*. I insisted on a product-driven image to contrast with the standard beauty campaign that typically featured a twenty-year-old model caressing her face while tubes of lipstick and vials of perfume hovered in a bottom corner. Flush was the star of Reveal's first ad. We photographed a single bottle of Flush lit from behind and below, so it shimmered with mystery. A thick stroke of Flush oozed across the page, temptation in cosmetic form.

A medium-sized cosmetics group reached out wanting to buy Reveal from me. "Wait until we have more to give them," Ellen instructed. "Never take the first offer you get." At the time, that *we* made me feel supported. I wondered where her assurance came from, though given her investment, I didn't feel able to question it.

I was fully enmeshed in Ellen's daily routine. She woke every day at 7 a.m., regardless of her plans. Donald woke at five to ride his bike in Central Park with some buddies before work. One morning, I was up early and Donald passed me in the kitchen; he was in his cycling clothes, his helmet hair matted to his head with sweat. Normally, Donald ignored my presence as he had when I first encountered him in Ellen's boudoir. Ever since his argument with Ellen when I moved in, he had been silent, so far as I knew, on the topic of my living arrangement. He was either on his bike, at the office, or at a social engagement with Ellen. He spent so little time at home, I wondered why he had even cared that I was there. The guest room was in a separate wing of the apartment, near the servant entrance in the back. I had taken to using this door, unprompted by Ellen, to avoid run-ins like this.

I expected Donald to continue to his bedroom. Instead, he paused at the granite island.

"You're up early," he remarked. "Ellen doesn't so much as blink until seven."

"Yes," I said. "There's coffee." I gestured at a pot by the stove. "But I guess you've already had some."

"I have," he said. His bushy eyebrows crinkled. "This business of yours—"

"Reveal."

"—yes, Reveal. You're serious about it?"

"Of course I am. It's my calling."

"Your calling?"

"Yes. I've been doing people's makeup my whole life. It's what I was born to do."

"Founding a business is not the same thing as an artistic calling."

I fingered the rim of my coffee mug. "I can learn how to build a business. Talent and passion—those aren't things you can teach."

A reluctant smile spread over Donald's lips. "I would agree with that," he said. "Still, in my experience creative talent and business acumen rarely coexist in the same person."

"If you feel that way, why would you invest in Reveal?"

"I did it for me. For my personal brand. These days, people like a power couple. It gives you a social edge. Trophy wives have lost their currency. We can't be a power couple if my wife's spending all day in the hair salon while her candles collect dust." Donald cleared his throat. "Ellen thinks this is her investment and her business. You won't do anything to change her mind."

"Sorry?"

"Ellen is not a businesswoman. There's no harm in letting her think it, though, for the sake of appearances. Make no mistake: I am running this show." Donald leaned in closer to me. I could smell his dried sweat. "Image is everything, Maxine. Don't you ever forget it."

Donald's message about appearances didn't scare me as it should have. I was a beauty founder: Who knew more about the importance of that than I did? At the time, I thought his concern was for how his marriage to Ellen looked, how it reflected on his own prowess as a man and a financial titan. I was too young to recognize that the image he referred to also included me. As for the revelation about his role in Reveal, my age protected me there, too. At twenty-three, I believed that I could handle, with ease, the injection of a little male involvement—and money—into the skin of Reveal. I was a visionary. The company didn't exist without me. Naivete and hubris are the vertebrae of youth; they gave me a conviction that my inexperience didn't merit.

By 6:45 a.m., Donald was gone from the apartment. Ellen seemed to see him as infrequently as I did. She would wake and press a buzzer next to her bed. A maid in a full uniform of a black dress and white lace apron, straight out of a movie, would enter her room, draw the curtains, and set the newspapers on the end of her bed. The maid would then leave and return a few minutes later with black coffee, toast, fruit, and one soft-boiled egg on a silver tray. Most mornings, I kept Ellen company.

After my encounter with Donald, I watched her eat breakfast from my usual position in a stuffed armchair. The room smelled of newspaper ink and of Ellen's extra-dark toast. A paisley silk robe was wrapped around her pajamas; reading glasses were perched on her unmade-up face. I wore the striped cotton pajama set Ellen had loaned me on my first night and that I had slept in ever since. As a child, I had never sat and watched my mother read the paper or eat breakfast. I couldn't recall my mother ever enjoying a leisurely morning meal.

The newspaper rustled as Ellen turned the page. She considered me with her penetrating gaze.

"I'm very proud of you," she said.

My body seemed to float out of the chair.

"Thanks, Ellen."

"I mean it, Maxine. You are so disciplined and devoted."

I had no social life, no friends, nothing except for Reveal and Ellen—I wasn't so much devoted as I was a monk, the occasional night out aside.

"You remind me of myself," Ellen continued, which I understood to be a high compliment, narcissism being the pinnacle of praise. "You will do anything to succeed. It's thrilling to watch."

"Thanks, Ellen," I repeated, at a loss for any other reply.

Ellen smiled.

"Keep up the good work," she said, then returned to her newspaper.

Ellen, I realized, lived a complete lie. She wasn't a businesswoman or a hardcore achiever. She had a Park Avenue existence paid for exclusively by her husband. The closest she had approached success was a defunct candle business. In that respect, she wasn't so different from my mother. Though there was a crucial distinction: my mother wasn't a fool; she was aware of how imbalanced her circumstances were. That's why she was so dissatisfied. Ellen was too delusional to recognize her unhappiness.

I could feel that Ellen's praise was sincere. It warmed me. Unlike my parents, she saw my ambition and rewarded me for it. She wanted Reveal to succeed. So did Donald, even if he only cared how that success appeared. On the surface, our agendas were mostly aligned. If I probed beneath that surface, though, I felt a deep sadness for Ellen. Donald had said trophy wives were no longer in fashion, but to my eyes that was still exactly what Ellen was.

I negotiated a deal to sell Flush at the Bloomingdale's and Henri Bendel department stores—without any help from my estranged father, I should add. Since I only had one product, Reveal didn't merit a full counter setup, like the ones I had operated behind during my Macy's days. Each store erected a small display, a table piled high with Flush bottles, now boasting Reveal labels, adjacent to signage with our ad, overseen by a saleswoman whose job it was to paint passersby with my concoction. If they liked what they saw, she slipped them a free sample. The Flush tables were located at the front entrance to the Bloomingdale's and Henri Bendel cosmetics departments, the better to maximize customer contact.

One day, I visited the Bloomingdale's outpost on a reconnaissance mission. Anonymity shielded me, despite the *Vogue* article. A single magazine story didn't equal widespread recognition. I would inspect how the store was representing my product, get a feel for who my customers were. The Reveal station was a mirrored hexagon with tiered white shelves that held bottles of Flush, like a champagne-glass tower you see in Las Vegas.

Back then, the Bloomingdale's cosmetics department existed in a perennial state of bustle. Today, it is like a silent wing of a library. Everyone goes to Sephora or shops online, as the Board loves to remind me. Sephora existed back then, too; the first US store, in SoHo, opened the same year that Reveal launched. Still, department stores threw around their weight for a while longer.

Each cosmetics counter at Bloomingdale's had multiple staffers and those people worked for their commission. To walk across the cosmetics department meant tolerating borderline assault. There were the perfume men in their black slacks and skintight button-down shirts, their straightened hair gelled back from their ample foreheads, wielding atomizers like weapons as they spritzed a person with an array of florals and cloying vanilla finishes. The lipstick women were equally aggressive, charging after prospective customers in their three-inch heels.

Then there were the bullies, whose preferred strategy was to browbeat people into requiring services. *That foundation looks all wrong! No one with your lips should wear that shade! Is that really how you want your eyes to look?*

The woman who oversaw my Flush display at Bloomingdale's was an emaciated blonde in black pants and a black long-sleeved top. Beauty brands are generally responsible for hiring their own sales associates, even in department stores, and Ellen had chosen this woman on the recommendation of an acquaintance. I paused beside a nearby handbag display to observe the action from afar. The woman was tall and she exploited her height to box in potential customers, then swipe their wrists with stripes of Flush before they had a chance to decline. Repeatedly I watched this scrawny yet towering woman throw herself into the line of oncoming pedestrian traffic. It was hard not to admire her determination—until she added heckling to her repertoire.

"Ma'am, are you feeling okay? You look awfully pale . . ."

"How's your circulation, miss? You could use a little perking up."

"When was the last time you flushed with pleasure? Not lately?"

The tall blonde followed these insults with her combo attack of ". . . try some Flush today—I guarantee you'll never leave home without it." She was a one-woman good cop, bad cop routine. It seemed to work. The customers she offended halted, taken aback by her insults. She quickly converted their horror into pleasure at the effect that Flush had on their complexions.

Still, I didn't want the success of Reveal to rely on a woman's low self-esteem. Flush was an elixir of confidence; this hack was treating it like a bandage for a woman's sins.

I strode in the direction of the saleswoman. She took the bait, thrust herself in front of me with all the zeal of a religious acolyte. Go ahead, I thought, give me your best insult.

The woman paused for the first time since I had watched her. That's right, lady—I'm perfect. I already wore my daily dose of Flush. Her eyes careened over my cheeks and lips, then she went in for the kill.

"You're looking sickly today. Try some of this—it will perk you right up."

I smiled widely, which immediately threw her off. She wanted her customers indignant so she could pull her one-two punch. Now that I was closer to the Flush station, I saw there was a printout of my *Vogue* story resting against some Flush bottles with an *As Seen In . . .* frame around it. This woman had been standing beside my photo the whole time.

"Listen, do you need glasses or something?" I nodded at the

framed *Vogue* story and watched the color, Flush and all, disappear from her face. "That's me and this product is mine. I will not have you criticizing customers to sell it."

This woman couldn't muster a worthy retort.

"Get going," I said. "You're fired."

"I don't work for you!" she sputtered, finally locating her vocal cords.

I glowered at her.

"Yes, you do. My product, my decisions. Go."

The woman clomped away. Without her, I would lose a day of potential sales. Until we found her replacement, I would do her job.

The first woman to stroll my way was a practiced New Yorker; she swung so wide, you would have thought she was avoiding a sinkhole. A pair of women came toward me from a different direction; they had the tough, pointy faces and minimalist ensembles of corporate-ladder climbers. I watched their eyes move curiously over to the Flush display, though the speed of their strides remained steady.

"Do you have a second?" I asked, my tone reticent, overcompensation for my predecessor.

The older of the two women, a redhead, tossed me a look of deep pity, like she couldn't believe this was how I earned a living.

More women passed me by, women with strollers, women loaded down with shopping bags, bored women, stressed women, women with somewhere else to be. Each time, I held out my hands and did my best to catch their eyes. No one paid me attention.

It was an unfamiliar feeling, this complete disinterest from other women. I was accustomed to being judged and disdained, not ignored. What was happening here? I knew I possessed charm; Caroline and Jessica and many other women were evidence of that. When the occasion called for it, I could turn it on. The reason my charm had worked in those instances was because it came wrapped up with sex. Extricated from lust, my charisma didn't know what to do or where to land. It required the insinuation of physical attraction, like a base note in a complex perfume, to ground it and lend it power.

If I was going to land any future customers, I needed to flirt.

"Excuse me, ma'am, would you like to try some orgasm in a bottle?"

The forty-something brunette in a pink Chanel suit stopped short.

"What did you say to me?"

"I asked if you wanted to try some orgasm in a bottle."

The brunette stared at me in disbelief.

"What does that even mean?"

I angled a bottle of Flush so that the store's fluorescent lighting cut a quick line of transparency through the red liquid inside.

"Maybe you saw my story in *Vogue*," I said, nodding at the framed article. A woman in Chanel lived and died by the pages of *Vogue*. "I created this. It's called Flush and it makes a woman look like she had the best sex of her life. Care to try some?"

I unscrewed the bottle's metal top and offered its built-in brush to the Chanel woman.

"Okay," she said. She pushed up one of her pink tweed sleeves and showed me the underside of her wrist.

I dipped the brush back into the bottle's rosy pool and applied a gentle stroke across her inner wrist. Her dark eyes burned into my forehead. I suppressed a small smile. The woman looked down at her wrist. Then she glanced back up at me, her eyes lingering on my face longer than common courtesy permits. I noticed her gold wedding band. The light in her eyes told a different story than that token of convention did. The stale department store air between us was suddenly alive.

I cannot explain how or why I knew that she was different from what her appearance would suggest. Caroline was correct when it came to "signs." You develop an extra sensitivity to the world when you experience firsthand its more covert and complicated layers. This sixth sense is a means of survival as much as it is a language of connection.

"This is meant for . . ." she said, gesturing at the bottle of Flush.

"Your cheeks and your lips." I paused. "But you can put it anywhere you want."

My eyes settled on the woman's lips as I gauged her reaction. Her mouth was like a slightly deflated croissant. I can work with that, I thought.

"Will you show me what it looks like on?"

I beckoned the woman over to a stool on the other side of the Flush display.

"It would be my pleasure."

The Chanel woman's name was Cheryl. Later that day, after I had painted the inner wrists of too many women to count, I met Cheryl at her Central Park West apartment. She had a view of the reservoir and the Bridle Path, not unlike the one I have today. In fact, my current building is a block from her then home. I wonder if she still lives there.

Cheryl served us ice-cold gin martinis, garnished with little cocktail onions on thin silver skewers. We drank them as we sat in her chintz-filled living room, redolent with the scent of gardenias and roses. Cheryl's husband was out of town on business, clearly lucrative going by her surroundings.

Halfway through her gin martini, Cheryl plucked her glass coupe by its slender stem and carried it across the living room, down a long hallway, and into her carpeted bedroom. I followed her. There, she downed the remainder of her martini in one elegant take and placed the empty coupe on her dresser. She took my coupe, swallowed its contents, and settled it next to her glass. Then she kissed me. In bed, I made it clear that where orgasms are concerned, I am better than anything you'll get from a bottle, even one of my own design.

Afterward, we lay on her massive king bed, her sheets satiny against my bare body. An extravagant chandelier hung above us; its faux flames emitted a sepia light. The curtains on the room's picture windows were defiantly open. Cheryl lived on a high-enough floor that there was no danger of anyone seeing us. Outside, the sun had already set, and the sky's dusky light wafted in.

Cheryl was on her stomach. She was a slender woman and her long, graceful back crested across the bed majestically. In the dual lighting scheme from the chandelier and the window, her skin had the radiance of crushed pearls.

"Your skin," I whispered.

"What?" said Cheryl, her large dark eyes on me.

"Don't move," I begged her. Even if I had snapped a photo of Cheryl's back, I doubt it would have captured the effect that so mesmerized me in that moment. The only choice was to memorize what I saw and do my best to re-create it in another form. I stared at Cheryl's back, for how long I can't say. By the time I left Cheryl's apartment that image of her gleaming back, like a crescent moon fallen to earth, was imprinted on my brain.

Be a Boss

Reveal needed a home base now that we were an established operation. Ellen—and Donald—had a friend who was the landlord of a cast-iron building in SoHo. He gave Ellen a sweet deal on a fifth-floor open-plan space. The area's scrappy, artist legacy would set Reveal apart from the saccharine fluff of the beauty world. We retained the suite's openness and set up desks that faced each other so that each worker could see everyone else on the floor. Full transparency was Reveal's touchstone from the start, like the makeup we were selling. An architect cordoned off a corner of the suite with glass walls. That was for my office. Reveal wasn't a socialist enterprise, after all. Besides, everyone could see into my office. I was more on display than anyone else.

Those desks in suite 506 required bodies. Ellen reached out to her various acquaintances across her social network and asked them to send her the résumés of any young, talented women interested in "getting in on the ground of the next great beauty revolution." That was how she put it.

"We need to discuss new hires. I'm thinking six employees to start," Ellen informed me one afternoon over lunch at a French bistro she frequented on the Upper East Side. Until then, it had been me and a rotating cast of eager interns Ellen had exploited from her friends' children. I was drowning in restock requests, press inquiries, raw materials sourcing, and quality control struggles with various factories. Ellen speared a dainty bite of her chicken paillard, light on the oil, no butter. "We can build from there."

"Okay," I said. "I can set up some interviews."

"Don't you think I should handle the interviews? It is my investment, after all."

I wanted to remind Ellen that it was technically Donald's investment. "They'll be reporting directly to me, not to you. As the founder, I should do the interviewing—at least initially. You can meet them once I've vetted them." After the saleswoman incident at Bloomingdale's, I needed to have serious oversight of Reveal to ensure that it adhered to my principles.

"So you want to take ownership here," said Ellen, her voice sharp. "A bold stance for someone your age." She cocked her brow. "I suppose I should be impressed."

I felt my face pale at Ellen's reference to my "age." Had she known all this time how young I was?

Ellen smiled like she could guess my thoughts. "I would never invest in a business without a background check. But I guess someone who dropped out of college might not be as devoted to doing their homework."

I swallowed hard. "Ellen, I'm so—"

"Don't." Ellen shook her head sternly. "You did what you needed to do to get ahead. I can respect that kind of cutthroat determination, more than you'll ever understand."

My throat tightened with dread, which didn't make sense since I should have been relieved. I swallowed hard again. "Right. Thanks, Ellen."

Ellen placed her fork and knife gently on her plate and reached across the white tablecloth to pat my hand with her chilly, soft palm. "If you're serious about taking ownership, you need to be a boss. This isn't some school project. It's a business. Who you hire will make or break you. What is the point of all the work you've put into Reveal if you can't get those products onto as many women's faces as possible?" Ellen retracted her hand. "What is the point of all the money I've invested if this brand doesn't explode?"

"I get it, Ellen. You don't need to worry about that."

Before Reveal, power to me had been synonymous with artistic autonomy. Now I understood that to execute my vision I would have to depend on others, and those others were people I needed to manage. I couldn't just be the creative visionary of Reveal. I had to be a boss, too. In the business and beauty worlds, anything less than conventional power, which is to say masculine dominance, was a display of weakness.

I hired those new employees, among them a marketing manager and an entry-level Jane-of-all-trades who functioned, in part, as my first assistant. I don't remember her name. I was too controlling to give her any task that allowed her access to my private life. She kept my meetings schedule at the office, filed expenses for my corporate Amex, and answered my phones. That nameless assistant had no information on where I went or what I did outside work hours. So far as she and my other Reveal employees were concerned, I disappeared into a black hole the second I left the office.

A few weeks after our lunch, Ellen took me to a party at a friend's apartment. Donald didn't join. In all the years I lived with Ellen, I don't think I ever saw her go on a date with Donald or sit down to dinner with him. He only socialized with her when there was a clear benefit to his image, preferably one that could be captured by a society photographer. When Ellen brought me to parties, I accomplished two goals for her: I acted as a platonic substitute for Donald, and I reminded her friends that she was now an angel investor, a professional pursuit that was superior to their less splashy knitwear-line and capsule-jewelry-collection endeavors.

This party was at the Park Avenue apartment of a woman named Francine. I don't remember what the occasion was, someone had just returned from somewhere or was headed somewhere or had published a book somewhere. I was in a cluster with Ellen, Francine, and a couple of other ladies. I had attended enough gatherings with Ellen that her friends were familiar with me. We stood around and sipped our flutes of champagne.

"I look so tired." Francine sighed as she glanced at herself in a nearby mirror.

"No you don't," said Ellen.

"Fred has been stressed at work. His tossing and turning is driving me nuts," Francine continued.

"I have this fantastic concealer," offered another woman. "I can give you a tube."

Usually, I kept quiet at these parties. I rarely had anything to add to the conversation. My epiphany with Cheryl from a couple of months ago tugged at my lips.

"What if there was another way to appear rested besides concealer?" I asked.

Francine and the other women all looked at me, as though they had forgotten I stood there. Ellen eyed me curiously.

"What are you talking about, Maxine?"

Excitement tickled my tongue.

"Something that could make you radiant, like you are surrounded by candlelight. Everyone looks good in candlelight. That's why all those fancy dinners you attend have candles as their centerpiece." I paused. "And why people always light candles before big sex scenes in movies."

"Go on," said Francine.

"The reason candlelight—or moonlight—is so flattering is because it makes everyone glow. The light is soft; it buffs away any harsh lines or shadows."

"How interesting," said Ellen with a close-lipped smile. "And you could bottle that?"

"No, but you can re-create it with a highlighter that makes you look like you're in a candlelit love scene. A liquid highlighter."

The women's eyes narrowed in contemplation. Then Francine smiled at me widely.

"It's genius, Maxine," she said.

"It is," Ellen concurred, mirroring Francine's expression.

I could tell from the crinkle near the bridge of her nose that Ellen was not on board with the postcoital implications. However, she wasn't going to verbalize her prudishness after her friends' enthusiasm. Back then, I believed that Ellen could differentiate between her personal values and best business practices. I believed, too, that if the product was unequivocally good, as Flush had been, it would convert Ellen's bias, that capitalist achievement could change hearts and minds.

Ellen turned back to her friends. "Remember this moment. Reveal is going to be everywhere."

Even with the establishment of Reveal's offices, my breakfasts with Ellen continued. She liked the comfort—and power—of knowing she was my first so-called meeting every day. It was a time for us to check in, to discuss any meetings on my schedule, to review events on our respective calendars. Truthfully, I didn't mind this ritual. There was a cozy domesticity to it that contrasted with the hardcore demands of entrepreneurship. Ellen was my investor, yes, via Donald, a fact I never forgot. She was also my support system, a high-society fairy godmother who had transformed me from a college dropout into a *Vogue*-approved beauty changemaker. I pitied her at times, still I trusted her to elevate me to greater heights.

It was a few months after my highlighter pitch. I had been living with Ellen for almost two years. My weeks had been occupied with a brief round of market research—brief because there were no other liquid highlighters to use as comps—and testing with the lab. We were up to formulas ten through fifteen. One was too chalky. Another too glittery. Yet another was so shiny, I referred to it as "Crisco." I was showing Ellen the latest iteration when, between nibbles of toast, she presented me with a contract.

"What's this?" I asked. The pages were dense with small-point font, a few sticker tabs indicating where I should sign.

Ellen glanced up from the highlighter test bottle in her hands.

"I thought we should formalize things beyond what we've already committed to together." She smiled. "I am your investor, after all. I've taken a big risk in financing Reveal. It's important that I feel protected as we expand."

"Okay," I said. "That requires all these pages?" I flipped through the contract. The teachings from my abandoned business major were useless in real life. The contract may as well have been written in a foreign language.

"Yes. We are doing big things together. You are the face of everything, the vision, and I am the money. I don't want to get lost in the shuffle."

"You won't. I'm so grateful for everything you've done, you know that."

"Yes. Well, you can show me your gratitude by signing this."

Ellen's face was eerily calm for someone who claimed concern about her stake in Reveal. There was a hollowness in my throat, but I ignored it.

"Do I need a lawyer or something?"

Ellen patted my hand with her chilly palm.

"This is about protecting me. You have all the power here. I'm the one who needs a lawyer." She smiled. "But of course, if you would like to have a lawyer review it on your behalf, I'd be happy to recommend some people."

This will likely sound unbelievable: I was so touched by Ellen offering to set me up with a lawyer that I took it as confirmation that a lawyer was unnecessary, because why would Ellen suggest this if she had something to hide. Plus, I didn't want to appear ungrateful to Ellen by taking her up on her kindness. This was as much from ignorance of the business world as it was from blind trust of Ellen. I had no reason to doubt her motives. Dummy that I was, I didn't even read over that stupid document. I wouldn't have understood it anyway. I may have been a newly minted boss, but Ellen had all the power, financial or otherwise, in our relationship. She possessed an emotional control, too, something most men, including Donald, would never understand. Male power always seemed like a form of intimidation, the proximity of Donald's sweat, for example, when he lectured me about image-making from his kitchen island. Ellen's emotional control hit a deeper note. She didn't overwhelm my space; she welcomed me into her home. I wanted to please Ellen. My desire for her continued approval was the biggest reason why I signed the contract that morning.

As for that bottle of highlighter in Ellen's hand, it was too Studio

54 to make the cut. Many more iterations followed before I finally released Glow, a luminous champagne lotion, in 2000. Every time I dab it onto a woman's cheeks or brow bone, I am transported back to that evening in bed, when Cheryl was my own personal lunar eclipse.

DAY FIVE

Morning

I shut my laptop thinking of Ellen, who is now Reveal's illustrious chairwoman of the Board. I can't attend the Board meeting four days from now. That only happens in movies and television shows. On that fateful day I will await a call from my lawyer Sandrine to inform me of their verdict. It's not a legal "verdict" as there is nothing judicial about the process. There is no opportunity to defend myself. I can elect for arbitration after the meeting, should things not go my way.

Sandrine insists on a visit to my apartment this morning. We have only ever communicated by phone or email. It wasn't my idea to hire Sandrine. When you're a founder, your interests are the same as your company's interests. Until they aren't. I met Sandrine in 2012 when Elizabeth recommended I hire some legal help for a minor issue. Elizabeth's husband, Arthur, referred me to Sandrine. If only I'd known about Sandrine in 1999 when I signed that contract in Ellen's bedroom.

Sandrine arrives at 6:45 a.m. Her chestnut hair is in a low ponytail. She wears a terra-cotta pantsuit whose rust tones accentuate the light tan of her skin. I am in a silk robe belted at the waist over those cashmere sweatpants and a matching knit T-shirt.

As she explains it to me, Sandrine likes to anticipate how her clients will react to the heated exchanges that could transpire in scenarios such as the hypothetical arbitration for which she is girding us. That way, she can intervene as needed, before someone says the wrong thing.

"This all assumes I'm terminated and that we go to arbitration. Isn't there bad karma associated with prepping for a disaster that may not happen?"

"Tell that to hurricane victims in flood zones," Sandrine cuts back.

"I'm the flood zone in this comparison? Or the victim?"

"Well, you're not the mansion on the hill. This is the plan."

"Got it."

"And if we go to arbitration, it's important that you maintain your composure."

"You don't need to worry about that. I am the most compartmentalized person you'll ever meet." I sip my fair trade, organic coffee from a porcelain cup. It tastes more bitter this morning. I must have brewed it too strong. A silver tray holds some assorted pastries I ordered from a local bakery I'd heard about. I still haven't left the house. I keep thinking today will be the day, but some mixture of anger and exhaustion prevents me.

Sandrine sips her coffee, black with sugar, and eyes a particularly well-endowed croissant like it is a bomb about to detonate. "All due respect, but we wouldn't be here if that was entirely the case."

The woman makes a good point. I like Sandrine. She is forthright and though she is a bit butch for my taste, with her boxy clothes and designer wing-tip oxfords, under a different set of circumstances I would consider sleeping with her.

Sandrine is undeniably gorgeous, with feline eyes, sharp cheekbones, and a small cherry of a mouth. She could have been one of those ethnically ambiguous catalogue models that are all the rage now if her legal interests hadn't panned out. Sandrine is young, I would guess mid-thirties, and she is probably one of those women who has never used eye cream or sunscreen and yet somehow looks perennially fertile.

So Sandrine and her lineless face talk at me for a billable hour, making this coffee and these uneaten pastries one of the most expensive breakfasts I've had. She runs down her strategy for arbitration; with each tidbit, its hypothetical status seems more inevitable.

"Amanda's lawyer is going to make you look like a power-hungry monster," she tells me bluntly.

"Don't you mean *if* this happens, she *will*?" I reply. "I'd appreciate some conditional phrasing."

Sandrine ignores my comment. "He'll try to goad you into an angry outburst."

"He." I snicker. "Miss Feminism has a male lawyer?"

"That's your takeaway from what I said? The gender of Amanda's lawyer, not the fact that he's going to paint you as a power-hungry monster?"

"I heard that part. We both know it's ridiculous. Why should I worry he'll say something so patently false about me? What moron would believe such an absurd statement, that I'm a monster?"

A deep sigh—an involuntary one, to go by her facial expression—escapes Sandrine's throat.

"Max," she says, softly and patiently, like she is talking to a first grader, "arbitration isn't about what's true or false. It's about who tells a better, more convincing story." Sandrine sips from her cup of coffee. "Knowing what kind of story the other side is going to spin is crucial to understanding how to make our story stronger."

"You're saying I should be scared? Defensive?" Anger burns my tongue. "Defensiveness is not my modus operandi."

"I'm not asking you to be scared. I'm asking you to be smart.

Don't let your anger get the better of you even when, especially when, someone accuses you of being a monster. We're going to focus on your vulnerability."

"You mean on my weakness."

Sandrine's lineless face hardens.

"Softness isn't weakness."

"Sure it isn't," I spit out. "I have no doubt the Board or a judge will see it that way."

"You need to consider the possibility that they will. Because the alternative, going in on the attack, emphasizing your strength and power, will not play well, not in this room or in this world."

Tightness grips my throat.

"I don't know this world," I tell Sandrine.

"I know you don't," she says calmly. "But I do. That's why you hired me. You need to trust me when I tell you the strategy we will follow. You need to behave as though the worst will happen, even if it doesn't come naturally to you. Okay?"

"Yes."

"Good."

"This is ridiculous," I can't help adding. "I bet Hillary Clinton doesn't get counseled to emphasize her vulnerability."

Sandrine gives me a pitying look. "You're not running for president," she says. "You're fighting to survive." She pauses. "And you're wrong. I bet people tell her to soften her image all the time."

Sandrine swallows the dregs of her coffee and throws one more tentative look in the direction of the croissant. Then she tells me she'll be in touch and excuses herself to make another meeting.

Absolute Devotion

As an entrepreneur you exist in a perpetual state of development. You are always only as good as your last product launch. In that sense, entrepreneurship is not so different from acting or fashion: you can have a hit movie or collection and still you must always think about what is next. Let me tell you, it is exhausting.

Flush made Reveal a name to watch; Glow established Reveal as a player. We continued the product-centric ad aesthetic we had begun with Flush in our Glow campaign. The ad showed a clear curved bottle of Glow nestled in an abalone shell, a trail of highlighter leaking to the edges of the image.

During the eighteen months I spent developing Glow, we added three more shades of Flush to create a proper category thanks to another round of cash from Donald. I fine tuned a lighter peony color, a blood-orange iteration, and a mauve berry that wore like a faded sunburn. Some customer feedback had suggested that Flush's staying power was limited, so we revised the formula to last longer. I tweaked the packaging, too, refined the original nail polish bottle shape into something closer to a perfume vial with lean curves, an Art Deco Lucite vessel whose silhouette a woman could showcase on her vanity. We released a more portable rollerball model that was the perfect size for a purse. All Reveal's packaging would be transparent like its company's ethos.

"Gird yourself," Ellen cautioned me in one of our morning sessions. "When we release Glow, people will go nuts."

Nothing could have prepared me for my success, not even Ellen's sage warnings. Glow sold out of every department store in Chicago, Los Angeles, Boston, and New York within a day. Flush sold out, too, in all four shades. A shortage of raw materials created delays, which only whetted appetites further. *Vogue* did another story on me. So did *Allure*, *ELLE*, and *Harper's Bazaar*. A writer from *W Magazine* asked me about the ingredients in Flush and Glow. I told her, "So long as women look good, they won't care what they put on their faces." It was 2000 and everyone declared Reveal the cult brand of Y2K. "Greet the new millennium with a face gleaming in Flush and Glow," *W Magazine* instructed.

Ellen had a friend—she had so many friends in places I wouldn't have known to look—who worked in brand marketing. He pitched Reveal to all the retailers and soon we were in boutiques across the country.

I celebrated by moving out of Ellen's guest room. Three years into living with her, our situation had grown stale. I was tired of tiptoeing around to avoid Donald. It was like living with my parents all over again, but worse. Whereas my mother had been resentful of my father's financial control over her life, Ellen operated from a position of make-believe, the fantasy being that she was a serious businesswoman. My mother's anger was preferable to the sadness that Ellen's delusion inspired in me. I was willing to accept Donald's money and

Ellen's charade; I just didn't want to be confronted with this arrangement after hours.

I asked Ellen if we could have a drink together at home. Five p.m. rolled around and I sat in Ellen's chintz living room, staring at one of her Cubist paintings. Ellen swept in a few minutes later. Even in her own home, she liked to make an entrance. Her maid darted in with some glasses of chardonnay, ice cubes on the side, Ellen's preferred beverage. Glass clinked against glass, and we sipped our drinks.

"I hope you know how grateful I am that you've let me stay with you," I said as Ellen placed her glass atop a leather coaster on the coffee table.

"Of course," Ellen said. "I enjoy our morning meetings. It's good to have you close by."

"Reveal is doing so well," I said, as I fingered the stem of the wineglass. "I thought it might be time that I get a place of my own."

Ellen and I had agreed that I could start paying myself a salary now that the company was in a profitable place. Ellen took her investment cut and I received a modest income. The rest of our earnings went back into growing Reveal. Ellen assured me it was normal that her investment cut was exponentially higher than my salary. She had put money into this, while I had only contributed my labor and my vision.

Ellen flinched, nearly imperceptibly. "You think you can afford your own apartment?"

"If I scrimp by, yes."

"Why not stay here and save the money?"

I sipped my wine. It was so cold and diluted, there was barely any flavor. "It's important that I spend time on my own," I said. "To recharge."

"You can't recharge here?"

At this, Ellen cocked her brow and I wondered if she had an inkling of my nocturnal activities. After all, she had known about NYU and my age. Ellen probably wondered at my lack of interest in a boyfriend at twenty-five years old. I always returned home directly after any rendezvous. Occasionally, I dropped asides about my absolute devotion to Reveal to stave off concerns that my single status was anything more than standard-issue workaholism. As I crept closer to my thirties, I wasn't sure that my efforts would do the trick.

"It's better for Reveal that I have space from it when I'm not at the office," I said. This was a lie; there wasn't a second of my day when I wasn't thinking about my company, it didn't matter where I was. "Besides, I'm sure you and Donald will appreciate having the apartment back to yourselves."

"Of course," Ellen said sharply.

I realized then that I had been more of a buffer for Ellen than I had previously understood. She lived a fantasy of success, yes, but it wasn't magical enough to exclude loneliness. Our morning sessions were her closest approximation of affection. My announcement was, to her, a form of abandonment.

Despite her chilly reaction to my news, Ellen set me up with a real estate agent. We saw upwards of twenty apartments, the majority of which were well outside my budget. Like most super-rich people, Ellen had no concept of an average woman's household spending. Half the places she had the agent show me were on the Upper East Side. I asked the agent if we could venture farther south.

"How much farther south?" he replied.

"Below Midtown would be great," I told him.

The morning I walked into the Flatiron studio it was ablaze with light. The poured-concrete floors brought the city's sidewalks indoors. The vast casement windows framed the Sixth Avenue views like artwork. I could already imagine the low-slung Italian furniture I would eventually scatter throughout. The studio was somewhat outside my budget, but if I kept my expenses extremely frugal, I could afford it. Entertainment and vacations were not part of my repertoire, anyway. This, I thought, is what success looks like.

Barneys New York, the chicest department store in the city, hosted an event at which I could meet some of its top customers and talk up Reveal. These personal appearances with prospective high-spending clients were part of the job of being a founder. You would think that after all the practice of Ellen dragging me to her parties and lunches, I would be a pro at such endeavors. I excelled at one-on-one interactions. They were extensions of my work as a makeup artist and, frankly, my work in the bedroom. They were intimate, energizing. Personal appearances were the opposite. They required that I stand before a room of people and charm each person, simultaneously, as though they were all the same.

The Barneys event was in the store's basement-level restaurant. This was 2001; today, the restaurant is on the store's windowed top floor. The original subterranean location was cool and clubby. The Barneys PR person had reserved an area of the restaurant for our private lunch. There were twenty women in attendance. I arrived fifteen minutes before the start time and somehow I was late.

"We've been trying your cell for over thirty minutes," the Barneys PR person hissed when I met her at the restaurant's entrance.

"I always forget to leave that thing on," I told her, having never been one for technology.

She dragged me to the long table where twenty women were already seated with expectant and vaguely annoyed expressions on their tightly pulled faces. The women looked to range from forty to fifty-five years old, but I was still adjusting my age perception to the surgical interventions of the Upper East Side. I plastered on my widest, most charming smile.

"Hello, ladies," I chirped. "I'm excited to meet you all and introduce you to Reveal."

Stoniness greeted me. Apparently these women didn't like to be kept waiting.

"Maybe I should tell you about Reveal's origin story." I chose an empty seat in the middle of the table and shared my childhood Popsicle anecdote and how that inspired Flush years later.

"It's a cute story," said a tough blonde across the table from me. "And I know Reveal is the 'It' brand right now." I smiled. "But I'm not totally convinced I can pull off a Popsicle-lip look. Is this really for adults?"

"It's definitely for adults," I said. "I actually call it an 'orgasm in a bottle.'"

Nervous tittering filled the table.

"That's catchy," said another tough blonde. "How did you come up with that?"

"Reveal is about liberating women, aesthetically and spiritually," I told her, my face beginning to warm. "It's about making women feel beautiful showing their true selves, including their sexual vibrancy, as opposed to masking their radiance with heavy makeup. We also have a liquid highlighter called Glow."

"It's a lovely idea," said a brunette. "What are you, twenty-nine?"

"Twenty-six," I said. She wished she looked like me at twenty-nine.

"Right," said the brunette. "I don't mean to be contrarian here. It's just we have concerns you're too young to understand. Wrinkles, sunspots, visible pores—when you're our age, coverage becomes necessary. There are things you want to hide."

"I disagree," I said. "Women should never hide themselves, no matter their age. All women are at their most beautiful when you can see them naturally."

The first tough blonde laughed ruefully.

"My husband has never seen me without full foundation. We've been married for over thirty years. He probably wouldn't recognize me if I walked around with so little makeup on," she said. "What does your boyfriend think of your barefaced cheek-tint-and-highlighter look?"

"I don't have a boyfriend," I said, swallowing hard. "This isn't about men. It's about you and your face and what makes you happy."

"I want to feel attractive to my husband," said the brunette. "That makes me happy."

"Really?" I said.

"We are all married to men," added tough blonde number one. "How could this not be about men?"

Her question hung in the air. I couldn't imagine making decisions about how I should look based on what men wanted. Why would I care about a man's opinion when I had no interest in being with one? I thought back to Christine and how she had allowed Ted to cajole her into a fuchsia lipstick. Christine had been a child then and these were grown women. Still, they couldn't discount men, or they weren't ready to. Not for the first or last time, I realized how sad it was to be straight. Yes, I had a don't ask, don't tell life. Yes, this ate at me, slowly, in ways that I can now admit were harmful. This robbed me of the full range of human experience. But I wasn't stuck with a man's version of beauty. In that one significant way, I enjoyed a freedom that the women gathered at this table would never know. I didn't resent tough blonde number one. I pitied her.

When she realized I had no plan to answer tough blonde number one's question, the Barneys PR woman took over the proceedings. I didn't sell very many Reveal products at that lunch. However, my vision for Reveal had never been stronger.

I wasn't downtown the day the towers fell. A routine doctor's appointment near my apartment spared me from that. I stopped at my Flatiron studio before heading to the office, and was home when I realized what had happened. There was screaming and yelling outside my window. I switched on my television set and saw it. Pure, utter horror.

I stayed inside the rest of the day; the television played the news the whole time. There was no reason to leave. I was afraid of how the air might smell, of what I might see. My parents tried to call my cell, I learned this days later, but they couldn't reach me, the cellular networks and phone lines were overwhelmed. I spoke with Ellen, though. Of course, she managed to get through when no one else could, how I will never know. It was the only time I ever heard Ellen's voice tremble, which sharpened the terror of that day. Ellen offered to have me come "home," as she put it, to move back into the guest room. I considered it, I really did. But even amid that chaos, I held tight to the independence that had propelled me out of her apartment.

It is crazy to me that the youngest employee at Reveal today was only eight years old back then. Do they remember anything? Do they remember how people were scared to enter tall buildings after that, in a city teeming with skyscrapers? How people refused to go downtown below certain streets? Can they understand how it suddenly felt like your life could be ripped from you, any second of any day, because you had the fatal misfortune of being in the wrong place at the wrong time? Of course, this possibility was always there—it is part of the bargain of being alive. But before the trauma of that event, most people could comfortably suppress this knowledge as they navigated daily existence. Afterward, there was no comfort to be had.

The thing I remember most from that day is not the footage of those stricken towers—though that footage will never leave me. Nor is it the sense of a world forever reconfigured. Nor the unimaginable loss and the penetrating fear that would wake me in the middle of the night, for weeks after, with no warning, and leave me shaking and drenched in sweat. The thing that I remember most is the news reports, on television and in the next day's papers, about the throngs of people roaming the city, cell service down, searching with desperation for their children and husbands and wives and girlfriends and boyfriends and colleagues and friends. There was no one on those streets searching for me. I was alone, in my apartment, ice-cold bottle of vodka by my side, the news loop my only companion.

I don't say this out of self-pity. What I'm trying to express is a sense of clarity that emerged from the tragedy of that day. I had made a choice of absolute devotion to Reveal, at the expense of everything else. Instead of questioning that, I doubled down.

Investor Relations

Many businesses fled downtown after 9/11. To Ellen's credit—and Donald's—Reveal remained in SoHo, though the motivation wasn't altruism. It was about appearances. New York needed to project resilience and so, too, did a New York–based company. Besides, Ellen was able to renegotiate our lease and, suddenly, our rent was a fraction of the price.

Money was on her mind. My performance at the Barneys lunch had convinced her that we required image-maintenance help, which would in turn demand more funds.

"I would like you to interview some public relations candidates," Ellen told me one afternoon at lunch in early 2002, between bites of a Nicoise salad at a Madison Avenue canteen.

"Isn't that something we can outsource? We've had plenty of press already without one," I replied. Ellen frowned as I chewed my steak frites. It was increasingly evident that my days of French fries were numbered.

"Barneys did not go well," Ellen said. "I don't want something like that to happen again. In our current climate, we must be extra careful. You need someone to shape Reveal's messaging and keep it consistent."

"That Barneys lunch was an outlier," I argued. "Those women were angry that I was late, even though I was actually early, and they were an older demographic. Not everyone thinks like they do."

Ellen narrowed her eyes. "Older women, as you put it, have money to spend. We can't just rely on youth. An experienced PR person would understand how to reach both groups without alienating anyone."

"Fine. I'll start interviewing people," I said, as I sliced a bite of steak and shoved it in my mouth.

"Good. And speaking of money, we really need to bring on some new investors," Ellen continued, her frown returning. "We are running out of funds to grow Reveal and pay these new employees. There's no way I can continue this situation single-handedly. I was chatting with the financier Chip Adler the other night at the breast cancer research gala. He expressed interest in Reveal. He's noticed all the celebrity fragrances coming out and those two big indie acquisitions a couple of years back. He believes that in times of great stress, women will turn to beauty as a salve. Chip could bring on some other people, too. He wants to meet with you first and get to know your vision better."

"Okay," I said. "No problem."

"He mentioned Thursday evening would work."

A waitress approached our table to clear our plates. Ellen had barely finished half her salad. As the waitress reached across me to remove my steak frites, I caught her eyes and smiled. I watched the waitress's retreating figure clandestinely. Or so I thought.

"Careful there," Ellen said pointedly.

I could feel my cheeks reddening.

"I don't care what you do in the privacy of your home," Ellen said sternly, "but if we are continuing this journey together, you must promise you will remain discreet. Not everyone is as open-minded as I am. You're a founder. This brand will live or die on your image."

I nodded.

"We are in a different league now. There's no room for sloppy mistakes. Compartmentalize—that's what leaders do. I know you have what it takes." Ellen flagged down the same waitress, who paused at our table. She glanced in my direction, and I stared down at the white tablecloth. "We'll take the check, please. Just the check."

I had committed yet another youthful mistake by allowing Ellen a glimpse at my vulnerability. Sex is a basic human need, but investors don't want to see you as human. Neither do customers. To them, you must be aspirational. A woman of any sexuality who fulfills her basic need isn't aspirational, she isn't a leader, she's out of control. Our society believes that, unlike men, women are incapable of having sex without emotions. Nobody wants an entrepreneur who feels things; they want an entrepreneur who earns money.

Ellen was right: leadership requires strength and a sense of priorities. The reality was—still is, frankly—that the particulars of my personal life would have negatively impacted business, should such particulars have come to light. Hers was a tough-love approach, no arguments there. As a twenty-seven-year-old, I felt protected, like she had my best interests in mind. Today, I wonder whether "love" was ever in the mix at all.

Chip Adler asked to meet for a drink at a hotel on Park Avenue. Dark and clubby with oversized leather armchairs and brass sconces, the hotel's lounge was a bastion of clichéd masculinity. Ellen had instructed me to *wear a dress and heels—but not too high, Chip's on the short side*. I obeyed her orders and had on a long-sleeved black jersey dress that clung to my hips as I waited for Chip in an armchair. He arrived a few minutes after me, in a cloud of cologne and entitlement. I greeted him with a handshake and he held my proffered hand far more tightly than professional decorum dictated. He was, indeed, petite.

Chip flagged down a waiter.

"The usual," he told the guy, then gestured at me. "And the lady will have—"

"Thanks, I'll have a Johnnie Walker Black neat," I cut in before Chip could order for me.

The waiter glided away. Chip's eyes traveled the length of my bare shins. He met my gaze and his wrinkled face settled into a smirk.

"So you're the famous Maxine."

"Feel free to call me Max."

"I prefer Maxine. It's more elegant, don't you think?"

I shrugged to show him he couldn't rattle me, though my jaw started to throb. "Up to you."

The waiter returned with our drinks. Chip's order was a smoky single malt, whose peat I could smell from three feet away. He clutched his cut-crystal tumbler.

"Cheers," he said.

I clinked glasses with him. Butterscotch filmed my tongue.

"I'm glad we're doing this. Ellen has told me so much about you. I had to put a face to a name."

Though he must have been barely forty-five, Chip's hairline was departing briskly. He had combed his gray-streaked mop to the side of his face, mitigation for this recession.

"Ellen tells me you'd like to invest in Reveal and that you have some friends who would join you."

Chip guffawed. He sipped his single malt.

"Cutting right to the chase, aren't you? I might. Depends on what you're offering."

My jaw still throbbed, but I kept my voice even. "Our first product was Flush. It sold out of Bloomingdale's and Henri Bendel within a month of its release. We introduced more colors of Flush and also Glow, a highlighter, that's doing the same all over the country. And I have plenty more ideas to expand."

"Impressive."

"We've been called a cult brand. Unlike our competition, we're purposely maintaining a very minimal lineup. Keeping our offerings tight."

"Just how I like it."

My stomach clenched and my molars ground against each other.

"I'm more interested in you," Chip continued. "Tell me about yourself, Maxine. Where are you from? What do you do for fun?"

I reached for my tumbler of whiskey and gulped a mouthful.

"I'm all about my work," I said. "What's fun for me is watching Reveal succeed."

Chip leaned forward. Beneath the table he placed his small, manicured hand on my upper thigh. He ran his hand down it, then patted my kneecap.

"Relax, honey. I want to know you. We'll get to your little business, I promise."

I was tempted to slap him or toss my drink in his face, get up from that stupid armchair, and leave the hotel. Reveal's future kept me in my seat. We needed money; Ellen had made that clear. For all his sleaziness, Chip ran in powerful circles. He could be a help—or a hindrance.

I rested my hand on Chip's tiny paw.

"I have a boyfriend," I said.

Chip's paw tightened its grip. His gold wedding band pressed into my knee.

"Of course you do."

"He's a heavyweight boxer."

The fingers of Chip's hand stiffened.

"He has a bit of a temper. I wouldn't want you to get in trouble."

I widened my eyes a smidge, in mock concern. I removed my hand from Chip's paw, and he retracted his arm immediately, and sat back in his chair, like he couldn't get far enough away from me.

"Understood," he said. "Thank you for letting me know. So about this Reveal of yours . . ."

Back at my apartment, the phone rang while I was changing. I freed myself from the black jersey dress and picked up the receiver.

"Chip was very impressed," Ellen cooed. "Whatever you did, it worked."

"He's a sleazebag," I shot back.

"He agreed to invest in Reveal and pitch it to his friends."

"Ellen, he felt me up at the table. He clearly wanted to sleep with me."

There was a pause on Ellen's end. I could hear her shallow breaths. When her voice returned, it had an edge.

"As I said, whatever you did, it worked."

"I didn't sleep with him!"

"I never said you did."

A realization came over me.

"Why did you tell me to wear a dress and heels to drinks?"

"I wanted you to look presentable. Chip is more old-fashioned, as you likely gathered. He doesn't react well to a woman in pants."

I squeezed the phone's handset so tightly, I thought it might shatter.

"Ellen, did you know he was going to hit on me?"

There was another pause and more breathing. This time, I filled the dead air for her.

"Jesus, Ellen. How could you not have warned me? You sent me in there like a sacrificial lamb."

"If I had warned you, you wouldn't have shown up. I couldn't risk that. We need the money. Besides, I knew you would handle yourself. You're such a strong girl and you'll do whatever it takes. I'm proud of you, Maxine."

Ellen hung up the line. I placed the handset in the phone's cradle and sat on the edge of my bed. Ellen's cavalier attitude terrified me. Though I had never mistaken our relationship for a bond between equals, it hadn't occurred to me that I was disposable.

I could stand up to Ellen, make her promise never to do anything like this again. Threaten to take my company elsewhere if she refused to apologize. However, just as with Chip, pragmatism intervened. I needed Ellen's connections, her money. One call from her and the entire city would turn its collective back on me.

It was more than necessity, though. Her final words, "I'm proud of you," settled in my chest. My father and mother had never said the same. I had no doubt that when neighbors asked after me, they hung their heads in shame. Ellen had sent me into a lion's den with full confidence that I would emerge unscathed. I had fulfilled her very high expectations. Leaders were supposed to be tough. They were supposed to compartmentalize. These were Ellen's lessons. I saved Reveal and I made Ellen proud. To my younger self, that was a worthy reward.

So once again, I accepted Ellen's tough love. I accepted Chip and his buddies, too. The irony is not lost on me that a company founded on beauty through a female gaze was now, thanks to these new investors, a brand funded by men. If I'm honest, it had been this way before Chip came on board, I just hadn't been willing to acknowledge it. As a child, I had vowed never to make myself reliant upon men. Adult Max broke this promise many times over.

The morning of her interview for the public relations job at Reveal, Elizabeth Sanders strolled into my glass-enclosed SoHo office in one of the dowdiest outfits I have ever seen. She wore a beige skirt suit made of an awful rayon material that managed to look cheap and overwrought at the same time. The jacket was too tight in the shoulders. The skirt puckered and ballooned in places with extra space that Elizabeth's proportions didn't require. I almost sent her packing on the spot. How could I delegate the messaging of Reveal's public face to someone who couldn't style an inoffensive outfit?

Ellen had raved about Elizabeth to me. Elizabeth's résumé, spackled with an Ivy League degree and stints at the best PR agencies in the city, spoke to this confidence.

"Nice to meet you," Elizabeth said, as she reached across the desk to shake my hand. Her grip was firm and her face was bare. Bold move, I thought, to show up to an interview at a beauty company cosmetics-free. There was a genius that I respected. Elizabeth needed to sell Reveal's story to the outside world. Her ability to do that didn't require that she partake of the goods. I'd bet money there are nicotine executives who have never smoked a cigarette.

"You're probably wondering what kind of lunatic shows up for an interview at Reveal with no makeup on," Elizabeth continued as she sat in the chair across from me.

"No, of course not," I replied.

Elizabeth grinned, a mischievous parting of her lips that was at once all-knowing and playful.

"I won't pretend that I'm a cosmetics expert or that I understand beauty. I couldn't care less what lipstick a woman puts on." Elizabeth paused. Her shoulder-length brown hair was in desperate need of a trim.

This was either the dumbest or the most brilliant sales pitch I had ever heard. "Go on," I said.

"What I care about is Reveal's messaging. If you hire me, I will do everything in my power to ensure that the face Reveal shows the world is exactly the look you want."

I leaned back in my desk chair, which creaked its displeasure at my shift in position.

"What I offer you is consistency and transparency. I am telling you who I am. My place is by your side. I am essentially a professional wingwoman."

Elizabeth walked me through some of her previous PR campaign successes, then it was her turn to lean back in her chair. She crossed one beige nylon leg over the other—did I mention that she was wearing stockings—and flashed me that same grin. She had nailed the interview. It was merely a question of how soon I could make her a proper offer.

Elizabeth officially signed on as the director of public relations for Reveal within the week. Thirteen years later, she is now part of the company's executive team, too. Hiring her was one of the best decisions I made throughout my career, not only because she is loyal and unflinching in her assessment of what is needed. She is also my friend, one of the few people to whom I would apply that term. I can say with some certainty that when another disaster befalls this great city, Elizabeth will search for me in the streets. For that, I am forever grateful.

DAY FIVE

Afternoon

Following Sandrine's rousing visit earlier, I finally have the motivation to leave my apartment. Amanda's lawyer thinks I'm a monster, a creature who should be locked up under house arrest. Well, I'm no monster, I have nothing to fear. This is my narrative and in my narrative, I save the document of my life story, and I go for a run. Besides, my wrists need a break from the keyboard.

It is my first time outside in five days, since that ill-fated sunset reservoir stroll. The air smells like burnt caramel. I wear my usual workout uniform of black leggings and a zipped black pullover. My hair is in a low, neat ponytail. A baseball cap shades my face, which is slathered in SPF 50+. I don't normally run in the middle of the day, at a peak-UV-strength hour. Still, what little of the sun makes its way onto my skin feels calming.

I avoid the reservoir path—too soon, as they say—and elect for the concrete of the main park drive. I am struck by all the random people out at this hour. They walk their dogs. They ride their bikes. People frolic on grassy knolls in plaid shirts and denim jackets, earbuds in, books on a blanket or bench beside them. Who are these people? The perpetually unemployed? The genetically wealthy? Not all these idlers, I imagine, can be the victims of corporate accusations and Board treachery like me.

The repetitive movement of my run shakes loose the anger from my meeting with Sandrine. What was a dense wall of fury slowly transforms into a pile of benign rubble, bits and pieces scattered here and there until they are indistinguishable from the gravel of Central Park.

I am on the east side of the park drive, three miles into the six-mile loop, when a young Asian girl, maybe four or five years old, dashes in front of me. Her shiny dark hair is in two uneven pigtails tied with pink bows. She has on a matching pink plaid dress with a white turtleneck underneath. I am wearing earbuds, though the 1980s new wave station is playing at such a low level, I can easily hear the conversations of nearby pedestrians, runners, and cyclists. My environmental awareness is not impaired. The girl comes out of nowhere. I try to swerve, but she is so close to me, I end up accidentally kicking her in the shin—lightly, so lightly—with my left foot.

The young girl begins to cry. Her little face scrunches up like a used tissue. I scan her leg for blood and find none.

"Are you okay?" I ask her. "You really need to be more careful," I add. "You can't run out into the street like that."

An Asian woman, presumably the girl's mother, runs toward us.

"Esther," she admonishes the child, "what were you thinking? You could get hurt. You never run into the street like that!" This is my type of mother, one who blames her reckless child, not the grown adult minding her own business. Too many parents today coddle their children like they're made of handblown glass. I have no doubt these children will grow up to become insufferable wimps in the office, whining about working long hours and unable to weather criticism. A decade from now, we'll reminisce about the days when we thought millennials were the problem.

"That's exactly what I just told her," I say.

"Mooommmmy," the girl cries.

I thought Asian kids were always quiet and well behaved.

"I'm sorry about this. She knows better," says the mother. She turns to me. "Wait. You look so familiar. Have we met?"

My skin suddenly feels cold. The evaporating perspiration and slowing heart rate, I assume. "I don't think so," I say.

The mother stares at me. The young girl stops crying. She stares at me, too. I watch the mother's eyes narrow, her long thin brows angle downward. I step away, ready to finish my run.

"I should go," I say. "I'm glad she's okay."

"Reveal," says the mother. "You're Maxine Thomas." She clutches her daughter's hand and pulls her closer.

"You're a fan of our products?" I ask, my voice shaky.

"Get up, Esther," she tells her daughter. "Now." The mother stares at me. "You stay the hell away from me and my child," she yells. "You racist bitch."

My skin is frigid now. People around us stare. My lungs are so tight, I can't breathe. I start to run. To sprint. I don't stop until I am at the front door of my building.

I don't know what this woman read or heard about me, as I dismantled the Google alert for my name when I saw the first round of abhorrent headlines. I've avoided the internet altogether in the previous five days, my search for Caroline aside. Did this mother read a newspaper story? A social media post? She recognized me; that means there was a photo involved. What photos are people publishing? I'm sure the media is probably picking the most hideous photos imaginable—ones where my bare arm is shot from such an angle that it appears twice its actual size, or ones with stark overhead lighting. Perhaps they're even painting horns and a trident on me for good measure.

Thank god this mother didn't get a picture of me, though that may not stop her from a Facebook post of her own. I can see it now. Status update: *My daughter was attacked in Central Park by the beauty mogul Maxine Thomas. She is evil incarnate.* Should I warn Elizabeth? Call Sandrine?

All I know is there will be no more Central Park visits until this ordeal is over. When it comes to controlling my narrative, typing is far safer than running.

Friends and Family

The end of my twenties sprinted by. Reveal continued to grow, with new hires in design, R&D, sales, and marketing. We expanded from suite 506 to half the fifth floor of our SoHo office building.

Product wise, we expanded, too, though we did so at a very measured pace. The idea was to treat Flush and Glow as verticals; we would go deep within each category instead of building out new ones. If a customer liked Flush, they'd want everything associated with it. "Highly selective" was our business motto.

There were more shades of Flush—the range now included ten colors total. We offered them in three different concentrations, Watery, 50/50, and Potent, like cocktails, so customers could decide how strong their look would be. We added tinted lip balms, Flush for Lips, in the same range as Flush, and released copper, rose gold, bronze, and silvery iterations of Glow. We celebrated Reveal's fifth anniversary with Glow and Flush for Nails; they referenced the original vessel I had used for the concoction that became Flush. Our packaging designer dreamed up expensive, double-sided Lucite compacts that contained a cream-solid Glow and Flush for Lips. Ellen convinced Donald, Chip, and his buddies that they were worth some extra cash—appearances mattered as much as the contents. It was an adage Donald understood well.

The early aughts were a sea of earnest girliness and strip club sexuality, an unholy pairing that only American culture could produce. Grown women coated their lips in ultra-shiny lip gloss that was so sticky it caught any blowing strands of their hair like they were human Venus flytraps. Runway and editorial models trended toward girls with enormous, innocent eyes and cherubic features. Meanwhile, Tom Ford, who was the creative director of Gucci, debuted an ad campaign featuring a model whose pubic hair had been shaved into the brand's logo. Average women wore the waistbands of their jeans so low that their pink lace thongs poked out at the top. Eyebrows continued to be pin-thin to a degree that many women now regret. Beneath those perilous tightropes sat frosted eye shadow that gave the effect of zero-Celsius conjunctivitis. Tacky, shameless, balding, frozen: by comparison, Reveal makeup was the portrait of subtlety.

Fortune put me on the cover of their Innovators issue in 2003. A well-known conglomerate had expressed interest in acquisition and, though we turned them down because Ellen—or Donald—thought the company had undervalued Reveal, that it would be worth far more after some serious years of growth, the rumor garnered us much-welcomed heat. For the cover, I wore a white pantsuit from Helmut Lang, its lapels hanging off the front like first-prize ribbons.

"You look like you're waving a flag of surrender," Ellen chastised me over the phone when she received her subscriber copy of the issue. "We need you to project strength."

"It's a reference to the suffragettes," I argued, though the real motivation behind my fashion choice came from a sinewy saleswoman at Helmut Lang's SoHo boutique.

"Oh, come on. What does the right to vote have to do with Reveal?"

"Autonomy," I pushed back. "They both express female autonomy." I had stumbled upon an old issue of *Ms.* magazine at a vintage store a few weeks back and was happy to recycle an argument I had read there if it suited my cause.

"I don't think our customers will get the reference," Ellen said. "And white isn't exactly a slimming color, you know."

"Noted," I said.

"You'd do well to run these things by me first."

There was a new tension in my relationship with Ellen. She accepted my decisions with increased reluctance. A layer of distrust seemed to undergird her words. Hadn't I done everything she had asked when it came to Chip and my sexuality? I had swallowed my pride, kept Reveal afloat, maintained discretion. By her standards, I was the consummate leader.

I wondered if Ellen was simply trying to claim relevancy. So long as there was something about my choices that required critique, she could convince herself that she had an important role to play in my life. My decision to move out continued to sting. Ellen was lonely. Most of her friendships with those other Park Avenue ladies were empty games of one-upmanship and Donald was hardly a true partner.

My twenty-ninth birthday was in November of the same year that Reveal turned five. Ellen threw me a dinner party at a brasserie in the Meatpacking District to celebrate this final gasp of my twenties. We were seated at a central banquette, surrounded by the din of inebriated chatter, platters of icy fruits de mer scattered before us. Ellen was at the center of the table. She clinked a salad fork against her flute of champagne and stood up.

"Thank you all for joining me to celebrate Maxine's birthday!"

There was gentle clapping from the gathered guests, among them Elizabeth, who was seated beside me.

"Reveal has had a banner year. Here's to the next five."

More scattered whooping.

"To Maxine," Ellen intoned, as she held her flute outward and looked me dead in the eye, "to Maxine, on your twenty-ninth birthday. You have accomplished so much."

A few awws circled the table.

"You are so devoted to Reveal," Ellen continued with a crisp smile, "When I was your age, a woman's priority was finding a husband. How lucky you are to have other options. Anyway, I know you will never allow *anyone* to distract you from our mission. Your toughness makes me proud."

While I appreciated Ellen's sidestepping of the husband issue, the mention of "anyone" felt gently threatening. Was I supposed to be celibate now, too, on top of emotionless? I don't remember whether I said anything in response. Most likely, I plastered a grin across my face. Next to me, Elizabeth's eyes narrowed.

In the year and a half since I had hired Elizabeth, she had become a confidante. This surprised me as much as it did anyone else. True to her interview, Elizabeth had little interest in aesthetics. Her first couple of months on the job were a montage of terrible outfits: scratchy and boxy skirt suits in a palette that can only be described as "dystopian landfill." One evening, I left the office at the same time as Elizabeth. In the glaring light of the building's elevator, my fashion feedback was uninhibited.

"Where do you like to shop?" I asked Elizabeth.

That professional, capable smile spread across her face. "Nowhere. I don't like shopping, at all."

"I can tell," I told her.

"I'd be happy to buy my outfits from Helmut Lang or Dior

Homme if you give me a separate clothing allowance. I'm not spending what little I earn on fashion."

I was shocked that she knew where I bought my suits.

"Don't mistake disinterest for ignorance," she said. "I know my stuff. I choose not to participate."

Elizabeth's answer impressed me. When the elevator dinged at the lobby, I realized I didn't want our conversation to end.

"Are you doing something right now?" I asked.

"I'm not," said Elizabeth.

"How about a post-work cooldown? On me."

"Lead the way."

We went to a bar a few blocks from the office. Elizabeth ordered a gin and tonic. I had a Scotch neat. We stayed for two rounds. Over the course of those drinks, there was nothing notable, from the outside, in our exchange. I asked Elizabeth about her background, what she had studied in school, experiences at previous jobs. In turn, she inquired about my creative development, my passion for beauty, the challenges I faced as a woman entrepreneur. The topics we covered went no deeper than a surface interview.

However, Elizabeth was anything but superficial. She really listened. I could tell from the concentration across her forehead. She didn't glance at her watch or at our surroundings, not once. There was none of the insecurity that so many women have, the concave slouch of the shoulders or the stiffness of a neck that ossifies into a posture of preemptive attack. Destroy another woman before she has the chance to uncover your weaknesses. Elizabeth didn't operate like that. She was confident because she was free of artifice. She didn't pretend to be better than she was.

That first night became a weekly routine. Drinks turned into phone calls and text messages and meals on the weekends. Benign conversations about work and outside interests meandered into more personal territory. I didn't worry that my friendship with Elizabeth would confuse our professional interactions. She was an adult and I trusted that she would never spend time with me out of pity or corporate advancement. Her demeanor was so open, so completely at ease. I was safe with her.

In that initial elevator ride, Elizabeth didn't just upend my expectations around who she was. She showed me another way to function: you don't have to live and breathe your job to care. Still, Elizabeth's example of a healthy work-life balance is not one I have ever mastered. I don't believe that a person in my position has that option. My work resonates with customers because of how much I pour into it. The image of an artistic founder is part of Reveal's allure. Flush and Glow and everything else we offer—they are extensions of me. Rather, they are extensions of who the public and my investors wish me to be. Who I am really is another matter.

My father called me a few weeks before my thirtieth birthday. He had a new cell phone, whose number I didn't recognize, so I couldn't screen his call as I had others over the past few years.

"Maxine," he said when I answered.

My stomach clenched at the sound of his voice.

"It's been a while," he continued. "How are you?"

"I'm fine," I said icily. Like he cared how I was. "How are you?"

"Good, good. I'm planning to retire in a few years." My father was sixty. "Slowly winding things down now."

"That's good," I said. "I should run. I need to get to an appointment." It was a Sunday morning and I was still in my pajamas.

"This early on a weekend?" he asked.

"No days off," I told him briskly.

"I meant to call last year when I saw that *Fortune* story," he offered. "You looked good. It sounds like work is going well."

I felt a flush of pride, though it hardened into anger. "Yes, contrary to your prognosis years ago, I'm doing very well on my own. Turns out I didn't need that college degree or corporate career. My ideas are better than anything that already exists."

"I've only ever wanted you to succeed," said my father, a quiet pain filling his voice. "For you to be happy."

"You wanted me to have your version of success, your idea of happiness. I wanted something different."

"Are you happy?" he asked.

"Of course," I said. "I have a thriving career and I'm changing the beauty landscape. The pursuit of creative excellence makes me happy."

My father cleared his throat. "Who do you share this happiness with?"

"Myself," I said fiercely, though I was curious about his question. Unlike my mother, my father had never pushed the idea of a boyfriend or a husband. I wondered if he knew who I was and if his avoidance of the boyfriend-husband issue had been his expression of this hunch. In another world, he and I might have had a conversation about this. What did I have to lose? I was already estranged from my parents. What further harm could my revelation have caused? But in this world, Reveal's entire existence rested on my shoulders and my primary investors had made clear that my image was the most important factor of success. I couldn't afford to trust someone who had previously doubted my choices.

"Your mother and I would like to take you out for dinner to celebrate your birthday," my father said.

"The last dinner didn't go so well," I replied.

My father sighed. "Think about it," he said.

"Maybe we could do something for Christmas," I relented. "I really do need to go."

"Okay, Maxine. I'll call you again in a few weeks." He sighed again. "We won't be here forever."

On Christmas Day that year, I met my parents for lunch at a restaurant in Midtown. We pushed our food around our plates in circles. My dad asked polite questions about Reveal. My mother asked pointed questions about my perpetual singledom and my preference for pantsuits. They both looked smaller and more lined than I remembered. When we parted ways outside the restaurant, my father patted me on the shoulder.

"Let's do this again next year?" he asked.

"Sure," I said.

I imagined that other world, the one in which the three of us had open and nonjudgmental communication and I could trust that my parents would love me no matter what. That world was a fantasy and I saved my dreaming for Reveal.

Ahead of the Game

There is nothing that compares to the sensation of a woman's face beneath your fingers. It is the most miraculous feeling on earth. In that moment, a woman is a vessel of vulnerability, trusting of your skills. She believes that the makeup you will rub, brush, pat, blend across her skin will make her shine. Your touch will render her whole.

The continued rise of Reveal brought an end to my private makeup artist business because the payoff was too slim to justify the time. Relinquishing this aspect of my selfhood was painful. Those hours with my clients were a form of love.

Severed from this formative part of my identity, I poured myself even further into Reveal. Over the next couple of years, we moved into fragrance, something Chip insisted on because he had been advised that perfume equaled sales. The margins were so high because the perfume's synthetic ingredients were cheap; the packaging cost more than the product itself. Two blond celebrities, Paris Hilton and Britney Spears, had launched signature scents to great success. Reveal followed their lead in 2005 with a range of musky eau de parfums, inspired by the nether regions of a frisky ballet dancer, not that this is public knowledge. The scents were a hit. We also launched Glow for Body, a moisturizing cream highlighter in multiple shades that women could daub on their clavicles and shoulders and down the ridged line of their shins. For the holiday season, we created a limited-edition dry oil spray that combined the shimmer of Glow with the heady musk of our fragrances. It was so successful we added it to our permanent lineup. By 2006, Reveal was a total-body operation.

At the same time, I was testing formulas of Glow for Eyes, a cream eye shadow with a mica-inflected powdery finish that I hoped to package as a stick. I handed out samples to all the girls in the office and made them wear it to dinner, on the weekends, out dancing, even to the gym to see how well it held up to sweat and oils on the eyelids. We had yet to land on a formula that didn't crease.

I needed a new hero, too, separate from the Glow category. The marketplace was now saturated with copies of Flush and Glow. I was feeling the pressure for my next hero to innovate. The harder I strove to dance around the idea of a skin-toned product, the more I realized that my avoidance was the biggest indicator that this was where I needed to focus. There's a reason that flesh-colored makeup is called "foundation" or "base": it is the crux of a woman's entire routine, the first layer of defense a woman has between her unadorned self and the public, which is eager to pounce on any perceived flaw.

In 2006, fake tans proliferated courtesy of beet-dyed lotions and full-body airbrushing sessions. Tom Ford had left Gucci and had just launched his own beauty line with a single fragrance heavy on patchouli, vanilla, and black truffle. That same year one of the only out lesbians on television signed a two-million-dollar contract for a daytime talk show with a clause that required she keep her hair long. The messaging was clear. Women needed to be jet-set bronzed, high-end edible, and very, very straight even when they were very, very gay.

Elizabeth and I had drinks one night at a bar on Mercer Street that was a favorite neighborhood watering hole because of its unexpected 1990s-bachelor-pad decor. Cowhide rugs. Boxy leather seating. Mirrored tables. SoHo in the mid-aughts experienced a major luxury boom. Big-name European brands consumed the independent boutiques and galleries that had filled the area's cast-iron buildings through much of the '90s. A thin film of artistic grunge remained in pockets of the neighborhood, but it was one swipe of a designer mop away from extinction, replaced by the sanitized shine of new money.

We sat across from each other at one of the cocktail tables in the back. Elizabeth clicked through emails on her BlackBerry, between sips of her gin and tonic. I had tried, in vain, to convert her away from this collegiate go-to beverage. My BlackBerry was on the table. I couldn't look at another email about quarterly numbers, sales projections, and vendor lists. The struggle to procure enough raw materials to fulfill our manufacturing needs was a constant headache. I caressed my glass of whiskey and let my eyes wander.

A woman sat on a leather barstool, alone but seemingly not lonely, and flicked through messages on her own smartphone. Her long legs were bare; her tanned calves gleamed against her suede minidress. Her dirty-blond hair was in a messy bun at the nape of her neck. She was deep in thought over whatever message was on her phone. When she finally glanced up, I made sure her dark eyes went directly to mine.

Elizabeth's eyes landed on me, too.

"Did you see that email from Ellen about Saks?"

I ignored her and Elizabeth followed the direction of my gaze.

"Hmm," she said. That was Elizabeth's way of saying, *I don't approve, but there is nothing I can do so expressing disapproval would be a waste.* It wasn't the source of my interest that bothered Elizabeth, rather it was my refusal to choose one woman, to settle down and approximate a monogamous, committed lifestyle. Elizabeth was single herself because she found dating exhausting, though she hoped to marry a worthy man eventually and build a child-free partnership with him. The issue she took with my extracurricular activities was the extent to which they drained my resources.

"It's an ongoing distraction," she'd lectured me once.

"Exactly," I told her. "That is the point, to distract me from life's suffering."

"I'm not suggesting you become a spinster like Ellen demanded. Isn't it time to find one person and stay with them? Quality over quantity."

I shrugged in reply. It was a rhetorical question anyway. Elizabeth knew I had spent my most recent birthday in a Lower East Side hotel room with three bottles of champagne, a tin of caviar, a bag of Frito-Lays, and two naked thirty-something women whom I would never see again.

"Think of how much more productive you would be," Elizabeth had pressed, "with the extra time you waste on whatever it is that you're doing."

"What makes you think I'm not productive in bed? Glow would not exist without my nocturnal endeavors. Neither would our fragrances."

"If we had a product for every woman who cycled through your bed, you and I would be multimillionaires."

On this night at the Mercer Street bar, Elizabeth followed up her "Hmm" with a deep sigh and a toss of her brown hair. She reached for her half-empty gin and tonic and finished it.

"I guess this would be my signal to depart."

"You don't have to leave right now," I protested.

"Are you inviting me to join? Because otherwise, I'll postpone the inevitable."

"Would you accept the invitation if I extended it?"

Elizabeth glanced again at the dirty-blonde, then back at me.

"She's gorgeous, but you are not my type."

A more honest wingwoman there never was.

"I appreciate that. Your drink's on me."

"I should hope it is," Elizabeth said. She stood up from the table, slung a purse over her arm. "See you tomorrow, killer."

Elizabeth disappeared out the bar's door. A server came by to clear her glass and she indicated my near-empty tumbler.

"Another round?"

I looked at the dirty-blonde to see if she was watching me. She was.

"Yes, I'll take another, thanks. And I'm changing my seat."

The server disappeared and I walked over to the woman. She was enveloped in the scent of vanilla and tobacco.

"I thought I'd come introduce myself before you leave. I'm Max."

The woman held out her smooth hand and I shook it.

"Sasha. I'm not leaving. Why don't you join me for another round?"

An hour and one cab ride later we were at my Flatiron apartment. The frenetic glow of New York beamed in through my windows as I eased Sasha out of her suede dress and tried to guide her through the otherwise dark studio toward my bed.

"Let's stay here," she murmured.

We were pressed against my bare walls. Goose bumps rose on my arms, from Sasha or the cool plaster against my skin, I'm not sure. She had the firm body of a fitness acolyte because she taught Spin classes to help pay her way through law school. She kissed me and tugged at the waistband of my pants. I pushed her gently in the direction of my sofa, a few feet away.

Sasha lay across its firm seat, haloed in the blurry light from my windows. Her matching bra and underpants were a beige mesh. I imagine they were likely sold to her as "nude," but they were a couple of shades too light to ever be mistaken for her faux-tanned coloring.

Still, the effect was mesmerizing; the mesh had a glossy finish and Sasha's skin shone through its hazy filter. Instead of sitting on top of her body, blocking its natural vibrancy, her sheer lingerie imparted an otherworldly sheen.

"Are you just going to stand there and stare at me?" Sasha asked.

"Do you really mind being looked at?"

"No." Sasha sat up on the sofa and unhooked her bra. "But in that case, let me get a bit more comfortable."

"Fine, I guess I'll join you," I said, in mock exasperation. I had already gotten what I needed from this encounter.

The following year, we made our first foray into international waters, pairing with the Harrods department store in London as the exclusive UK retailer of Reveal. We launched Glow for Eyes there and Ellen wanted me to fly over for the occasion. Much to her consternation I was too consumed with the countless development rounds of Whisper, a tinted serum laced with essential oils and a dash of opalescence to lend women's faces the same gauzy luster of Sasha's lacy underpinnings. We went through twenty-five iterations—too sticky, too oily, not enough coverage, etc.—before we arrived at the perfect formulation. The debut of Whisper coincided with the ten-year anniversary of Reveal.

Unlike the more traditional tinted moisturizers on the market, Whisper was thinner. It hearkened back to the clean, minimalist skin of an early 1990s runway model, but it was less "recently showered" and more "freshly baptized" in finish. Whisper was my antidote to the flat, matte foundation that persisted in 2008 and the late-aughts more generally—well, that and the full-body bronzer of which Sasha had likely partaken. Her underwear was more the muse than her faux-tanned epidermis. I even nodded to her lingerie in the campaign: we shot a bottle of Whisper nestled in a froth of nude French lace.

Elizabeth booked me a television spot for the launch. The morning of the interview, I sat in the show's greenroom, Elizabeth on the sofa beside me. By then, her attire had improved marginally. Her suits fit better and she had traded in that horrid polyester for the natural wonders of cotton, wool, and, occasionally, cashmere. No one would mistake her for a fashion lover, though; she didn't care enough. But she cared about Reveal and me and she could sense across the tight air between us that something inside me was awry.

"You okay over there?"

I turned my face, gleaming with Whisper, toward her.

"Why? Does my makeup look okay?"

"Forget your makeup."

"Elizabeth, Reveal is a makeup company. Did I put on too much Flush? Does my face look too pink?"

"You are perfect, as always," Elizabeth replied, with no pause to consider my face. "I meant that you seemed quiet. Are you nervous? It's not like you."

"I haven't slept well the past few nights."

"Whisper is great. You know that. Don't give it another thought."

"Three minutes, Maxine." A woman with a headset and clipboard motioned in my direction.

"Got it."

"Maybe you should take a vacation," Elizabeth pressed as she raked her brown hair into a low ponytail. "After we finish the launch of Whisper."

"Where would I go? What would I do? Lie on some beach in the Caribbean?"

"There are worse fates."

I patted Elizabeth's shoulder. "Maybe for others."

Out I went into the bright klieg lights of television, with Elizabeth's confidence propping up my shaky self-esteem. The television appearance went swimmingly—or so I thought. In my mind, the pancake-faced anchor looked like she wanted to lick Whisper off my cheeks, she was so excited. It turned out my nerves were justified, though. Whisper was a flop.

The downside of being a visionary is that on occasion, you are so far ahead of the game you lose a few matches. The comments were immediate, thanks to the internet and the advent of beauty blogs. *Greasy. Oil spill. Butter face.* That last one was creative. We had released Whisper in a tightly edited group of three shades. Our argument was that Whisper was so sheer, the shades didn't have to match a person's skin color perfectly, each of the three iterations could work on a wide array of tones. Apparently, that array was not wide enough. In addition to the greasy finish, Whisper's narrow-minded conception was a point of contention among diversity proponents. I can only imagine how much worse it would be now, with social media multiplying everything instantly. On second thought, I don't have to use my imagination at all.

Today in 2015, young women are obsessed with a dewy look. Entire companies are built on this premise, and I have no doubt they will ride my idea hard into the billion-dollar sunset. Face routines are predicated on achieving a glass-skin gleam. Where is the redemption for Whisper? I was seven years too early to the glossy party.

To make matters worse, around the time that Whisper debuted, the makeup tides shifted toward a chiseled, contoured face prompted by the explosive combination of online video tutorials and a certain curvaceous reality TV star. Everywhere, young women in clingy bandage dresses were baking and sculpting their cheekbones like they were clay vessels instead of human flesh. Whisper became a miscreant in a marketplace crowded with bronzer palettes and fluffy brushes and jars of translucent setting powders.

The final blow to Whisper had nothing to do with skin color or beauty trends. It was the market crash in September 2008. Ellen was livid when we spoke over the phone.

"This is a nightmare, Maxine," she practically snarled.

"It will be okay, Ellen," I reassured her. "We can tweak the formula, add some extra shades, relaunch it."

"Are you out of your mind? We look like fools. Chip and his crew are furious."

"Every business takes a hit here and there," I said, as defensiveness crept into my throat. "There's no way I could have predicted that contouring would return. Or a market crash."

"That is literally your job, to predict the future, stock markets aside. And to sell it. Otherwise, what the hell are we doing here?" Ellen inhaled audibly. "I don't know what we're doing here, I'm in over my head. We all are. Is this a real business?"

I was stunned. Ellen had never expressed anything less than utter confidence in her abilities as a businesswoman. Her question scared me more than her fury.

"Of course it's a real business. A highly successful one. This is a small setback, nothing more. The markets will rebound and we'll regroup and move on."

"We will move on, that is for certain," Ellen said, her voice crisp as starched Italian sheets. "We don't have a choice. We cannot continue as we are now. Things are going to change."

I wish I'd paid closer attention to those parting words. Though I'm not sure what good it would have done me.

In another unrelated jolt to my professional security, my assistant decided to quit nine months or so after Whisper failed its exams. I don't remember her name or what number assistant she was. My history with assistants before Amanda is a book of blank pages. I was always protective of my privacy, for obvious reasons; before Amanda, no assistant of mine had access to my credit card statement. Before Amanda: that should be the title of this document.

We were technically mid–hiring freeze for many months after the crash. The possibility of layoffs was floated. Elizabeth helped convince Ellen to let me replace the departed assistant. When Amanda Weston penetrated my life, I was coming off the biggest failure of my career. I was too low in spirits, too gobsmacked by her beauty to consider the potential danger lurking beneath her poise.

Amanda was a fresh college graduate, one month out of Sarah Lawrence. She didn't so much walk into my office as glide, like an invisible force cushioned her every step. She wore a dotted swiss skirt and a high-necked, Edwardian-style blouse, despite the late-June heat. It gave her an appearance of chastity. Her hair was a shiny dark brown, her skin a light tan. Amanda's eyes were both large and elongated. As with Caroline over a decade earlier, I struggled to locate her ethnic origins—I would never have asked her this directly, of course—though they seemed partially Asian. The way Amanda sat in the chair across from me, her posture ballerina straight and expectant, clicked something in my stomach I didn't know existed.

I glanced at the copy of Amanda's résumé on my desk, grateful for a prop that could prevent me from staring too long at her delicate face. Amanda had interned at three top PR agencies in the summers between semesters at Sarah Lawrence; she had done an eight-week stint at a larger beauty competitor.

For the first half of the interview, I grilled Amanda on her previous experience, her college extracurriculars, her educational background, not that these things had much bearing on her ability to perform the job. After all, I was a college dropout. Then I asked the same questions I posed to every Reveal candidate.

"Why beauty?" I asked. "Why Reveal?"

Amanda leaned forward in her chair, like the eager recent student she was.

"First of all, I am obsessed with your products. I'm wearing both Glow and Flush, in case that isn't clear. Whisper, too." Her face was ferocious with sympathy. "I love Whisper. All those haters have no taste."

She had the job on that comment alone.

"I couldn't agree more."

"The very thinking behind Reveal," she continued, "is so bold. That applying makeup can be an act of radical transparency. That beauty itself can be a revolutionary practice. In terms of why I want to work here, well, you are an inspiration. I've followed your journey since I was in middle school. Who better to learn from as I begin my own career?"

I know, I know. I should have stopped her right there. Red flags sprouted from her declaration about her "own career." Part of me was proud of her moxie. Here was a young woman after my own heart, one unafraid to declare her ambition from the outset.

"I appreciate your enthusiasm for Reveal and for me. You know this is an assistant role? You'll do basic clerical tasks, administrative errands, that sort of thing."

Amanda twirled a strand of her silky, dark hair. On anyone else, this gesture would have seemed like a nervous tic; when she did it, she oozed flirtatiousness.

"I fully understand the position. There is so much I can glean from you and I'd love nothing more than to spend the next couple of years getting you coffee. How do you take it, by the way?"

"Black, always," I replied. Willfully I ignored her mention of a "couple of years," as though she had already set an appropriate deadline for assistantship.

"Noted." Amanda smiled, not a wide-open grin of unbridled happiness, but a controlled lip parting, her teeth barely visible. "What about breakfast—should I get you breakfast, too?"

"You mean if you get the job?"

"You don't seem like someone who wastes her time on people you'll never see again." Amanda glanced down at the silver watch that encircled her slender wrist. "I've been here for almost twenty minutes. If you weren't going to hire me, you would have kicked me out by now."

It was like she could see through me from the very start. I was naked before her in ways that I have never experienced with anyone else.

"You might be right," I conceded.

There was that controlled smile again as Amanda leaned back in her chair.

"Excellent. When do I start?"

DAY SIX

Morning

Amanda seemed so innocent in that first meeting. She still looks innocent, with her fresh-faced aura, her girlie dresses, her small physique, and her pouty perfection. She is the sort of girl—young woman, I should say—who could walk straight into you at top speed and somehow you would be the one to apologize for the encounter.

Come to think of it, Amanda is not so different from that young girl, Esther was her name, who accosted me on my run yesterday. Their fragility shields them both from guilt.

I click out of my document and close my laptop. After yesterday's annoying kerfuffle, I can't stop ruminating on Esther's mother and what she must have seen online to provoke such a strong reaction to me. My brain spins out a demonic array of possibilities that are vile and sickening and likely untrue. Reality cannot possibly be as horrific as my dark imaginings. So after a cup of extra-strong coffee, I tap the Instagram icon on my phone.

My handle is @mtr11. Max. Thomas. Reveal. The month of my birth. I'm a Scorpio, as millennials love to inform me with the seriousness of doctors diagnosing a fatal illness. My account is private, and

I don't have a profile photo, just one of those blank bobblehead things. I follow four hundred accounts, among them @Reveal_Beauty98 and dear @AmandaWeston87.

I search for my name as a hashtag. The top result is from five days ago. The photo is, as suspected, criminal. My face is washed out, haggard; my hair is limp. I'm wearing a pewter evening suit. I believe the image is from a gala I attended a few years back. It was just after I returned from a work trip to Chicago that did not go well. I felt as though I aged about a decade in thirty-six hours and from the looks of this photo, I did.

I skim the caption. It is no different from the headlines I read days ago that prompted me to dismantle that Google alert. Anyone on social media knows the comments section is where the real fun happens.

Monster.

Racist cunt.

Send her fucked up ass to jail.

Queen of beauty? More like Queen of ugly.

This is why you can't trust women.

Fucking predator.

What did you expect from a dyke?

Can we bring back public stoning? Just for her.

No need to bring it back; public stoning never went away. I scroll and I scroll, and that strong coffee curdles in my stomach. I think I am going to vomit. What a fool I was to believe reality would transcend my worst fears. If my fate lay in the hands of public opinion, I would be on the guillotine come tomorrow. Who is to say that three days from now the Board will be any more rational than these trolls? For the first time since this nightmare began, I confront the possibility that I might lose.

After far too many minutes of spiraling, I tap away from my

search and scroll aimlessly through my feed. These young women on Instagram are something else. They all pose half naked or sometimes fully naked with their pouted lips and low body fat and neon bikinis and chests out to there. And their makeup. Cheesy, glossy mouths that look like they've been painted with bodily fluids. Eyes heavy with liner and shadow and fake lashes. Skin so doused in foundation and contouring it doesn't look real. I guess that's the point—to look unreal. To look like male fantasies.

Then there are their captions. So much complaining about how hard the world is, how tough it is to be a woman. I watch a five-minute video of a young woman *crying*. She is crying over some mean comments she received on social media about her appearance. People say she looks old, too thin. She decided to show her followers how unacceptable this treatment was by crying on camera, all while wearing a pink polka-dot bikini, rib cage visible beneath her obvious implants. She ends the video by flipping off her followers and stating, "The best revenge is looking hot." I almost scream, except what would be the point, there is no one around to hear me.

These young women today, with their pornographic sexuality and their nauseating sensitivity, they don't have a clue. No wonder a woman like me has to worry about being deemed a racist bitch or a monster; anything hardier than a doe-eyed Barbie shedding crocodile tears looks like a serial killer by comparison.

I wish I could point the Board to these nymphs' social media accounts. Do these women look like innocent victims, I want to ask them. Unfortunately for my case, Amanda is not like these women. Her feed is selfie-free. There are no bikinis, no gravity-defying implants. Her makeup is in keeping with the subtle perfection of Reveal. Her preferred dresses are buttoned so high on her neck, you barely get a flash of skin. If these other young women embody blatant provocation, Amanda is suggestion personified. She is smarter than those other young women because she recognizes the impact of understatement. That what you withhold is as important, if not more important, than what you show. When you refuse to give everything away, you spark an admirer's imagination. You create desire. Yearning. I know well the power of yearning because I've always driven toward the very things and people that the world tells me I can't have.

Money, Money, Money

The failure of Whisper remained a fresh wound in the years after the 2008 financial crisis. If my relationship with Ellen had been touchy before Whisper, after, it approached volcanic. The pressure was on to recover from this loss. The home fragrance category was picking up speed. Designer candles flickered in every boutique and living room. Ellen certainly relished the trend even if it arrived more than a decade after her failed ERA endeavor. As we entered the 2010s, Reveal released a collection of candles, room sprays, and diffusers, in our signature musks, and created a portable solid perfume in a chic compact so women could dab themselves on the go. Against my wishes, we finally took Whisper off the market. None of these moves assuaged Ellen's or Chip's concerns.

In the early months of Amanda's tenure, I was a very distracted boss. Normally, I was a paragon of self-sufficiency. I made my own doctor appointments and beauty upkeep sessions with waxing aestheticians, manicurists, hair stylists, facialists, and colorists. I booked my own restaurant reservations. I ordered my own personal care items. This may all sound obvious, but it isn't. Most people in my position have their assistants take care of these things. Their assistants practically wipe their asses when they go to the bathroom. Mine never did. I wanted my assistants to have the minimal amount of detail necessary to do their jobs. Anything extraneous—who I was having dinner with, how often I waxed my nether regions, what dermatological treatments I followed—offered them clues about who I was outside of my corner office. Those clues made me vulnerable. And vulnerability is a privilege that women leaders are not permitted, no matter what Sandrine might think.

The crack in my carefully constructed walls started with a taxi ride to Brooklyn. I was en route to a dinner date somewhere in the borough, which was not a place I frequented in 2010. Nor is it one I visit now. My date was "a Brooklyn-based artist" and she insisted that this restaurant in her neighborhood had the best tacos in the city. I could have cared less where or what we ate; she was gorgeous, and I figured the cross-county cab ride was the price of admission. That is, until the taxi halted on a block in the middle of nowhere.

"Here you are," said the driver.

"Are you sure?" I asked.

"This is Bushwick Avenue," he replied.

"Okay," I said, digging around in my handbag for my wallet. Nothing. I checked my coat pockets. Nothing. I tried my handbag again—still nothing.

"You going to pay or what?" said the driver.

"I'm so sorry. I seem to have forgotten my wallet. This has never happened to me before." It never had, not once in thirty-five years of life had I ever misplaced my wallet. "Can I take down your address? I'll send you a check as soon as I'm home, with a big tip."

"You must be kidding, lady."

"Look at me," I said, and gestured at my black satin Le Smoking. "I'm clearly good for it."

"I don't care what you're good for. You're not leaving this cab until you pay."

I was too embarrassed to call my date for help. She clearly expected me to cover dinner, given our differential in finances. If she knew I had no wallet, she'd probably cancel on me. The whole trip would be a waste. There was only one solution. I called Amanda. She answered on the third ring, and I explained the situation to her.

"I'm so sorry," I said. "I've never done this before."

"Don't worry," she said, her voice as soothing as Cortisone cream through my cell phone. "I'll get there as quickly as I can."

Amanda arrived twenty minutes later. I guess she lived nearby. I had called my date to let her know I was running late. Amanda pulled up in her own cab. She had changed since the office and was in a pair of slim sweatpants, a fitted sweater, and a parka. On her feet were Mary Jane slippers. She looked adorable.

"I'm so sorry," I repeated. She waved my apology away and paid the irate cabdriver. He drove off and she turned to me, her cheeks radiant in the streetlamp light.

"I did not take you for a Brooklyn woman," she said. That tight, toothless smile flashed across her face.

"I'm not. I'm meeting someone for dinner."

"Of course," she said. "Brooklyn has the best food scene."

"Yeah, exactly," I stuttered. Then I realized the taxi fare wasn't my only issue. There was my date and her artist budget. "I'm so sorry. I—"

"You need cash for your dinner," Amanda cut in. "I figured you might." She reached into her bag and pulled out an envelope of cash. "I stopped by the ATM before I came here. I don't know how much your dinners cost, but this should cover it."

"I'll pay you back tomorrow, obviously, and for your ride home, too," I said, as I accepted the envelope. "Thank you so much."

Amanda shook her head and smiled again. "Please don't worry. It's my job to take care of you. Have a good dinner."

She turned and walked toward a busier intersection, in search of a cab. Gratitude overwhelmed me as I watched her go. So this was how it felt to have someone look out for you. I had inadvertently let Amanda see me in a position of need. Instead of exploiting that weakness, she had fixed it. Amanda had saved me. I wanted her to do it again and again. The next morning, I paid Amanda back, as promised. I gave her something else, too, something no previous assistant had ever merited: access to my after-hours schedule and my personal appointments. It felt like the least I could do.

Amanda and I settled into a steady routine after that Brooklyn night. Every morning, I woke at 5 a.m. I went for a run down Broadway and across to the West Side Highway. I returned home. Showered, dressed for work, downed some coffee, the second of multiple cups throughout the day. I ate some fruit and downstairs, I hailed a taxi. I was at the office by 8 a.m. Amanda was already there with a porcelain mug of black coffee that she had brewed in the kitchen adjacent to my glass-enclosed office. Her desk was directly in front of my office, outside its doors, in the trenches of the floor's open plan. Her seat faced outward. Whenever I approached her from behind, I caught a glimpse of her screen. Not once in the many years that she worked beside me did I ever spy a non-work-related website or a Gmail window. It was always an Outlook calendar or a Word doc of a press release or an Excel spreadsheet of recent sales.

Once I was situated in my office, Amanda would sit across from me and run through my schedule for the day. This was my favorite part of the morning, that hush in the office before the meetings ramped up, before people were barging in every three minutes to ask me a question, to clarify my position, to demand my very divided attention. For these precious moments, it was just the two of us, together against the mayhem that awaited me. When I visualize what it would be like to wake in bed beside the person you love, to sit with them at a kitchen table, drinking your coffee, nibbling your fruit, reading the newspaper, a mighty team of two ready to fend off the outside world, my mind returns to this morning ritual with Amanda.

After our check-in, the meetings began to roll. I had ten a day, sometimes as many as fifteen. I won't bore you with their minutiae. They were usually divvied up by department: marketing might go first, then publicity, then sales, or customer experience—we had a crew of women devoted to training our salespeople in retail locations across the country. Supply chain conversations absorbed more of my time than I thought possible. Product development often came at the end of the day. Amanda knew that was my favorite, so she saved it for last.

Around noon or 1 p.m., Amanda would knock on my door and after I waved her in, she would place my lunch, a mesclun salad and a filet of grilled salmon, before me, mid-meeting, then leave the room as quietly as she had entered. Each evening, on the days when I didn't have an after-work event, Amanda would join me in my office for a final check-in to review any requests that needed to be pushed to the top of the next day's priorities.

Ellen was my final meeting of the day one evening a couple of months after the Brooklyn incident. She strode into my office and didn't bother to shut the door behind her. In a black silk evening coat over a matching shift dress, she stood before my desk, her lips a hard, thin line.

"Would you like to sit?" I asked, and gestured at the two empty chairs.

"I'm fine," said Ellen. "This will be quick."

"Okay."

"I need you to meet with a potential investor next week. Ross Palmer."

"Sure."

"We need him on board to help with the Whisper damage."

I suppressed the burn in my throat. Ellen never missed an opportunity to remind me of Whisper's failure. "I'll do my best."

"And you're going to Chicago in three weeks for a personal appearance at Nordstrom."

"Marketing already mentioned that trip to me. Amanda is working on my travel as we speak."

Ellen frowned. "Maxine, our sales are down in the region. Can't imagine why." A sneer crossed her mouth. "Chicago is the Midwest. They have values there, family values. Do me a favor and try to pretend that you have them, too."

"Excuse me?"

"None of this stuff about Flush looking orgasmic and women looking better bare. Or any of those feminist talking points you and Elizabeth love to go on and on about."

"Ellen, that is our brand. It's called Reveal. That is literally our MO: transparency."

"Well, it didn't work for Whisper, did it?"

Heat curled around my throat. "Enough, Ellen. I didn't cause the stock market crash. We are fine. I will charm Ross Palmer and I'll charm those Chicago ladies, like I always do."

"You overestimate your skills at the company's peril," Ellen snapped. She turned and left.

Amanda entered my office not long after. From the sharpness in her eyes, I could tell she had overheard our conversation.

"You okay?" she asked.

"I'm fine," I said.

"Should we go over your schedule for tomorrow? Or do you need a minute?"

"I said I was fine."

"Right. Sorry."

"No, I'm sorry," I said. Amanda sat in one of the chairs opposite my desk. "Thank you for asking."

"Of course." The sharpness in Amanda's eyes mellowed. "I think Ellen's wrong, though please don't tell her I said that."

For the first time that day, I smiled. "Your secret's safe. What do you think she's wrong about?"

"The part about you not mentioning that your products are sexy. Everyone wants to look desirable, sex sells. It's a cliché for a reason."

"It is."

"Another thing."

"Yes?"

"She's wrong about charm. Your charm, I mean." Here, Amanda's cheeks flushed. "I've watched the way you talk to people, in meetings, on calls. You have more charm in your pinkie than Ellen has in her whole body. She's jealous. There's a reason you're the face of this company and not her." Amanda's cheeks grew redder. "Sorry, I've said too much."

"No, I appreciate it. Thanks, Amanda." Her flush must have been contagious because I felt my own cheeks pinken. "Let's go over tomorrow's schedule."

Ross Palmer chose a private club in Midtown as the location for our meeting. His secretary—her term—informed Amanda that the club had a strict dress code.

"No denim, miniskirts, athletic wear, frayed hems, or sneakers," his secretary told Amanda, who recited the description to me verbatim from her notes.

"Who does he think he's meeting, a teenage girl?" I asked, as I smoothed the fabric of my gray flannel suit.

Before the drinks meeting, I went home to change into a sleeveless black shift dress, not wanting anyone at the office to see me in this uncharacteristic outfit. I undid my hair from its sleek side-parted ponytail and brushed it into a voluminous cloud. I patted on an extra helping of Flush and daubed some Glow on the peaks of my Cupid's bow. An angry pair of four-inch stilettos finished the look. Ellen didn't instruct me on any of these moves; I had internalized the messaging years ago.

The private club's lounge was identical to the hotel bar where I had met Chip Adler eight years earlier, in 2002: leather furniture, dark wood, clunky tables, meant to telegraph masculinity, though all I saw was overcompensation for the absence of real strength. Ross Palmer was not unattractive. He was tall and lean. Ellen had mentioned that he was a younger cycling buddy of Donald's. He had most of his sandy hair. His face was chiseled, his blue eyes sparkled. I will never fully understand the attraction of men, but if you're forced to sit across from one and make chitchat, you could do worse than Ross Palmer.

He stood when I approached the table, led there by a uniformed club staffer, and offered his hand. I braced myself for a needlessly aggressive shake, but his grip was light, respectful. His hand was well-moisturized, too.

"I've heard so much about you," Ross said, as I sat in the armchair across from him. A server approached. "What would you like?" Ross asked.

"Johnnie Walker Black neat," I told the server.

"Tonic with bitters," he requested. He noticed my surprise. "I'm training for an Ironman."

Ross was sober, polite, and borderline sincere. I didn't know how to behave. I shifted uncomfortably in the armchair and tried to cross my legs in a way that appeared dainty and the slightest bit coquettish, but it had been years since I'd worn a dress.

"Donald has told me so much about Reveal," Ross continued after our drinks arrived. "I'm impressed with the idea behind it."

"Thank you," I said. My body warmed at the unexpected compliment, even if it came from a man.

"My wife's a big fan of Flush."

"Then I'm a big fan of hers." I smiled as widely as I could. My shoulders, which had been tense all day, eased slightly. He had mentioned his wife. He wouldn't mention his wife and then make a pass. Men who made passes didn't like to think about their wives while doing so.

Ross chuckled. "I hear you're looking for more investors," he said.

"Yes," I said, and sipped from my glass. "We're continuing to grow and we need more funds to push us to the next level."

Ross smiled, revealing very straight and large white teeth. It was the smile of someone whose first solids were caviar and foie gras. "That's not what I hear."

"What do you hear?"

Ross sipped his tonic and bitters. "I hear you're looking to be saved."

I laughed in a way that I hoped sounded flirtatious, though I feared it came out as annoyed. "I don't need any saving. Neither does Reveal."

"After that Whisper business, you sure do," said Ross. "The way I see it, you have an inherent conundrum. Your brand's philosophy is based on minimalism, the essentials, a bare look."

I frowned.

"I do my homework like any good investor should. How do you scale an idea founded on minimalism? It's a challenge. I like a challenge." Ross flashed his teeth again. He reached across the table and, in full sight of the room, pinched my right nipple through my dress. Hard, like he wanted to tear it from my chest. I almost whimpered in pain. Tears came to my eyes though I refused to let them run down my cheeks. Ross registered my expression then released his fingers. He reached for his tonic and bitters as though nothing had happened. "Relax, Maxine. I'm not interested and from what I hear, neither are you. It's important that you know who is in control here. I will invest in Reveal and expect a return on my investment or there will be consequences."

I swallowed a large gulp of my whiskey as I glanced around the room. None of the other patrons registered our table. A server stood by the room's entrance. He was looking at me with a blank expression. Ross signaled to him for the check. The server dropped it off at our table, without a glance in my direction. I had the sense that Ross could have slit my throat in the middle of the room and the club's servers would have mopped up the blood like it was a spilled drink, then disposed of my body, no questions asked. Ross smiled at me as though in apology. "I hate to drink and run," he said, as he signed the check with a flourish. "It's been great meeting you. I look forward to working together. Stick around for as long as you like. It's a good whiskey, it should be savored."

Ross strode out of the lounge and I found myself longing for Chip Adler. I knew how to handle a Chip Adler with his under-the-table fumbling. A Ross Palmer, his younger iteration, was a different beast. I couldn't understand what had just happened. Ross had seemed so genuinely interested in Reveal. He had complimented it. His wife used Flush. Then there was a turn. Ross was smarter than

Chip, more charming, ultimately, more brazen and far more cruel. I thought of Donald, too, and how he hid behind the genteel shield of Ellen. Maybe Ross was who Donald sent to do his dirty work, so he could keep his precious image clean. He knew we'd accept Ross's money; I didn't have the power to say no. The players kept changing, their strategies shifted. The rules of the game never budged. Behind every great woman is a cluster of weak men, eager to suck her dry.

DAY SIX

Evening

I'm going to lose. That's the refrain ricocheting through my head. I played the game. I wore the stupid dress and the ridiculous heels and the ingratiating smile. I let the Ross Palmers of the world harass me. What do I have to show for it? A Board meeting three days from now at which they'll cry *Off with her head.*

Elizabeth comes by my apartment tonight for a drink. When was it that she dropped off the book? I don't remember. I am stuck in a time warp. Technically, Elizabeth should avoid me altogether. Her mere presence here could be misconstrued as a choice of sides. If she hopes to keep her job at Reveal, which she should, because she is great at it and she has equity in the company, the prudent thing would be to forgo any displays of loyalty in my direction.

Of course, Elizabeth is loyal. She is also a paragon of caution. She visits my apartment at 10 p.m., after a double-date dinner with Arthur, one of his legal partners, and her husband. Elizabeth has on a large pair of sunglasses and a dark bucket hat when I open the door. I point out that these accessories, worn at such a late hour, accomplish the opposite of their incognito goal. Elizabeth chortles at that.

"Why are you suddenly so worried?" I ask, as I take her jacket. "You didn't wear a disguise to drop off that book."

"Are you enjoying it, by the way?" she replies. I notice that she avoids my question.

"I haven't started it," I say. "I've been distracted."

"You should give it a read," says Elizabeth. "It's a guide for how women can climb the corporate ladder and balance their careers and personal lives through hard work and perseverance."

I want to ask Elizabeth if this book includes tips on remaining closeted at the behest of your angel investor, while being the aspirational face of a company. Is there advice in these pages on how to fend off the aggressive groping of male investors whose money you can't afford to turn down? Elizabeth doesn't know about the latter challenge. No one does, besides Ellen and the males in question. Sharing these stories with Elizabeth would make them harder for me to compartmentalize.

"I could write that book," I tell Elizabeth, suppressing a mordant laugh. "Why would I want to read it? Especially right now."

"I thought it might make you feel part of something bigger than Reveal," she says. "It might give you a wider perspective."

We sit in my living room, she on the blue tufted sofa, me on my preferred sun-worn armchair, and sip our Scotch. For the first few minutes we are uncharacteristically quiet. Then Elizabeth breaks the stillness with the simplest of questions.

"Are you okay? You seem more depressed than when I was here last. You look even thinner than usual, too."

I don't know how to answer. What is "okay"? I am sheltered, fed, hydrated, washed, and clothed. My body is swaddled in high-thread-count sheets and Egyptian-cotton towels. My skin is pampered with the best products on the market. I am not, in any shape or form, caressed or nurtured or loved. Does that make me okay?

"I'm fine," I reply.

"That's not the same thing as okay."

"Fine is better than okay."

"I disagree."

I swallow an aggressive amount of Scotch. It burns despite the whiskey's eighteen years in a European barrel. Some things are beyond the mellowing effect of age.

"What do you want me to say, Elizabeth?" I ask, heat rising in my voice. "That I'm crying my eyes out every day? I'm not."

"Okay."

"I'm scared." Saying it out loud makes it real. How can I come back from a loss like this?

"I was in a meeting with her yesterday. I absolutely should not be telling you this."

My throat tightens at the reference to Amanda.

"How did she look?"

Elizabeth's eyes are impassive.

"Did she look upset?" I clarify.

"She seemed tired, jittery."

"I won't ask what you talked about."

"I wouldn't tell you if you did." Elizabeth's sternness softens. "You will be okay, Max. Or fine, whichever you prefer."

"I don't know if I will." That tremor from days ago returns to my hands. "I'm nothing without this company. It's my whole life."

"I know, Max. Maybe it shouldn't be."

"Don't tell me you're choosing this moment to lecture me about work-life balance."

"Fair enough." Elizabeth sips from her glass. "Have you left the apartment at all? It might help."

"Now you want me to leave the apartment," I say, my voice growing heated again. "No. I can guarantee you it won't help."

"You should go outside, Max, walk in the park. Get some air."

"I don't feel safe going outside alone."

Elizabeth frowns.

"Why? What do you think is going to happen?"

I am too embarrassed to tell Elizabeth about Esther and her mother, that I let a random woman and her pre-K child make me cower and hide. "I'd consider it if you would go with me."

Elizabeth's eyes cloud with what looks like regret and she tucks some brown hair behind her ear.

"I don't think that's a good idea."

Neither of us says much after that. At some point, I refill our glasses and turn on some music. Top hits from the 1990s flow from my speaker system. I don't have the energy to find a more suitable playlist, so we sit there and listen to one woman's loneliness killing her and another woman's genie getting rubbed the right way. Eventually, we finish our drinks. Elizabeth stands to leave. In the vestibule, she wraps me in a big hug, and I give in, momentarily, to the sensation of being comforted. Then she pulls out of the hug and, hands resting on my shoulders, peers straight into my eyes. She still doesn't have on a scrap of makeup.

"I'll always be here, Max, in your life. I will never disappear."

She walks out the door, into the hallway, and presses the button for the elevator. It arrives and she gets on, without a glance in my direction. I close the door to my apartment and switch off the music. The tremor in my hands is still there. There is nothing I can do to change the future. However, my past belongs to me. I return to my computer and continue to type.

Building Trust

The Chicago trip was brutal. I was only there for thirty-six hours, but it felt like three years. The personal appearance was standard fare. The store hosted a cocktail event in its beauty department, where they set up tables with centerpieces of Reveal products surrounded by pomegranates, cherries, and strawberries. Ripeness was the not-so-subtextual message. A bar served sparkling-wine cocktails with pomegranate syrup, meant to mimic the color of the original Flush. Reveal makeup artists oversaw vanity stations where they dabbed guests with our fragrances, tinted lip balms, and latest shades of Glow, until everyone at the party shone like they'd been anointed.

My job was to mingle with the women. Make an impression. Anything to encourage them to buy, buy, buy. At first, I thought I was on a roll. I chatted to a buxom brunette about perfect highlighter placement. I cooed over another woman's manicure. A platinum blonde offered me restaurant recommendations for my trip. I did my best to manifest the considerable charm on which Amanda had complimented me.

I was mid-conversation with the platinum blonde when a young brunette approached me. Only an archaeologist could have unearthed her skin beneath her many layers of makeup. Dark brown contoured sections hollowed out her cheeks. I spied more contouring on the sides of her nose, which made it appear far thinner than what nature had gifted her. Her lips were swollen with what looked to be more than just gloss. Injectable filler, I assumed, something that was suddenly all the rage. At times it seemed the entire female population had embraced cosmetic surgery and needles with the casualness of swallowing vitamins and minerals. I had the feeling I often encountered with strangers these days: that I was speaking with a blow-up doll, not a live human being.

"I'm such a huge fan of Reveal," said the young brunette.

"Thank you," I said. "That's always nice to hear."

"When is Reveal going to release a foundation?" she asked. The platinum blonde took this as her cue to leave.

"That's an interesting idea," I said. "But we don't believe in foundation. You certainly don't need it." Flattery would save me.

"I love Reveal's products, so do my friends. We'd kill for a foundation by you."

"Women don't need foundation." I smiled. "It's the patriarchy that's made women feel that way. As I'm sure you know, Reveal is all about releasing women from that old-fashioned expectation."

"I don't wear foundation because of the patriarchy," the young brunette pressed. "I wear it because it makes me feel good."

"Sure you do," I said.

"That's a bit patronizing," the young brunette said. "You think I'm incapable of making my own decisions, that all my beauty choices are because of the patriarchy?"

"That's not what I said. I meant—"

"The problem with your older generation is you lecture us on wearing a lot of makeup, something we enjoy, and make us feel like it's anti-feminist. Meanwhile, you never examine your own choices."

"My choices?" Instinctively, I brought a hand to my cheek. I was thirty-five, but I knew I looked closer to thirty since I worked out every day and avoided the sun. I didn't smile enough to have crow's-feet.

"Yes, you're tiny. You must be a size zero, right? Is being a size zero feminist?" the young brunette asked.

"I don't see what my size has to do with anything. We're here to talk about Reveal products, not my body." Crow's-feet be damned, I smiled big and wide, the way you smile when you wish you could scream.

"You're the face of Reveal. You represent a beauty standard. Maybe you should consider how inclusive that standard is."

"Well, thanks for the feedback," I said. "We appreciate your business." Then I practically dove toward the bar. "Do you have anything harder than that?" I asked the bartender as she reached for a glass of sparkling wine. "Seriously, rubbing alcohol would be fine."

Somehow, in the nine years since the Barneys lunch, I had gone from being the young woman belittled as too naive to understand an older woman's beauty needs, to being the old lady at a Chicago Nordstrom, chastised for leading younger women astray. No matter what I did, I was never enough. Maxine Thomas couldn't be the woman everyone desired.

In my hotel room that night, a half-eaten tray of salad on the desk and a second pour of Scotch on the nightstand by the bed, I called Elizabeth. To vent, yes, but also for reassurance that I was not who that young brunette believed me to be. The call went to voicemail. Elizabeth had just started seeing Arthur. They had met on a dating website. She was probably out with him, so I sent Elizabeth a text.

> Nordstrom event was rough. Wish you had been there.
> These contour-happy 20 year-olds are killing me.

I swallowed a deep glug of Scotch. Then I called Amanda on her cell. Just to check in, I told myself. If she offers some moral support, all the better. Amanda answered on the second ring.

"How was the event?" she asked.

"Fine," I said.

"Only fine?"

"You know me, every Midwestern woman's shining ideal." I sipped again from my glass.

"Are you okay? You sound different."

"I was calling to check in about updates."

"Of course. Let's go over your messages and schedule."

I heard papers shuffling on Amanda's desk in New York. I wished I was in New York watching her shuffle those papers.

"You're still at the office?" I asked. "I should have called on the desk line."

"I had some stuff I wanted to catch up on," she said. "Okay, so you had a message earlier fr—"

"Do I look old?" I blurted out.

"What?" Concern filled Amanda's voice. "Max, that's crazy. You're not even forty."

"I will be forty in five years. So that makes me almost old, then?"

"No. Stop. What happened, Max? Did something happen at the event?"

"I'm done," I said. "I can't be the woman people want me to be."

"You don't need to be that woman, just be true to yourself."

I wanted to reach through the phone and shake Amanda by the shoulders. This younger generation and their belief that authenticity would set them free. That they could wear their insecurities to the office like a baggy sweatshirt and scruffy sneakers and suffer no consequences. Some of us can't get away with that. We wear sharply tailored suits for a reason. What did twenty-something women know about coming of age in a society that demands your toughness and that wants to eradicate your vulnerability as the price of success? What did Amanda know about having an entire company's fate reliant on your persona? Authenticity is a pipe dream. Women need to be more realistic to survive.

"It doesn't work like that. I am the founder of Reveal and that comes with huge responsibility. My story, my appearance, it all reflects on Reveal. I can't behave however I want. I'm a leader."

I thought back to years ago, when I realized I had to be a Boss, with a capital *B*, that it was my duty as much as being a visionary.

"You're a great leader, Max. I mean it," said Amanda. "You're the reason I wanted to work at Reveal. I admire you so much."

"Thanks," I said. "God, look at me venting to you. This is crazy. I'm sorry I bothered you."

"Bother me," Amanda said. "Anytime you want."

"Thanks," I said. "Good night."

That Chicago trip cemented my reliance on Amanda, a reliance that crossed over from the functional to the uncomfortable realm of emotions. Once unflappable, I angled for whatever boosts of morale she could toss me.

In the year that followed, Reveal focused less on product expansion and more on courting new customers. We did a series of special edition colors and packaging for the entire Flush and Glow categories with a slew of fashion designers. The goal was to make Reveal more appealing to a younger generation, the very cohort whose contoured ambassador had chastised me at the Chicago Nordstrom. To that end, we also made a big push into Sephora, starting with the New York flagship and working our way across Sephora locations throughout the United States. Young women no longer shopped at department stores. They demanded accessibility, and according to Reveal's sales team, Sephora, with its plethora of brands in drugstore-style gondolas, was the retail equivalent of a wide-armed hug.

One morning in 2011, I arrived at the office to find Amanda's desk empty. It was the first time this had happened in two years. She wasn't in the kitchen pouring me a cup of coffee. She wasn't in the bathroom. I texted her from my iPhone. There was no reply. In the kitchen, I brewed a pot of coffee for myself. While it gurgled, I riffled through the papers on Amanda's desk to search for any clues to her absence. Her appointment book listed all the day's meetings that we had reviewed the previous evening. Amanda liked to keep a handwritten hard copy of my schedule as a backup for the synced Outlook calendar on our computers, an analog quirk I found charming.

By 10 a.m., there was no word from Amanda, on my phone or otherwise. I was in my third meeting of the day, a deathly gathering to scavenge our monthly operating budget for cost-cutting opportunities. A young woman who normally worked in publicity sat at Amanda's desk. Elizabeth had loaned her to me as a temporary fix. Someone from accounting was mid-diatribe when I glanced through the glass walls of my office and spied a petite woman with dark hair leaning over the publicity woman from behind, gesturing at something on the desk. The publicity woman stood up with an aggravated shrug and walked away. The dark-haired woman took her seat. She looked over her shoulder in the direction of my office. It was Amanda. Her eyes were swollen and red and her normally even skin was blotchy.

"I need to cut this meeting short," I said, interrupting the accountant's monologue. "Could one of you please send Amanda in here?"

There was a scraping of chairs against my office's concrete floor as everyone stood up, gathered their pens and notepads, and exited through the doors. Once the accounting group had filed out, Amanda entered.

"Close the door behind you," I instructed her.

She did as I asked, then sat across from my desk. The underside of her nose was raw. Her hair, usually a silky curtain, was tangled. Errant strands stuck out in staticky clumps.

"I'm so sorry I was late this morning and that I didn't return your texts or calls. It will never happen again."

Amanda's eyes were trained on my desk.

"No, it won't, not if you want to continue working here." I paused. Amanda looked so mournful. A maternal instinct I had never felt seized my senses. "Are you okay?" I asked in a far gentler tone.

Amanda's lips began to quiver. Tears filled her dark eyes. She swallowed visibly, an effort, I assumed, to maintain control over her emotions.

"I'm fine."

"You're clearly not. I won't let you leave this office until you tell me what's going on."

Her face registered surprise at my insistence. She had obviously assumed that a meek apology and a promise of better behavior would suffice and that I would have no interest in whatever messiness was behind her negligence. Her eyes narrowed as she calculated how little she could reasonably tell me to extricate herself from this conversation.

"It's personal."

"I assumed as much."

"Do you really want to hear about it?"

"I need to hear about it. So I can judge for myself if we're okay to move forward."

"This is about gauging my productivity? You don't actually care if I'm okay?"

It was my turn to pause. An unfamiliar pang in my chest told me that I did care and that this wasn't simply an exercise in establishing my authority.

"I care. Amanda, tell me what's going on."

That little offer of softness opened a dam in Amanda. Shiny rivulets trickled down her cheeks.

"It's so dumb," she said between sniffles. "So silly."

"Doesn't matter."

"My girlfriend broke up with me last night." She let that hang in the air for a few seconds, then continued. "Sorry, that must sound so lame."

"No, no, not at all." I kept my face neutral as I processed this revelation about Amanda. She had a girlfriend. Past tense. Well, she was a Sarah Lawrence graduate.

"We were together for three years. I really thought that was it. Anyway, I'm sorry, I was up all night crying and I overslept this morning. That's why I was late. It won't happen again."

"Right, okay."

Amanda finally stared up from my desk, straight at me.

"Also, I'm not out, professionally. I would appreciate it if you didn't tell anyone."

"Of course, I would never." Heat surged up the back of my neck, to my ears and my hairline.

"I don't know why I'm sharing any of this." Amanda sniffled and rubbed her eyes. "I guess I trust you."

The heat at my hairline began to sear. Moisture threatened the skin above my upper lip and forehead.

"Thanks for telling me and I'm sorry about your girlfriend. We should get back to work." The three people slotted for my next meeting clustered, expectantly, outside my closed door. "Can you ask them to come in? Thanks."

Amanda stood. She attempted a tight-lipped smile, then opened the door.

"She's ready for you," she told the waiting colleagues.

The marketing trio clomped into my office. Soon their pitches for new campaigns drowned out the circling questions in my head.

Later at home, I was too exhausted to contemplate what had happened in my office with Amanda, beyond the obvious: Amanda was not straight. I was intrigued by her admission. Nothing about her appearance had suggested that she might be gay. She was almost a parody of femininity with her delicate, frilly clothes.

Given the advantage of hindsight, I realize the brilliance of what Amanda accomplished in that confession. She made herself vulnerable in the short term to encourage my future vulnerability. Sharing her sexuality wasn't a spontaneous act; it was a Trojan horse for her true aim of slowly dismantling my defenses. If only I had been wise enough to recognize the trap hidden behind her tear-streaked face.

London

Less than a year after Amanda came out to me, I flew to London for an important meeting with another rich man. A famous business titan, James Sutter, wanted to invest in Reveal. He was eager to enter the beauty arena, and Reveal was exactly the type of company to pop his cherry. That's what Ellen told me, not in those exact words, of course. The influx of cash from Ross Palmer in 2010 hadn't been enough to spur the growth we wanted. It was 2012 and the contouring trend persisted. Matte lipstick was back. Smoky cat eyes were all over runways. In SoHo, I saw women with eyebrows like tumbleweeds. This younger generation baffles me. They look simultaneously like cyborgs and like they're too good for a pair of tweezers.

Regardless of what they chose, it would end up online. Instagram had been around for two years. In the middle of crowded sidewalks, in restaurants, at bars, in bathrooms, women were aiming their phone cameras at flattering angles as they sucked their cheeks in and pouted for selfies. The audience for their faces wasn't just their horny boyfriends or their classmates or their BFFs. It was the infinite, anonymous followers clustered in their phones. Suddenly, iconic hairdos and trending fashion stopped emanating from celebrities in films or editorial spreads in magazines. They came from the millions of shares, likes, follows, and regrams pinging across crystal screens, all of it distorted to the point that it became a homogeneous mass.

I refused to accept that this was our future, that it was anything more than a phase. Women would become exhausted by their hyper-filtered faces just as they had tired of frosted eye shadow and that blond 1990s shag. When they were ready to return to the basics of natural, sexy beauty, Reveal would welcome them with a berry-tinted smile.

Until then, Ellen and Chip—and, I assume, Donald—decided that what Reveal needed was a small Board of directors to usher us into our next phase. I would be on the Board with Ellen and Chip by virtue of my CEO/founder position. They also wanted to add a big name, preferably one who would bring big cash; enter James Sutter.

Elizabeth would accompany me on the three-day sojourn, in her ongoing role as professional wingwoman. A week before we were slated to leave, I spontaneously asked Amanda to join us. She had been with Reveal for just over three years. Her one tardy morning aside, she had performed flawlessly. A business trip to London seemed a fitting reward. Plus, Elizabeth and I could use someone junior to manage our schedules, our dinner reservations, any extracurricular but fully necessary excursions. That's what I told Elizabeth when she enquired about Amanda's inclusion.

"Are you thinking of promoting her soon?" Elizabeth asked. "This trip could be a good testing ground."

"It hadn't occurred to me."

"You've never had the same assistant for this long before."

"Really? Wasn't the last one—"

"Molly."

"—Molly, right, wasn't she with me for four years?"

"Sixteen months."

"Oh."

"Amanda's clearly talented. She's not going to be happy making you coffee and answering your phone for much longer. You need to give her more challenging things to do."

"She seems perfectly happy to me, never complains about any task I give her. If she wants more responsibility, she needs to ask for it. She can't expect me to hand it to her."

Elizabeth frowned. "You can be a little intimidating, Max. She might be afraid to ask you. Managing people is about getting the best work out of them. You need to make them feel valued."

"Why else do you think I invited her on this trip?"

Elizabeth and I flew business class. Amanda brought up the rear in coach, as my generosity has its limits. We were booked at a hotel on Park Lane in the Mayfair neighborhood, one of the toniest postal codes. The hotel itself was dark and corporate, but my room had a view of the adjacent Hyde Park. Amanda's room was on the same floor as mine, four doors down, while Elizabeth was one floor below us. We would meet with James Sutter twice over the course of the trip, that afternoon at his Mayfair offices, and the following evening over dinner at an Art Deco restaurant a few blocks from his office, known for its ritzy clientele.

I will spare you the soporific details of our first meeting with James Sutter except to say that it went well enough that I emailed Ellen afterward to relay my enthusiasm for Reveal's potential partnership with him. There was no below-the-table fumbling or threatening innuendo; the entire meeting was aboveboard. Amanda sat in a corner of James Sutter's office and jotted notes in her spiral notebook. When my attention lagged during the meeting, my eyes drifted over to Amanda. Her posture was, as ever, straight like the handle of a paintbrush. She wore a Peter Pan–collared shirtdress that lent her juvenile primness. Her golden skin bore the lightest sheen of Glow and the faintest rosiness of Flush. Amanda was radiant, a bewitching flash in an otherwise stultifying room. I knew, without her telling me, that beneath that conservative exterior simmered the latent heat of ambition. She didn't need me to hand her a promotion. She would take what she wanted when the time was right.

Amanda had booked us a table for dinner at a bastion of modern British cuisine and social voyeurism. The room's mirrored columns, white tablecloths, and cane-backed chairs seemed better suited to a trio of mid-forties diners than a twenty-five-year-old assistant. I assumed Amanda had made this selection with her projections of my taste—and Elizabeth's—in mind, which served to remind me of my own age. I was thirty-seven and inching ever closer to the dreaded four-oh.

My body was as slender as in my twenties, though this required serious work now. French fries, pizza, burgers, ice cream, bowls of cheesy pasta: they were ghosts of my younger past. These days, I was all salad and lean protein all the time. My running mileage helped things stay tight and a combination of Retin-A, sunblock, and eye cream lent my pale complexion a boost of antiaging power normally reserved for those with far more melanin. I looked in the mirror and, generally, I didn't mind the face reflected at me. Chicago Nordstrom shoppers aside, I even felt a twinge of pride in my appearance.

As I sat in that London restaurant, though, and pushed around pieces of whole roasted sea bream, light on the oil, no butter, I couldn't help but wonder how much more time I had before my chemical and physical interventions into aging hit a wall. Plastic surgery was the next logical frontier, though for me, it was a nonstarter. I couldn't be the spokeswoman for transparent beauty and partake of a surgeon's knife.

Beside me, Elizabeth tucked into her miso-marinated salmon while across the table, Amanda cut her battered and fried cod into small, delicate bites. There was a pile of thick, browned fries—*chips*—on her plate. Amanda picked one up, bringing its salty goodness to her waiting mouth. I wanted to lick the grains of salt off her soft, full lips, the closest I would allow myself to any deep-fried food item.

Amanda caught me staring at her, mid-bite.

"Take one," she urged me, and gestured at the dwindling pile of fries. "Before I eat them all."

I shook my head vigorously. "No, no, that's sweet, but I can't."

Amanda's eyes glinted at me.

"Why can't you?"

"You'll see when you get older," I said, with a nod in Elizabeth's direction. Elizabeth shrugged in vague confusion and chewed a bite of her salmon.

"What's one fry going to do to you?" Amanda persisted.

"It's not about the one fry; it's the floodgates that it will open."

Amanda plucked a chip from her stack and extended it to me, like an invitation.

"I don't think the woman who wakes up at five to run and eats salad for lunch every day will be undone by a French fry."

Elizabeth smirked at that.

"She makes a solid point," she said. "You could use some meat on your bones, to be honest."

She and Amanda smiled, challenging me.

"Fine," I said. "Just one."

I received Amanda's outstretched fry and bit into its crisp exterior, which gave way to soft, fluffy insides. Salt and fat and starch flooded my mouth and I felt woozy with pleasure. I would have given up alcohol, caffeine, and possibly sex, if I could have French fries for the rest of my life without consequences.

"Jesus Christ," I murmured.

Amanda laughed and pushed her plate out of my reach.

"Remember," she said. "Just one." Then she pulled another chip from her stack and crunched it between her lips.

I had planned to tag along with Elizabeth on a morning of industry research visiting British beauty emporiums. After a trip to the hotel gym to work off that lone fry, I texted Elizabeth that I was abandoning her for the more inspiring, and to my mind necessary, environs of the Victoria and Albert Museum. I alerted Amanda to my change of plans, too. When I didn't hear back, I assumed that she had taken the notion of her morning off fully to heart.

At the V&A, I wandered beneath the spiky glass chandelier crowning the great entry hall, up a staircase, through rooms gleaming with silver, sparkling with reflections from stained-glass windows. I was in a gallery devoted to nineteenth-century British painting when I spotted a familiar figure one room over. Though I could only see her from behind, I knew instantly it was Amanda. Her posture and silky hair beckoned to me from twenty feet away. She stood before a wall of tiny works by a famous British artist. She was focused on one oil painting, in particular. As I moved closer to her, I saw it was a landscape scene, presumably set somewhere in the English countryside. At its center was a rocky hill; to the left, in the background, was a glimpse of a rough sea. The sky was the true star; its purples and grays spoke of barely restrained fury, waiting to unleash itself across a captive earth.

I watched Amanda from a few feet away. She didn't so much as shift her stance or tilt her head. She was stock-still. Eventually, my curiosity won out and I approached her quietly from behind.

"It's a stunning work," I commented.

Amanda turned her sweet face to mine. If she was surprised to find me standing there, she didn't show it.

"Do you see that little person in the left corner?" She pointed at a tiny white figure, a shepherd, staring off at the hill and impending rain. "That's how I feel, right now."

"You mean looking at this painting?"

"No, right now in my life." She looked at me. "Haven't you ever felt that way?"

Her gaze was so full of yearning, I almost forgot that she had asked me a question. I wanted to stare into her eyes for the rest of the trip.

"That shepherd doesn't look scared. If he was afraid, he'd run for cover."

"I didn't say I was scared," she said. "Sometimes storms clear the way for something better."

I was at a loss for a reply. It was like Amanda had scrubbed me clean of all artifice, like she alone could see my unvarnished self.

"Sorry I didn't respond to your text earlier," she said. "I had already planned to come here and I didn't want to not come here or lie to you."

"So you didn't say anything."

"It never occurred to me that we would run into each other in this enormous place."

Was she lying? Had she planned her visit to the museum after I texted her my change of itinerary? Even she wasn't psychic enough to orchestrate such a clever run-in.

I glanced at my wrist. It was nearly time for our lunch with Elizabeth.

"Should we head out?" I asked. When had I started asking Amanda for permission to leave?

"Yes, let's," she replied. We left the ominous painting and exited the gallery.

That evening, Amanda, Elizabeth, and I met in the hotel lobby ahead of dinner. Elizabeth wore an anonymous but easy-on-the-eyes black dress. Amanda was also in a dress, a long-sleeved navy number with a sharp pointy collar and a hemline that hit a teasing inch above her knees. Her shiny straight hair was in a low ponytail, her skin was incandescent.

"Everyone looks good," I commented, taking care to dole out compliments evenly between the two of them. I wasn't sure why I was careful at all. There was no way I was attracted to Amanda. That would have been crazy; she was barely an adult. Something had shifted between us, though, at the museum. Like her tearful confession in my office nine months earlier, Amanda's insights into the painting had opened another door into a cordoned-off room of my interior. I had no idea how many more doors it would take before I was completely unlocked, but I was viscerally aware that I wanted to know.

In the taxi ride to the restaurant, Amanda sat sandwiched between me and Elizabeth. The car hit a bump in the road along Piccadilly and Amanda's bare leg swerved into mine. I had never touched her skin before—of course I hadn't. I was her boss. It felt as I imagined freshly churned butter would when spread atop silk charmeuse.

We arrived at the Art Deco restaurant after James Sutter. A server led us across the dining room nestled beneath an arched ceiling crowned with an iron chandelier. James Sutter, in a smart navy suit, stood to greet us. Over icy vodka martinis for us and a double Scotch for him, he regaled us with tales of his various professional accolades, whose ranks we assumed we might soon join. A server set down our entrées, on porcelain plates with silver cloches.

"Bon appétit," said James Sutter. He sliced into his juicy pink steak, covered in an unctuous béarnaise sauce.

Elizabeth poked at her filet of salmon, and I did the same with my no-butter, light-on-the-oil lemon sole. Amanda had ordered the schnitzel. The idea of crunching on its golden, battered exterior made my insides churn.

"So you wish to remain the CEO of Reveal in the long term?" James Sutter asked me.

I swallowed an acidic bite of sole.

"Of course, it's my company. I founded it."

"Yes, I know," said James Sutter. He may have graduated from Eton and Cambridge, but he chewed with his mouth open like a child raised in the wilderness. "Founding a business and running it are not the same thing."

"Flush is one of the top products on the market. We sell a bottle every five minutes."

"You should be aiming to sell a bottle every minute, especially to this younger generation. You need someone who can help you do that."

I glanced in Elizabeth's direction. Her expression was unperturbed, but a wariness lined her eyes.

"What makes you think I need someone else to do that?"

"I spoke with Ellen and Chip before I left for dinner. I mentioned the names of two gentlemen in New York who could be a good fit."

"A good fit for what?"

"They're King's College boys, like me. You can't go wrong with a Cambridge man."

A flash of heat streaked across my face.

"Are you trying to replace me?"

"Now don't get so hysterical."

"I'm not—"

"You'll always be the founder. I just made some suggestions of men who could help you prepare Reveal for acquisition. That's the goal here."

I placed my fork and knife gently on the side of my plate. Two-thirds of my fish remained.

"I appreciate your concern, but we have things handled. As you'll see when you join our Board. We haven't even discussed acquisition."

James Sutter's fork and knife clanged as they hit his plate. He had annihilated his béarnaise-covered meat.

"You misunderstand the situation. One of my recommendations will become CEO of Reveal, which we'll sell when the time is right. If you want my money and my presence on your Board." James Sutter grinned at me.

I shouldn't have been shocked. Nothing we had done in the four years since Whisper and the market crash had placated Ellen or Chip. I realized that this had been the plan all along. James Sutter wanted to place a puppet president at the company's head and unload Reveal to a future buyer. I was tempted to stand up from the table, walk through the restaurant's rotating doors into the damp London night, and phone Ellen with my anger. Issue her an ultimatum: him or me. The businessman or the founder. The money or the creative brain. With a stab of discomfort, I knew that Ellen would choose the businessman.

I swallowed a sip of my martini. Elizabeth stepped in to cover my frustration before it exploded into a regrettable outburst.

"That's enough shoptalk for tonight," she said, like a wife admonishing two workaholic husbands.

James Sutter chuckled, his eyes on me.

"Looks like we're done here. Let's see a dessert menu."

After a banana split for the table, another nod to James Sutter's questionable sophistication, our trio bid farewell. The restaurant's doorman hailed us a cab and we sat in the back of the car, the whooshing traffic outside our window an understudy for chitchat. Amanda hadn't spoken since James Sutter's big reveal. I regretted her presence at the meal; I was mortified that she had had a front-row seat to my debasement.

In the hotel elevator, Elizabeth pressed the buttons for our respective floors. She slung an arm around my shoulders and gave them an affectionate squeeze. It was all I could do not to rest my head on her arm. Elizabeth exited the elevator first. One floor up, it was my turn. Amanda's room was closer to the elevator banks, but as we approached it, she made no motion to pause.

"How about a drink?" she asked, her face luminous with pity.

"Why not," I replied. "Come to my room? We can scope out the minibar."

We continued to my door. With a swipe of the key card, we were inside my dark chamber. The minibar was well stocked.

"Whiskey?" I asked.

"Sure," Amanda replied as she sat in the room's sole dining chair.

I poured our whiskeys into two stemless wineglasses and handed one to Amanda. I sat in the room's scratchy armchair and leaned back. Amanda crossed one slender leg over the other. Her shins gleamed like polished nails.

"That was some dinner."

"I'm sorry you had to be there."

"Why?" she asked, her eyes dark pools.

"To witness that. It was humiliating."

"You didn't do anything wrong. That guy was an asshole."

"That asshole is our new boss."

I stared sorrowfully at my whiskey.

"*You* are my boss. Period." Amanda's gaze was ferocious now.

"Thanks, but that's not actually true."

"It is."

Amanda's indignation lit something inside me, deeper than the whiskey could reach. Unlike James Sutter and Chip and Ellen, she was on my side. This blazing young woman wanted me to succeed as no one else ever had. She wasn't embarrassed on my behalf; she was furious. Not even Elizabeth had expressed such anger over my treatment.

This fury only made me more resigned. I was parched of all outrage. I had lost the top position at my company and eventually I'd lose the company, too. How could anyone else do what I did? Who else could be what Reveal needed?

"It's still yours, you know," Amanda went on, as though she had a peephole into my thoughts. "Just because someone new will be president, it doesn't mean the company is his. You will always be Reveal."

"It's only a matter of time. Once they sell it, they'll axe me. They always toss the founder out like trash."

Amanda drained her wineglass. She set it on the desk behind her and walked the few feet over to my perch. With one of her hands, Amanda patted my knee.

"It will all be okay. You just need to have some self-belief."

Her hand drifted farther up my leg, kneading my thigh as it moved.

"What are you do—"

"Shh," Amanda said as she leaned over me. Her face was above me now.

I have replayed this moment so many times in the last three years. I watch it on the screen of my mind now. Amanda smothers the air between us as her lips kiss mine and her hand caresses its intended resting place. I whisper, "No." "Please don't." "We can't." I resist her kiss. At first. But the combination of the whiskey and the dinner and the sadness shatters my self-control. I am weak against the heat that surges from Amanda's hand.

"I can't," I murmur in one last attempt to halt the inevitable.

"Yes, you can," she says. Her hand is inside my underwear. "And you will."

Against all better judgment, I do.

DAY SEVEN

Evening

I slept with my half-Asian, decade-plus-younger female assistant. At least no one can accuse me of being a cliché.

The optics aren't great. What about the other dynamics at play? I was depressed. Beaten down by the misogyny of my industry. I had just lost the top position at my company. Amanda pounced on that weakness. She spotted her opening and made her move, with the goal of rendering me dependent on her. She sought to bind herself to my professional status, the better to climb to a higher eventual position without the work of creating something of her own. Once she saw me falter, she threw me to the wolves instead. Yet all the public sees, all the Board will see, is a monstrous white dyke who groomed and violated a fragile minority girl. The real context will always elude them. Don't they realize how insulting that narrative is to Amanda's agency in all this? She is too smart to be a victim.

I can't continue reliving this scene. It will drive me mad, so I click out of my document and turn on the television in search of distraction. After scrolling through the abundant yet lackluster streaming options, I switch over to cable and put my entertainment in the hands of a television network programmer, like in pre-internet days. A biopic of a famous musician has just started. Though I'm not very familiar with her song list, I settle in. It's addictive to consume the rise and fall of anyone, especially a stranger; you're free to root for them or wish secretly for their demise, unburdened by the constraints of familiarity.

This musician had some life. Abusive uncle. Drug-addled teens and twenties. Abusive first husband. More drugs. Second husband died after a year of marriage. Rehab. More drugs. And so on. She managed to find time, in all of this, to write and record hit after hit after hit. I watch this movie and wonder, What would the greater public think of my full story, the one I've been typing, if I were to actually share it?

Insecurity slaps me in the face.

I think about the Board, about my inability to defend myself to the people deciding my fate. There's the inevitable arbitration and Sandrine's directive that we excavate some vulnerability or trauma, to help a hypothetical judge see that I am not a power-hungry predator, that I am, instead, a victim of an unfair society. Perhaps I've internalized Sandrine's strategy because I've been doing exactly that. I've tapped into the homophobia I faced, the loss of Caroline, the relentless misogyny of doing business, Ellen's ongoing betrayal, Amanda's impending betrayal. That's a ticker-tape parade of victimhood ready for a captive audience. Then I switch on the television and suddenly I wonder if all those obstacles I've dredged up amount to anything. Success is a handicap. People want to see the struggle.

I get the appeal of watching someone overcome immense hardship. It sends the inspiring message of *If [insert name of famous celebrity] can conquer [insert insurmountable obstacles] and succeed, there's no reason I can't do the same with my comparatively lesser challenges.* At a certain point, it seems like the number of barriers a person faces and the extent of their struggles are more important than the eventual triumph. To measure the value of a life by the quantity of suffering incurred seems like a sad way to celebrate human existence. In that case, why bother with achievement at all.

Clashing Visions

It's funny to consider that I closed on this apartment, my current sanctuary, in the first quarter of 2013, less than a year after I returned from that fateful London excursion. Usually a purchase like this marks a promotion or an engagement or the birth of a child, but I bought my dream residence after one of the most harrowing experiences of my life. A psychologist would have a field day analyzing this. I work in a superficial industry, so of course I confuse commerce with success. Or: I required the status of a top-tier apartment to bolster my flagging ego.

The truth is far simpler than either of those hypotheses. I loved this apartment from the moment I saw it. I wanted a residence that felt like a home, with nature outside my window and a doorman who could announce visitors and accept packages. Most of all, I yearned for the relief that comes when you walk out your door into a neighborhood full of living and breathing adults, people who don't care what cool bar opened on Houston Street or which influencer scandal is ricocheting from phone to phone. You'd be hard-pressed to find a group less interested in what's trendy than the residents of the Upper West Side.

I did not find my dream apartment via the standard channels, rather through Elizabeth's fiancé, Arthur, who had a friend who knew the owners of a classic six in a Central Park West address. The owners were planning to put it on the market, but figured they'd canvass their sizable Rolodex first and see if they could nab a taker.

"It's on the Upper West Side," Elizabeth warned me, as if I didn't know the location of Central Park West.

"I'm aware of that," I replied.

"I know you want to leave the Flatiron, but this is very uptown."

"That's the point."

"Not uptown like the Upper East Side."

Elizabeth and Arthur lived some blocks away on Columbus. She couldn't envision a world in which she and I would choose the same zip code.

"Thank god."

Elizabeth sighed at that.

"I warned you."

One of the owners, the wife, walked me through the apartment. Her hair had gray roots and her pants were in wide-wale corduroy and I thought, Okay, Elizabeth wasn't exaggerating. The place, though, was a thing of beauty. Its parquet floors had the patina of hard-earned love. Its public rooms were open and generous. The view of Central Park was nothing short of breathtaking. Within minutes of my tour, I knew this apartment was the only place where I would ever want to live.

Six reference letters, one co-op board interview, 180 pages of highly invasive questions about my finances, one mortgage, and seven months later, I closed on the Upper West Side apartment. The first morning I woke to a sunrise cresting over the Central Park reservoir outside my window and thought, If it all goes to shit, at least I will have this.

My premonition of Armageddon was hardly paranoia. When I returned from London in the summer of 2012, Ellen, anticipating my anger over James Sutter's revelation, confronted me with the details of the contract she had encouraged me to sign in 1999 after I pitched Glow. The one she had presented as necessary to protect her interests.

"I'm sure by now you're aware of the share-dilution clause in that contract," she remarked coolly over the phone to me.

"What are you talking about?" I asked.

"The share-dilution clause."

"I don't understand."

"The clause that keeps the percentage of my shares in Reveal steady no matter how many additional investors we take on, while yours grow weaker and weaker."

My body went cold. "So what you're saying is—"

"What I'm saying," Ellen cut in, "is that your shares are worthless compared to mine. And so is your voting power on our new Board."

For someone intent on controlling her creative vision, I had a real knack for relinquishing power. I wished I could reach back through time, grab my younger self by the shoulders, knock the naivete and hubris out of her, force her to seek a lawyer, and make her protect her creation. How dumb I had been to think that I could manage Donald and Ellen with ease, that my vision trumped their social and financial heft. Donald had begat Chip Adler had begat Ross Palmer had begat James Sutter and each of those men had drained my interests. Who knew how many more iterations awaited me in the future.

"I don't say this to threaten you," Ellen continued as I remained silent. "Only to dissuade you from any misguided notion that you can block this investment from James or the company's eventual sale.

I am doing what's best for Reveal. I have only ever done what benefits this company."

I called Elizabeth straight after in a rage. There was nothing to be done about the share dilution, but Elizabeth suggested that I work with a lawyer to negotiate a founder's agreement that would establish my authority with the new Board. Arthur recommended Sandrine, who put a deal in place, the exact terms of which I trusted to her expertise. Clearly, I knew nothing about contracts.

I never confronted Ellen about her betrayal of our long-standing business partnership nor her lapsed spiritual support. Nothing she could say would heal the wound from this revelation. Even if Ellen was merely a proxy for Donald in these decisions, she had still shown no remorse over the pain she had caused me. I realized that however tough and compartmentalized I had become, in service to her vision of leadership, at least I wasn't utterly heartless like Ellen.

The deal with James Sutter went through. Before Ellen had a chance to congratulate—which is to say, torment—me in person, tragedy struck her household. Donald died suddenly of a heart attack. I say "tragedy," but I'm not sure that's the correct word. The relationship between Ellen and Donald seemed about as warm as a cryogenic tank. Ellen inherited half of Donald's very sizable net worth. Between that and the extra security from James Sutter's investment in Reveal, she was thriving financially.

There was a price, though, there always is. Ellen visited the Reveal offices a few weeks after Donald's funeral. She appeared suddenly older than I remembered. Her hair was all gray of course, a beautiful white silver that she had tinted by a colorist. Her skin was patchy in spots. I had never seen her anything less than optimally moisturized. There were grayish bags beneath her eyes, visible through whatever non-Reveal concealer she had used.

In true form, Ellen expressed her misery by making others miserable. She strode into my office that day, her steps heavier than you'd expect for such a thin woman, and stood before my desk while gesturing aggressively.

"You need to change offices, Maxine," Ellen said.

"Excuse me?" I asked.

"This is the office for a CEO. You're no longer the CEO."

"I'm still the founder, Ellen." She looked so terrible, I almost felt sorry for her, despite everything she had done to me. "I'm not changing offices."

"We'll see about that," Ellen snapped.

"There are those two empty offices near publicity." A few employees had been poached by a rival company. "We could combine them and create something bigger than this."

"Fine," said Ellen. "So long as it's much bigger."

I almost laughed. It was like talking to a child, a very sad child.

Ellen lingered in front of me.

"Did you need something else?" I asked.

"I know what you think of me. What you've thought of me all these years. You're wrong."

"I don't know what you're talking about."

"You think I don't see it?" Ellen asked, her voice a dagger. "You think you're better than me, than all of us, because you're single and independent of a man."

I didn't speak.

"You think I'm some dumb wife. A fancy puppet for Donald to toy with behind the scenes. That he's been running the show all along." Ellen gripped the back of the chair tightly. "You're wrong. I let him think that. I let him think all these things—investing in Reveal, bringing Chip on, bringing Ross on, the Board—were his ideas. I whispered them to him at night when he'd had a few drinks. My father was a financier. He taught me everything there is to know."

"Then why was ERA such a failure?"

Ellen laughed sharply. "You think I'd have this life with a *candle business*? Please. I needed a husband and the wealth he could build. No one was going to offer me an MD job at a bank. So I propped up Donald's ego, gave him the credit, and I got what I wanted: stature and money. Women of my generation understand that this is how we amass power. You've never gotten that. You want to dispose of men. I know how to use them."

"In the process, you'll stomp on any woman who gets in your way, including me," I replied, anger shaking my voice.

"I don't see you pulling other women up with you," said Ellen. "You're no different from me."

"I empower women."

"You judge them. You're an authoritarian."

"I believe they can be free of patriarchal standards."

"And your standards are so much better?"

"Of course they are. My standards center female desire."

"You mean your desire."

"Same thing."

"Is it?"

"Anyway the power you describe isn't real. It's a mirage."

Ellen cocked her brow. "I'm chairman of your Board. That's as real as it gets."

Ellen was right on one thing: I had misjudged her and underestimated her role in the more egregious betrayals of the past decade. The men had always seemed to be the clear enemy. I had believed that Ellen's insistence on my stoicism as a leader had stemmed from her own powerlessness, however unacknowledged, in a patriarchal world. That she had turned me into a warrior to win the battles she was unable to fight. Now I realized that we had never been allies. We weren't enmeshed in the same war. To her, there was no war.

None of this is to exculpate the men—they were a vile and brutal lot—but the picture had been blurrier than I'd been willing to admit. Ellen's cruelty hurt more than their male transgressions because I hadn't expected it. She wasn't a pawn to be pitied. She was a queen married to a now dead king. If anyone was the pawn, it was me.

My new understanding of Ellen was the least of my concerns in the short term. Of the two New York–based Cambridge men that James Sutter had suggested for the job of president and CEO of Reveal, Alan Jeffries was deemed the more impressive. He was in his early sixties, a veteran of mass-market beauty brands, the type you were more likely to find in the cosmetics aisle of your local drugstore versus at a specialty beauty retailer. Reveal had always hovered near the middle of the indie prestige sector; it was more aspirational than a ten-dollar lip gloss but priced to undercut the ultra-expensive competitors in its same category. This positioning allowed us to be a special-occasion purchase for a mass-brand customer and a more casual buy for a luxury client. Alan's background with huge down-market companies did not inspire my confidence.

Alan began his reign of Reveal in late 2012, five months after the London trip, with the goal of preparing the company for eventual acquisition. I was demoted to chief creative officer, though they let me keep the "founder" title. Sandrine's contract saw to that. And so far as the public knew, I was still the face of and vision behind Reveal. One of Alan's first duties was an all-day, one-on-one meeting with me, what he termed "a download" of my activities at Reveal. *My activities,* I wanted to shoot back. *You mean the fact that I have devoted my entire adult life to this company's tight, discerning lineup while you oversaw cheap nail polishes and clumpy mascara for preteens?*

Amanda cleared my schedule. I sat through hours and hours of Alan and his bloated arrogance. There was, for example, the exchange where he interrogated me about Reveal's product roster.

"Why do you only have two heroes?"

Alan wore a wrinkled gray suit that strained to contain the paunch above his black belt. His skin was greasy, and he smelled like mothballs.

"Our heroes have deep, bestselling categories attached to them," I replied. "And it's more than two: Flush, Glow, our fragrances, Whisper."

"Whisper was a disaster," he replied. "The opposite of a hero."

I imagined stabbing him where it mattered with a pair of tweezers.

"Whisper was a hero the market wasn't ready for."

"You haven't answered my initial question."

"Product creation is time-consuming and costly. We only want to release things that are truly deserving of a woman's investment. We've iterated on Flush, Glow, our fragrances, and our home products many times to great profit. It's about depth and loyalty."

"That's absurd. How do you expect to make money by limiting the number of things your customers can purchase? You should flood them with options and take away the market share from your competitors."

"Reveal's philosophy is substance over quantity, a focus on the essentials. We earn our customers' trust by not overwhelming them with choices."

Alan literally laughed out loud at this, while I breathed deeply to suppress my rage.

"Beauty isn't about necessity or trust. I've been doing this since before you were born. The whole industry is built on convincing women to buy things they don't need. The products don't even matter. It comes down to marketing, not content."

Alan smirked at me. I wanted to punch that smug smile off his face. What did a straight man know about beauty? No one cared how Alan looked. He had nabbed the top position at Reveal in a state of total dishevelment. Meanwhile, I wore designer suits and worked out like I was training for the Olympics and I was still picked apart by customers and Ellen alike for every aesthetic choice I made.

"Historically, that might be true," I relented, trying to smooth out our rapport. "Reveal is a new model for beauty, based on instilling confidence in women, not robbing them of their self-esteem."

"That's fine on your own time. But you have investors. We have investors. A minimalist roster isn't going to cut it, I don't care how you justify it to yourself. I need ideas. I've already decided that we're going to add concealer, foundation—"

"Foundation! Absolutely not."

"—bronzer, setting powder, a makeup primer, lipstick—"

"Lipstick? Have you lost it?"

"—gloss, and lip liner to our offerings. I want a new product release for Reveal every six months going forward."

"That's insane," I sputtered. Rapprochement was officially off the table. "We go through twenty or thirty iterations before each launch. It takes us eighteen months to two years to develop a new product properly."

"Not anymore. There's no way you need that much time. Labs can churn out a formula in weeks."

"Next you'll want us to sell products online."

"Yes, that's exactly what we'll do: build our own e-commerce business."

"Customers need to test the products in person. We should open a brick-and-mortar store."

"Reveal can open physical retail on a future owner's dime. Digital is the future. Technically, it's the present. Look at all these new companies that sell directly to consumers. They cut out the middlemen and maximize their profits. That's what Reveal needs to do. Take it from a veteran."

"You've already decided on products you know are against my wishes and a digital plan that I oppose. Why are we even meeting?"

"You're the face of this brand," Alan explained. "Customers love a founder narrative. They still believe you're in charge, so we need you to get in line."

"I don't make any product decisions going forward?"

Alan smiled. "Of course you do. We'd like to build out the eye category. Mascara. Eye shadow. We need a true hero there, not just Glow for Eyes. Something special that no one has done before. I want you to spearhead that while I roll out everything else."

As awful as the onset of Alan's tenure was, the silver lining to that tragic London trip was Amanda. Sweet, beautiful Amanda. After our entanglement in my hotel room, Amanda declined to spend the night, a decision I believed spoke to her discretion. The next morning, we met Elizabeth in the lobby and shared a car to the airport. Amanda didn't so much as blink in acknowledgment of our rendezvous. There were no smiles, close-lipped or otherwise. By the time we landed in New York, I had convinced myself that what had transpired between us had been merely a blip on the otherwise static radar.

I worried, briefly, that she might go to HR. Intraoffice relations, however meaningless, are always a tricky business, no less so when they're between two women. But she didn't, not that I was aware of. I decided this was a sign of her maturity. She was an adult. If this had been a concerning development, she would have said something. Adults speak up when they're uncomfortable. Her silence, to me and to the greater world, was the clearest message she could have sent.

As for me, well, I was completely unchanged by our London night. I didn't look at Amanda differently because I had seen her naked. Because we had kissed. Because her fingers had slipped inside me and seized control of my body. Of course I didn't. When I glanced at her across a desk and handed her my corporate receipts and said good night to her at the end of a long day, I didn't imagine her beautiful skin, how soft it felt against mine, how her silky hair tickled my stomach as she kissed her way down my torso. No, I saw her as my assistant. Someone who was good at her job. A person I could trust with my life.

We settled back into our pre-London routine. She was as detail oriented as ever. Anticipatory. She brought me lunch before I knew I was hungry. She called me a car before I had to ask. She RSVP'd yes and no to exactly the correct events. There were no injured looks. I saw no hesitancy in her body language. She was as even-keeled as she had always been. Not a hair was out of place. There were only meetings and more meetings and the constant churning that was and is Reveal.

A Fresh Pair of Eyes

Six months after our return from London, Amanda and I were the last two people in the office, a not irregular occurrence. It had been a long day of twelve meetings. Outside my window, the sky had been dark for hours. Amanda knocked on my glass door out of habit. She sat at my desk, her leather diary open, and pulled up a digital copy of my schedule on her phone. I noticed that she wore a high-necked black maxi dress with a chunky, oversized cardigan. I had never seen her wear such baggy clothes.

"Are you cold?" I asked.

A light flush spread across Amanda's cheeks. "It's chilly in here and freezing outside," she said, as she hugged her cardigan tighter around her torso.

"It's these old windows," I said.

"Yeah, they get so drafty," said Amanda. "You have Elizabeth at nine a.m. tomorrow. Then accounting. Then HR wants to chat more about Alan's transition. Then—"

"I don't think I can do this." I rubbed at my temples, which ached like someone had stabbed them with needles.

"You want me to move HR?" Amanda's brow furrowed as she

examined the rest of my schedule. "Maybe we could ask marketing to switch with them for the four p.m. spot?"

"No. I mean this, right now."

"Oh, sorry. I can come back later if you need more time." Amanda made a motion to stand up from her chair, but I waved her back down.

"No. That's not what I meant. Are you doing anything right now? Do you have anywhere to be?"

A look I had never seen teased at her rosy lips.

"No plans."

"Want to get out of here? Go get a drink somewhere? On me."

"Sure, sounds good."

Amanda walked back to her desk and slipped on her peacoat. It made her look collegiate. On our way to the bar I had in mind, we passed a Sephora.

"Do you mind if we duck in?" I asked Amanda. Why did I ask her if she "minded" things? "I'd like to see our latest gondola."

"Of course not," Amanda replied. "I never turn down a trip to Sephora."

The place was abuzz, like those department store floors used to be. Young women flitted from brand to brand, swiping lipsticks onto their balmed pouts, tugging pencils across their lash lines, spritzing their necks and inner wrists with the latest and greatest ouds. A few salespeople in all black tended to customers seated in director chairs beside mirrored vanities. Most of the Sephora staff either fetched inventory or roamed the store desperate for a task. Their beauty expertise was in short demand.

All those many years ago as a student, I had wielded my cosmetics knowledge like a magic wand to make women feel beautiful and yes, to make at least one of them come. Beauty and seduction danced cheek to cheek in my world. I had met Caroline from my perch behind a counter. My makeup acumen landed me in her bed. In today's landscape, we might never have crossed paths. What place did charm and talent have in a store whose customers knew what they wanted without the aid of an expert? What place did I have in an era where instant gratification had supplanted seduction?

"This is a site of discovery," Amanda chided me when I raised my concerns to her, absent the Caroline anecdote and sexual subtext. She patted some expensive moisturizer on the back of her hand from a golden jar. "Department stores are so intimidating and exclusionary. Here, people feel uninhibited to try things, case in point."

"I guess," I said.

"Sephora has been amazing for brands like Reveal. All those indie start-ups can get a foothold here in a way they never could with a department store."

"Great. Sephora is giving my competition a leg up," I said. Nearby, two young women were sucking in their cheeks and pouting their lips as they dusted their faces with dark powder. They looked like dead fish. "Will the contouring trend ever die?"

"I don't know, but it's fascinating to watch."

"Fascinating? More like deforming."

Amanda's eyes narrowed. "Drag culture is part of the reason contouring is so mainstream now. It has roots in the LGBT+ community."

"So, I'm required to like it then?" I asked. "And what about that?" I nodded at a woman a few feet away who was using her finger to tap layers of green-glitter eye shadow across her lids. Her lips were already coated in an ultra-shiny magenta gloss. "She looks ridiculous."

"She's having fun," said Amanda.

"It's completely unnatural," I said.

"That's the point," said Amanda. "It's self-expression. She doesn't care if it's conventionally beautiful. Haven't you ever worn glitter?"

"No," I said, as I watched a young woman in leggings and Birkenstocks dot a two-hundred-dollar serum beneath her eyes. When did women start walking around like it was perpetually laundry day? "The elevated part of cosmetics is missing. This experience doesn't feel special. It's like you're playing with makeup at a glorified slumber party."

"Exactly!"

"That's a good thing?"

"Yes," Amanda explained patiently. "Accessibility is more important than rarity. Who wants to feel so excluded they never buy anything?"

"Reveal is a cult brand," I reminded her. "Cult status isn't found in a sleeping bag."

"How many cults do you know that have ended well, Max?" she asked.

I couldn't take the crush of people anymore, so I ushered her out the door, to SoHo's crowded sidewalks, and farther out to a nearby bar.

Amanda was right. I was now on the wrong side of beauty business history. To these young women, I was the equivalent of traditional. In Amanda's eyes, I'm on the wrong side of other histories, too. The unfairness of that makes me want to scream. Don't you know what I have been through, I wish to tell her. Don't you understand that I had to suffer so you could exist?

I steered Amanda in the direction of a little hole-in-the-wall on Bleecker Street that had dim lighting. We found a table in a back corner. Amanda ordered our drinks, two bourbons neat, from the bar. She smiled at the tattooed male bartender a beat longer than necessary and I wondered about her relationship history. She seemed like someone who never needed to return home alone from a night out, but often chose solitude over others.

We sat at the rickety cocktail table and sipped our whiskey. In the bar's amber glow, Amanda's face beamed at me.

"Are you doing okay?" she asked.

"I've been better."

"Is it Alan?"

"Yes." I ran my finger across the edge of my drink's glass.

The cocktail table had a rough, splintery top. An entire history of past patrons was carved into its mottled surface. It reminded me of the bar where Caroline had broken up with me.

"You need to stand your ground."

"It's a lot easier to say that when you're a spectator."

If Amanda was taken aback by the rising sharpness in my delivery, nothing in her expression suggested it. Her face was pristine like a fresh bullet of lipstick.

"I'm not just a spectator here. My job doesn't exist without you."

"If you needed to find something else, you would be fine."

"Is that where you see this going?" Amanda's dark eyes welled with concern. I remembered that I was the adult here, the boss, and it was my job to reassure and lead.

"No, definitely not. I meant that purely hypothetically. Everything will be fine. Don't you want to move on to something else anyway?"

"I'd love to discuss that. I've been thinking—"

"You must be bored by me. I don't blame you."

"Oh. No, of course not." Amanda's eyes widened. "We can talk about it another time. Maybe I could put something—"

"I don't know what I'd do without you." I let the rest of my glass's contents slide down my throat.

"You don't have to worry about that."

"Another?" I glanced pointedly at Amanda's almost empty vessel.

"Sure." She downed the rest of her whiskey.

"Maybe a change of setting?"

I believe this is what people call an inflection point. My first night with Amanda was something a person could write off as a poor decision made in the heat of shock. This moment could not benefit from a similar generosity. Yes, I was depressed over the state of my professional authority. Still, I wasn't drunk or blindsided. My vision was as clear-eyed as could be on two inches of whiskey and a half-empty stomach. The one important note I can issue in my defense is that, as before, Amanda consented. On the topic of "signs," there is no stronger indicator of mutual desire than that.

Back at my apartment, I lay on my duvet as Amanda hovered over me. I unhooked her black silk bra and reached for her breasts, small and golden with dark pink-brown nipples. They reminded me of Caroline's chest, but they were smaller. Amanda caught my hand before it caressed her right breast.

"No touching unless I say so."

Oh, we were going to play like that now, were we? Fine. Her long stare sliced through me. Then she offered me her lips with faux reluctance and I knew that I would be a cooperative participant in any game she chose.

This time, Amanda slept over. My alarm sounded at 5 a.m., per usual. I glanced at Amanda's sleeping form. She appeared even younger in repose, her sharp intelligence no longer swooping in to complicate her innocent features. Not for the last time, I questioned how I had graduated from conquests in their thirties and forties to someone more than a decade my junior. As I admired her in the overcast light of day, her chest rising and falling, I understood that what I gained from Amanda, what attracted me to her nubile shores, was not the sizzling heat of sex—though make no mistake, she was dynamite in bed—but the embrace of hope. Amanda was the future wrapped in one delicate body. To be with her was to court an ageless, fresh start.

The next year was a roller coaster with far more lows than highs. At Reveal we released a new product every six months, per Alan's directive. First came lipstick, in a range of fifteen shades, each one more cringe-inducing than the next. At least they were in a creamy finish. I girded myself for the future meeting where Alan would enthuse about the return of matte. I wasn't so lucky in the concealer department, the second product launch under Alan's reign. The formula he approved was so thick and pasty, it could have doubled as plaster on a rental apartment's walls.

"Why don't we just send women to the hardware store? They can buy some cement instead," I told Alan. "Reveal makeup is supposed to be sheer, so you can see the woman underneath it. That's our MO."

"It's called 'concealer.' It's supposed to cover things up," said Alan. "Women want makeup that does its job. I did this for decades—I know what works."

I wanted to cement his mouth shut with that concealer, seal it tight, so I didn't have to hear another self-important word.

After that night at the bar, Amanda and I fell into a routine: We were together two or three nights a week. Sometimes, we would leave the office separately and meet for drinks—always at a place far from work—before we headed to my apartment. Other times, Amanda would go directly to my apartment, separately from me; if she arrived there before I did, my doorman knew to send her up. Amanda had a key, and she could let herself in, fix herself a drink, settle down in the living room, relax until I returned home. She had no possessions at my place, no extra pairs of underwear or change of clothes. Whenever she wanted to freshen up, she used my face wash and shampoo. I did give her a toothbrush, though. One night, I handed it to her wrapped in tissue paper with a ribbon, after we had finished in bed.

"What's this?" she asked. She slipped her black cotton underwear back on. I noticed that her hip bones were more prominent than when we first began sleeping together regularly. The lines of her rib cage were visible, too. Amanda had lost weight. I took it as a compliment. She wanted to look her best for me, not that she had ever been chubby.

"Open it," I said.

Amanda tore the paper. She held the pink toothbrush in its plastic packaging, confusion wrinkling her brows.

"A toothbrush?"

"For when you stay over. You're often here so late."

Amanda glanced at the time on the digital clock by my bed. It was after midnight.

"I guess it is late," she said. "Thanks, Max. This is nice of you."

Occasionally, we went to dinner together. Amanda was a cheap date; she had become accomplished in the art of pushing food around her plate. We dined at restaurants where we wouldn't run into people we knew. It wouldn't have mattered. She and I were never affectionate in public. There was no hand-holding or kissing, no hugs or shoulder squeezes or errant caresses.

We weren't a couple, of course, not in a romantic sense. I did stop sleeping with other women once I began having sex with Amanda, though it wasn't misplaced monogamy: juggling multiple schedules was too complicated. Any avoidance of public touching with Amanda wasn't because I thought there was something wrong with our affair, specifically. As I've said, this was a consensual situation. The care we took in the outside world, that was a question of privacy. We could both guess what people would say about her if they knew she had sex with her boss. As for me, well, I had enough to deal with professionally, thanks to Alan; I didn't need my sexuality to complicate matters further.

At the office, Alan did everything in his power to undermine my leadership. There was the packaging meeting where I was at one end of the conference table while he sat at the other. We had gathered to discuss a special edition of Flush for the next year's holiday season. I contemplated a glass vial stamped with mini-snowflakes, too cheesy for my taste.

"Why don't you offer Flush in a stick form like so many other companies are doing now?" Alan asked. "You go to Sephora and all the blushes are sticks."

Alan slouched back in his chair, stretching his legs out in front of him, like he was in his living room. All the eyes in that meeting landed on me to gauge my reaction.

"Because Flush is a liquid product. It blends better that way. Besides, we have a tinted lip balm. If a woman wants to use that on her cheeks, she's welcome to."

I smiled and clenched a fist beneath the table.

"You'd rather ask women to find innovative ways to use a different product than give them what they want?"

The heat of collective breath was focused on my answer.

"Our lab technician tried a solid for cheeks, and she couldn't achieve the same seamless flush. The product works best as it is."

"Customers won't notice. They're not as particular as you."

"Women notice everything," I said, my gaze lingering on the roll of fat above his waistband. "It's my job to be particular."

"You should also do a powder version of Glow," Alan pushed on. "All those girls on YouTube use powder highlighters."

My employees' eyes pinged back and forth across the room.

"Reveal doesn't believe in powder highlighters. We're all about dew. I really appreciate your feedback, Alan. This is a packaging meeting, and these are questions better suited for a product development conversation."

Alan smirked.

"Of course. We have that meeting at four p.m. We'll discuss it then."

His litany of inane queries continued a couple of hours later. Why didn't Glow come in the same trendy purplish pink that other brands were offering their highlighters in? Because we didn't believe women should look like victims of extraterrestrial colonization. Why didn't you focus on an entire range of foundations, the one cosmetic product women are most loyal to? Because we didn't tell women they needed to cover up their skin to feel beautiful. Why, why, why, why, why? Every question Alan threw my way could be answered with one simple reply: because that is not what Reveal does and if you took two minutes to care about this brand, you would know that.

He hadn't been inducted into Reveal's leadership to understand the brand, however. He had no interest in Reveal or me beyond future acquisition. Even his insistence on using the word *you* in all his questions made clear the divide between what Reveal put out and his corporate ranking.

Ellen agreed when she phoned one morning to check in.

"Alan mentioned on our call yesterday that you are being hostile to his suggestions," Ellen said.

"That is blatantly untrue," I replied.

"You are his direct report."

"My understanding was that I answered to you and the Board."

"We are aligned with Alan. If you answer to him, you are also answering to us."

I gripped the arm of my desk chair so tightly my knuckles turned white.

"This is still my company."

"It is *our* company," Ellen shot back, with a ferocity I didn't expect. Her tone was calmer when she continued. "Maxine, we are all on the same side here: the success of Reveal. Why do you have to put up these walls?"

"I don't want to expand Reveal with products that aren't true to our brand."

"The only truth here is numbers. You'll do what Alan says."

Ever-loyal Elizabeth provided little solace during this period. Her frustration with me was palpable.

"Alan asked me to remind you that he needs to see some pitches for eye products," she told me as we wrapped up a weekly publicity one-on-one.

"Creativity doesn't happen at the push of a button," I snapped.

"I know, Max. I want you to be aware of the directive coming from above."

"Consider me aware."

"Not all his ideas are terrible. He's right that digital is crucial to any business today. Instagram, YouTube, all those younger women are online. I watched an influencer makeup tutorial that my assistant sent me. Have you seen any? They're pretty addictive."

"They're crass, that's what they are. A makeup routine is intimate, not something to be whored out for views or whatever."

"You know, not every woman wants an ultra-natural look," Elizabeth continued, like I hadn't spoken. "A lot of women today see cosmetics as a medium for shaping identity. It's almost a performance."

"Then they can get it from a different brand. When did you become an expert on what women want from makeup?"

Elizabeth popped up from her chair and strode to my office door. I thought she was going to leave, but she paused.

"Max, I'm not saying any of this to upset you. I care about you." She lowered her voice. "I'm worried, Max, for you and Reveal. I'm on your side." She glanced at Amanda through the glass door. "Maybe we should ask Amanda what she thinks."

"Why? She's an assistant—she doesn't make business decisions."

"She's part of this next generation, it would be good to have her insights." Elizabeth frowned. "And she's not going to be an assistant forever. You're going to promote her eventually, right?"

"I asked her about it a while ago. She didn't express any interest."

"Maybe you should bring it up again."

"Did she say something to you?"

"No, but it's been over four years now."

"Has it?"

"She started in the summer of 2009. It would be good to get some younger people moving up in the company. Helps keep us relevant."

"I'm perfectly capable of keeping this company relevant on my own, thanks."

Amanda was the only saving grace during that period. On a call with Ellen or Alan or any number of other grating individuals, I would glance up from my computer and see Amanda's shiny, dark head. Lightness would bloom in my chest.

Despite Elizabeth's suggestion, I never raised the question of a new position with Amanda after that one time at the Bleecker Street bar. Amanda was a grown woman, too old to be handed things she didn't request. It's true, moving her to a different role would have been a huge loss for me, so I did what any boss would have done in my place: I incentivized her to stay with multiple generous raises. She was the best-paid assistant in all of Manhattan. No one would leave a gig like that.

Amanda and I were at my apartment after work one night in early 2014. We were reviewing my next day's schedule—and yes, she would stick around for a while after that. On the coffee table was Amanda's leather planner and two half-empty tumblers. Amanda liked to unwind with a few rounds before we moved on to the intimate portion of our evenings. She scrolled through the calendar on her phone as she enumerated my various appointments the following morning.

We sat on the same low-slung sofa from my Flatiron apartment, which I have since replaced. There was maybe a foot of space between us in our seating arrangement. A thrill shivered across me as I waited for Amanda to finish her assistant duties and transition to my willing playmate.

"You have marketing at six p.m. Ellen plans to call you at six thirty-five on the dot. I'll knock on your door at six twenty-five to make sure they're out in time."

"Sounds good."

No matter how many nights I spent with Amanda, I could not get over her face. It was like Caroline's, but as seen through a buffed filter. There were no sharp edges across Amanda's swollen lips, her rounded nose, her full cheeks. Everything about her was curved and inviting. And those eyes, they teased you, like an upturned hand extended in your direction, just out of reach. I had always believed that the bigger the eyes, the more beautiful the girl. Women of my generation were desirous of a wide gaze, the better to exude the innocence that has always been the hallmark of female beauty. A round stare was the perfect counterpoint to the growing strains of feminism.

Amanda's eyes did the opposite. They foregrounded a woman's

sensuality. They were wide enough at their center to appear open; meanwhile, the tantalizing taper at their corners said, *Not so fast, I'm in charge here.* They were generous and withholding in equal measure. They captured the heart of womanly contradiction: vulnerability and flintiness in one graceful look. Imagine, I thought, if every woman could achieve such a sensual balance.

"Are we all good?" Amanda looked at me expectantly.

"Do you use anything on your eyes?"

"Like eyeliner you mean?"

"Sure or shadow. Anything?"

"No, I never have." Amanda placed her phone face down on her planner. She leaned back against the sofa and stretched her legs out onto the coffee table, her thigh inches from my lap. "Why do you ask?"

I leaned forward and reached a hand toward her face.

"May I?"

"If you must." Her tone sparkled with mischief.

I cupped my hand beneath her chin and her skin nearly melted into my own. I tilted her face down. She stared at me the whole time, refusing to release me from her visual spell.

"They are the perfect shape."

"Thanks. I guess."

"Why the 'I guess'?"

"It's not like I had anything to do with it."

"I want them."

"How—you want to clone me?"

"No, I—"

But Amanda cut me off with a kiss and the rest of the night faded into an ecstatic blur.

DAY EIGHT

Morning

This time, I don't bother with pastries for Sandrine. No need for such pleasantries since we both know they're going to remain untouched. It is another crack-of-dawn appearance by my lawyer. I barely have time to shower before the doorman is buzzing the intercom to announce her arrival.

I sit in my sun-faded chair with my hair wet, little droplets dotting my neck and back. Sandrine is in another one of her boxy suits. Today, it is a tart cranberry. It's not the worst thing having a lawyer who's alarmingly hot. When my throat tightens and my vision blurs as Sandrine and I discuss the finer points of my seemingly inevitable firing, I can distract myself with her silky face. I bet she has a little black book that's even thicker than mine.

My gaydar has its limits. With Amanda, I never thought to question her sexuality. The way she dressed, moved, spoke: it was an award-winning performance of straightness. That should have been a glaring hint that things were not as they seemed. Sandrine, however, exudes a deep confidence that only manifests when a woman knows her value exists completely independent of men. No straight woman I've met, however evolved, has achieved this same aura.

Sandrine sits there and sips her coffee and walks me through the various hypothetical outcomes of tomorrow's Board ordeal. Her words flit in and out of my ears, like hair-dryer static. When she has covered all her concerns, she places her cup back on the coffee table. Her gaze warms with curiosity.

"We have a game plan and we'll stick to it depending on what happens in the meeting. But have you given some thought to how you'll process everything? No matter what they decide, it's important that you're ready to move forward. That requires coming to terms with the past."

Who is this woman, the Zen Buddha of legal practices?

"Why do you care?" I reply. "If I win tomorrow, your job is done. If I'm fired, which we both assume is inevitable, then you have your work cut out for you. My understanding has nothing to do with it."

A frown appears on her face. It would harden the expressions of most women; on her, it deepens her beauty.

"Max, I would never have taken this case for the money." She laughs wryly at this. "You don't pay as well as most of my other clients."

"Thanks a lot," I say. "Happy to give you some beauty products as extra compensation."

"Reveal is a little femme for me," says Sandrine. "No offense."

"None taken."

"What I was saying," she continues, "is that I find your case intellectually challenging. You've had to build yourself up in a way men don't need to. I have empathy for that. You also fucked your Asian assistant. Complicated doesn't begin to encompass things."

"Always happy to provide complexity," I say.

"Anyway, it's not my job to judge you. It's my job to win. But this Amanda business, it's not going away after tomorrow, even if you win. You need to get your story straight—for yourself—so this doesn't happen again."

"Isn't that how you lawyers make so much money—repeat offenders, appeals, all that?" I ask. "If everyone behaved perfectly, you'd be in the poorhouse."

Sandrine smiles. "Again, my incentive here isn't financial, it's intellectual. And I hate people who waste my time."

Sandrine departs soon after that and here I sit, blue light illuminating my face, pondering her words. Do I have my story straight? What does that mean? I know what happened. Everything I've written has been an exact recitation of events. I haven't gotten overly emotional. Ellen would praise my stoicism.

If only Sandrine knew how devoted I am to the art of honest storytelling.

Sly Part One

My first eye hero veered from the pattern I had created with Reveal's other products. Isn't that how innovation works? The Flush, Glow, and perfume categories contained tools of enhancement. Sly—a portmanteau of *slinky* and *eye*—crept closer to transformation. It made the most of your natural features through an illusion of shape and reflectivity. It sculpted your raw potential into something special. Sly made the average eye striking. Still, everything I have done with Reveal, Sly included, has been motivated by the organic. I have never encouraged women to seek a look that conflicts with who they are naturally. My gift to them is not artifice, but flattery, and imitation is a form of flattery.

I assumed that Amanda would be gratified by all this. Every woman wants to be a muse. After that night on my living room sofa, I asked Amanda to set a meeting with Alan. I pitched him my original idea of Sly, a metallic, water-resistant gel eyeliner. Unlike a traditional pencil with its pointed end used for enhancing the upper and lower lash lines, Sly would be shaped like the chisel tip of a highlighter pen. Its wearer would create a long, thick, tapered line at the outer corner of the eye, slanting it up toward the end of their eyebrow. Using the flat wedge of Sly's tip, they would draw in a small triangle at their eye's inner corner. The goal was to elongate and narrow their overall eye shape so that it appeared squinty like the ultimate bedroom eye. You could even call the effect "foxy," as I did when describing it to Alan.

"You told me to come up with something no one has done before," I explained. "Sly will be unlike anything else on the market, the happy medium between sexy and natural."

"It could work," Alan conceded. It was evident that while he wanted the company to thrive, he didn't want it to be courtesy of my brilliance.

"It will work and you know it."

Alan's thin lips refused to budge.

"The name? Sly?"

"It's slinky, like a clingy evening dress. A slinky eye is a sexy eye. It's perpetually withholding."

"So it's clingy, but also withholding?"

"Yes. It's purposely contradictory because women are complex."

"Is the term 'sly' a compliment? It's normally more of a put-down."

"Why don't you let the copywriting team take care of the naming?"

Alan held his hands up in melodramatic surrender, but I didn't care. I had nailed it. He would be a fool to dismiss my idea.

"Very well, Maxine. I appreciate the pitch. I'll chat about it with the Board and let you know."

"Shouldn't I be there, too?"

A smirk finally parted Alan's lips.

"Not to worry—I'll make sure you get full credit."

While Alan took my pitch to the Board, I continued to sleep with Amanda. The Board approved Sly in the first quarter of 2014. Amanda was fully aware of the idea for Sly, though we never discussed its point of inspiration and Amanda never commented on Sly either way to me. I assumed this was out of professionalism. I had never asked her to weigh in on a product before; there was no reason for her to do so here. It took eighteen months to perfect Sly's formula with our lab, to nail the shape of Sly's tip, to perform stability testing, to approve the packaging, etc. Alan wanted it faster, of course, but I insisted that a hero required more care.

He also wanted the unveiling of Sly to coincide with the debut of our redesigned website. He had become obsessed with online sales and social media. As we developed Sly, we hired a self-described social media guru to assist the publicity department with promotion. In every meeting, Alan would drone on about the new direct-to-consumer brands that were remaking the beauty landscape by forging intimate relationships with customers through their online communities. There was one female-led brand he was especially fixated on, a start-up that had begun as a blog devoted to interviews about people's beauty routines and that launched in the fall of 2014 with four products. "Just you wait: in less than a year, they're going to accomplish more than Reveal has in its entire life," he would tell me. I wanted to inform Alan that I knew more than he ever could about forging intimate relationships with women, no online community necessary.

In mid-2014, I promoted Amanda from my assistant to a junior publicist. It was her five-year anniversary at Reveal. A role opened in Elizabeth's department and Elizabeth explicitly asked if she could hire Amanda.

"She has the perfect disposition for PR," Elizabeth told me.

"What disposition is that?" I asked.

"Diplomatic, but persistent," said Elizabeth. "People think good PR is about aggression. It's not, or not entirely. Relationship-building, strategy—those are the real keys."

"I don't know," I said.

"You have to let her go at some point," said Elizabeth. "It's a waste to have someone that talented doing busywork."

When I told her about the job, Amanda reacted with atypical emotion.

"Really?" she said. "This is really happening?"

"Yes, of course it is," I replied. "I wouldn't joke about something like this."

"Thank you," she said, tears forming in her eyes. "You have no idea how grateful I am."

"You earned it," I told her. "I know you have been reluctant to take the next step, but don't worry, you will be great."

I hired a new assistant, a competent recent Columbia graduate. The new assistant was smart, efficient, friendly. Her face seemed plastered with a permanent smile, more so than Amanda's ever was. But something was missing. When she brought me lunch, it was like she was crossing off a task. Her morning and end-of-day check-ins with me felt similarly routine and obligatory. I didn't get the sense that she truly cared about my well-being. To her, this position was simply a job, a stepping stone to something better. Nothing she did inspired me to remember her name.

What I'm trying to say is, I missed Amanda. She infused every action with care. I thought back to that contentious meeting with Ellen four years ago, after which Amanda bolstered my ego. That Chicago hotel room was instantly cozier when Amanda answered my call. She mellowed the sting of London and Alan and countless other slights. Amanda didn't just make my life easier, she nurtured me.

It's not the same thing as nurturing, but we were still sleeping together, though the frequency of those encounters diminished considerably after Amanda's promotion. Once she was situated in her PR position, I sent her a totally professional text message requesting a meetup.

> Would love to chat about your first few weeks in publicity. Let me know if tomorrow night or Thursday evening works for you.

Amanda didn't reply. I gave her a week, then sent her another message.

> Following up on the above. Could you let me know what nights in the next two weeks work for you?

Still nothing. Finally, I timed my departure from the office with hers so that we shared an elevator ride. Alone.

"Did you get my texts?" I asked as soon as the doors closed.

Amanda flushed, with embarrassment, I assumed.

"I did," she said. "Sorry for not responding. This new job has been great, just very consuming."

"Of course," I said. "I'll save you a text. Why don't you tell me now what nights you're free?"

"My schedule is so up in the air. I wouldn't want to make a date and then cancel."

Amanda tugged at her dark hair. She was so nervous about the prospect of canceling on me, it was adorable.

"Please," I told her. "I'm the boss. If Elizabeth or someone puts something on your schedule, I'll get them to move it. There would never be a reason to cancel on me."

"Won't that look like favoritism?" Amanda's voice was pleading. She was so good, so unwilling to accept special treatment.

"I know how to handle these things, don't you worry. How about Friday night? You're unlikely to have a work conflict then."

"Friday?"

"Unless you have other plans." I winked.

Amanda flushed deeper.

"No plans. Friday it is."

"Great. So glad we ran into each other."

As a member of the publicity team, Amanda was fully aware of Sly's conception and development. Like everyone else on the Reveal staff, she was excited about the company's debut ocular hero. I asked her to be the star of Sly's campaign—the first time we would feature a model in the images. Sales had suggested we pivot from product-only ads, so I pitched the idea of using a staffer instead of a traditional model, to keep things fresh. When I approached Amanda about the shoot, she was visibly enthusiastic.

"I'd love for you to model Sly in our campaign," I told her, having called her into my office without preamble. She sat across from me in our timeworn configuration.

Amanda's marigold cheeks pinkened.

"Are you sure I'm the right person for this? Don't you want a model?"

"You're the only person for this. Stop being so modest. Anyway, it's going to be a tight shot. No one will know it's you unless you tell them."

"Okay, that sounds good."

"Elizabeth will email you all the details for the shoot."

"Is there anything I need to do in preparation?"

"I wouldn't go binge drinking the night before. Other than that, show up as your gorgeous self."

It wasn't just that Amanda's role at the office or the infrequency of our meetups had changed. Now that she was no longer my assistant, she was much friendlier toward Alan. On multiple occasions, I saw her interacting with him in a manner that could only be described as delighted. I walked by the kitchen one day and they were standing by the coffee machine. A wide smile, one that showed teeth, split open Amanda's face, while Alan laughed at something she said. Another time, I saw Amanda enter Alan's office with a stack of papers, presumably press materials for him to review. Instead of merely placing them on his desk and quickly leaving, she stood there and chatted with him. Alan gestured at one of the empty chairs and she sat down.

What could they have to discuss, I wondered. I tried not to give it too much thought. The possibility that Amanda had suddenly switched from my side to Alan's, as a matter of protection, occurred to me. The friction between me and Alan, between me and the Board, was an open secret. The safe bet was to get behind the higher-ranked executive. But I brushed this idea away. Amanda was not duplicitous. She was ambitious, sure, but she had integrity. She would never betray me. Joke's on me, I guess.

DAY EIGHT

Evening

After I purchased my Upper West Side apartment, I turned the second, spare bedroom into an enormous walk-in closet. The room is pale and clean, with oak cabinetry and a speckled taupe carpet. A central island holds my jewelry, evening clutches, scarves, and other accessories. One wall is devoted to handbags and shoes, all in neutral tones. The shoes are primarily loafers and low-heeled models, save for the black stilettos I maintain for investor meetings. I suppose I won't be needing those anytime soon.

There is an area for jackets and matching pants. Another wall has my coats and various outerwear. My button-down shirts—what my mother would call "blouses"—comprise their own section, too. Open shelves hold my cashmere and wool sweaters, my knit shells that occasionally whisper beneath suits, the odd silk T-shirt for casual days. Then there is the lingerie section. I wear exclusively pastel lace underthings. Mint green, lavender, petal pink, sky blue. It's the one area of my life where I enjoy unnatural colors. I never tire of the look that crosses my conquests' faces when they strip off my sharp tailored suits to find the candy-colored surprise that hides beneath.

Is it a metaphor for my soft side? A form of perverse rebellion? I'm not one to linger on analysis.

My closet is my favorite room in the apartment. How's that for irony. When I stand in its confines, as I do right now, the sandalwood and lavender from the hanging sachets enveloping me like a warm hug, I feel at peace. My clothes give me complete control over my image. I have hand-selected every item in this room for its potential to render me strong, protected, elegant, and, yes, beautiful.

I walk over to the wall of jackets and pants. My hand glides over a favorite ensemble. A black suit with angles so sharp they could draw blood. I run my fingers across the jacket and down the pants. The silk satin is decadent, intoxicating. I could be touching human skin. If I could attend the Board meeting tomorrow, this is the suit I would wear.

I slip my T-shirt over my head. Those cashmere sweatpants are on the floor. I don't bother with a shirt. On go the pants. They slide up my legs. Sparks of electricity ripple upward. The jacket caresses my shoulders, my clavicle, my breasts, my stomach. Beneath the lapels, my nipples are hard. Who needs a phallus when you have a suit as virile as this one.

There is a mirror on a nearby wall in which I examine my reflection. I am lean, polished, impossible to ignore. I do not resemble a monster. I look like I could make your night.

The public hates me and the Board may fire me. Still, Maxine Thomas will always dress the part of a woman who gets what she wants.

Sly Part Two

The shoot for Sly went off without a hitch. On set, the makeup artist created three looks, each in the same foxy configuration with the shades of Sly we planned to release, a champagne gold, a rose gold, and a steely pewter. As I promised Amanda, the shots were tight: a single eye with her eyebrow at the top of the frame and part of her under eye anchoring the bottom. A barely perceptible application of Glow added a highlight across her brow bone and at the apex of her cheek, like a fairy had left a trail of shimmery dust in her wake. The photo edit arrived. I included Amanda in the meeting, though her junior status did not warrant it. She was the star of the campaign, even if her role was anonymous outside the office; I thought she deserved to be part of the conversation. We made our selections. Amanda looked on approvingly. A week after Labor Day in 2015, Sly entered the world.

The initial reception to Sly was overwhelmingly positive. Elizabeth nabbed us full-page features in *Harper's Bazaar*, *ELLE*, *Vogue*, and *W* and even a story in the *New York Times* Style section. Editors raved about the shape of Sly's tip, the ease with which it glided across a woman's lid, the glimmering thick lines it left behind. Stores in the

US and the UK sold out of Sly within hours. So did our newly relaunched website, which crashed. We had a wait list with thousands of names by the end of the first day. Sly's arrival made the debut of Flush amateur by comparison.

The first sign that something was awry came on Sly's third day in the world. That afternoon, a user with the handle @AsianzRUS posted a collage of Sly's campaign and press clippings with the caption *When straight-up cultural appropriation earns you millions of dollars in sales.* @AsianzRUS tagged Reveal's Instagram account in the post. I didn't know this at the time. Amanda was the first person at Reveal to spy the post. She snapped a photo of it and sent it up the chain to Elizabeth with the subject line *FYI* and no additional comment. Elizabeth forwarded the email to me with the line *Amanda will keep an eye on this.* Pun unintended, of course.

If things had stopped with @AsianzRUS, all would have been fine. @AsianzRUS had a total of thirty-five followers and one of those digital bobbleheads instead of a profile picture. He or she was clearly a troll, likely some sad adult who lived in their parents' basement. The pushback did not stop with this subterranean loser, though. Within an hour, @BleachFreeBeauty had picked up @AsianzRUS's post. This is where the trouble began. @BleachFreeBeauty is a self-appointed digital watchdog whose mission is calling out beauty companies on the apparently limitless ways in which they are racist, sexist, and generally bigoted. The name @BleachFreeBeauty refers to their ongoing campaign against supposed whitewashing and appropriation.

On a side note, what is this millennial obsession with "calling out"? It is a distinctly abhorrent practice. Why has no one called out those who make a living calling out others instead of, I don't know, producing actual work of their own? It's as though an entire generation has decided that their defining feature should be criticism and public shaming rather than creation. What will they do, I wonder, when there is nothing left to demolish, and no one left to denigrate? When they wake up and survey the charred remains of our cultural landscape, the result of their relentless reaping, will they finally work up the courage to build something of their own? I doubt it.

So @BleachFreeBeauty picked up @AsianzRUS's post about Sly and added their own embellishing caption: *The true REVEAL here is how this whitewashing company has appropriated a stereotypical Asian eye shape as a selling point of their new Sly eyeliner. Yup, Sly. You couldn't come up with a more racist name for this eyeliner if you tried. How much longer are we going to suffer this ignorant shit?* It went out to @BleachFreeBeauty's one million followers, and next thing I knew, Elizabeth rushed into my office, minutes before Ellen and Alan clogged up my phone line. I closed the door behind Elizabeth.

"This is bad, Max."

"There must be something we can do. These accusations of racism are ridiculous."

The steadiness of Elizabeth's gaze wavered for a second.

"You don't believe what they're saying, do you?" I asked.

"How I feel is beside the point. We need to figure out a plan of defense."

"You're not a lawyer, Elizabeth. You can tell me how you feel."

She paused at that, as she always does before she delivers unwelcome news.

"I don't think their claim is completely baseless. I also don't think we or you did anything intentional."

"There's no *we* here, though, is there? It doesn't matter that Alan and the Board approved this. All the blame falls on me."

"You know this is how it works, Max. You're the founder—the public associates Reveal with you. I'm not saying it's fair."

Fury surged through my veins. I breathed deeply. The walls of my office were glass, everyone could see me. I had been an idiot to believe this level of transparency was a good idea.

"Even when I've lost full control of Reveal, it's still my fault."

"Consumers don't know your control has diminished. You're still the face of this brand."

"And what did I do? It's an eyeliner for god's sake. They're making it sound like I stole someone's eyes out of their face."

"Let's focus on putting together a statement," Elizabeth urged me. She started a blank note on her phone. "Obviously, we'll apologize."

"For what?" I practically yelled.

"It doesn't matter *what*—you just apologize, profusely, for doing wrong. You don't have to specify what it is, only that you did wrong."

"Jesus."

"So you'll apologize. We'll apologize," Elizabeth continued. "I need some info for myself. What was the inspiration for Sly?"

In the eighteen months since I had pitched Sly to Alan, I had been adamant about my idea's origin story: the hypothetical bedroom eye. Just as Flush lent an orgasmic flush and Glow mimicked a postcoital sheen, Sly extended a woman's ocular silhouette to its most seductive iteration. Reveal was predicated on the idea that a woman looked her best in the heat of sexual arousal, though I was not explicit about how I arrived at this information.

In this delineation, I had omitted Amanda's role in my thinking. Not because I was embarrassed of the part she had played, but clearly there were obstacles to my full honesty. I couldn't tell Alan or anyone else that her gaze had catalyzed Sly without sharing the reasons why I paid her face so much attention. All along, I had done this to protect her. Amanda wouldn't want the world to know of her relations with me—that type of disclosure called into question an employee's qualifications. Plus, I doubted she wanted to give anyone a reason to suspect the source of her recent promotion.

Elizabeth stared at me expectantly. I realized she wanted me to walk her through Sly's inspiration in earnest.

"I've told you how I came up with Sly."

"Tell me again."

"I thought of the ideal bedroom-eye shape and how to give that to women."

"How did you come up with that shape?"

"The same way I came up with Glow's gleam, I thought about how women look."

"In the bedroom?"

My phone rang and my assistant picked up the line from her desk. I watched through my glass walls as she typed a message on her computer before she placed the receiver back down. It was probably Ellen, with another furious demand that I call her back immediately.

"Max? Did you hear me?"

"Yes, sorry. I guess. Figuratively, of course."

Elizabeth powered her phone off. She placed it face down on my desk. Her voice came out in a deep whisper when she spoke.

"I need to know, was Sly inspired by someone you slept with? Was she Asian? Nod if your answer is yes."

I couldn't meet Elizabeth's penetrating look. A cold wave cascaded across me. I moved my head up and down in a barely perceptible nod.

"But not Asian," I said. "Not fully."

"What does that mean?"

"I don't know."

I would say the sigh that escaped Elizabeth's lips was overly dramatic, except it wasn't. She knew that we were in trouble.

"Elizabeth, I'm—"

She cut me off with a wave of her hand.

"No, Max. Please do not say that you're sorry."

"I thought that's what we were doing here. Apologizing."

"As a company, yes. You don't owe me anything. This is my job; I work for you. You are my person."

It was the closest I ever came to crying in the office. I couldn't tell you the last time I had cried at all, but with that declaration from Elizabeth, something inside me thawed.

Elizabeth stood. She retrieved her phone from my desk and powered it back on.

"I know what to say. I'll release a statement in an hour, I just need to run it by Alan first. Do you want to see it, too?"

"That's okay. I trust you."

Later that afternoon, Elizabeth sent me an email with a link to a story on *The Cut*, featuring the approved apology she wrote for me. I clicked on the link, whose headline read *Reveal Founder Maxine Thomas Says Your Criticism of Sly Speaks to* Your *Racism, Not Hers.* Hmm, I thought, what magic did Elizabeth cast here? I scrolled down to the part of the story that contained my so-called quote.

> *Maxine Thomas has issued an apology through a Reveal spokesperson. "I am deeply sorry to those who felt hurt or offended by our latest makeup release, Sly. Reveal and I did not intend to harm anyone, especially the Asian American community, whose long-standing devotion to skin care the American beauty industry owes an enormous debt to. Reveal was founded on the value of inclusivity, the idea that all women can feel their most beautiful when they reveal their true selves. My motivation in releasing Sly was to give women a tool to create a bedroom eye without all the extraneous devices that other companies require. The fact that some people have taken Sly's campaign and twisted it into a problematic depiction of a stereotypical Asian eye shape is deeply troubling to me. It speaks to the many erroneous ways in which American culture fetishizes Asian beauty. This*

country has a dark history of conflating Asian beauty with eroticism. I am stunned and saddened that Sly has become collateral in this ongoing narrative. Reveal will be making donations to our favorite AAPI charities—I would encourage anyone who is troubled by this to do the same."

Elizabeth was as brilliant as the first day I met her. Everything would be fine, thanks to her smooth intervention. It was barely 5 p.m., but I decided to leave work early and end the day on a high note. I asked my assistant to keep me abreast of urgent calls or emails. I walked across the bustling office; the din of phones ringing and keyboards clacking and desk-chair wheels squeaking on the concrete floor reverberated around me. That delicious soundtrack of productivity swaddled me. When the elevator arrived, I stood alone in its cavity and stared at the busyness I had birthed into being through my sheer determination. I had made Reveal. No one, not Alan or Ellen or the Board or some anonymous troll on the internet, could take it away from me.

That evening was the last time I set foot in Reveal's headquarters. In retrospect, I wonder if a deep instinct pushed me to a quick exit.

Elizabeth told me that, after I left, Amanda approached Alan's office. Elizabeth watched her knock on his door, enter, and close the door behind her. Like mine, Alan's office was entirely walled in glass. With her back to Elizabeth, Amanda sat across from Alan. Elizabeth saw Alan's face go from curious to horrified. Alan caught Elizabeth staring at him. He waved for her to join them. Then he picked up his phone and called someone else.

A woman from HR sat beside Elizabeth and Amanda in Alan's office. Elizabeth asked what was going on.

"Maybe you shouldn't be here," the HR woman told Elizabeth.

"Amanda reports to me. If she's upset, I should know," said Elizabeth.

"All right," said the HR woman. "To be clear, though, you're here in the capacity of a concerned manager, not for crisis management."

"What crisis are we managing?" asked Elizabeth.

"Tell her," Alan directed Amanda, with perhaps a tinge of excitement.

Amanda nodded. Her cheeks were blotchy with reddened patches. "This is really hard to tell you."

"I appreciate you coming to us with something so difficult, whatever it is," said Elizabeth.

"I want you to know how grateful I am for everything you've done for me. I feel lucky to work under you."

"We are lucky to have you."

Amanda flashed Elizabeth a sad smile.

"It's about Sly. I was the inspiration behind it."

"In what sense?"

"Max copied the shape of my eye for Sly."

"You mean at the shoot?"

"No, before that."

"Did she tell you this?"

"She didn't have to. She pitched it to Alan the morning after we were together."

"Together—how? At the office?"

The blotches on Amanda's face grew darker.

"At her apartment."

"You dropped something off for her?"

Alan cleared his throat. Elizabeth turned to look at him. His face bore the traces of poorly masked glee.

"No. We went over her schedule. We had something to drink."

"Alcoholic?"

"Yes. And . . . we had sex on her sofa."

"Max had sex with you."

"She's been sleeping with me for years."

The Aftermath

There it is. Elizabeth vacated Alan's office quickly after Amanda's revelation and retreated home where, glass of vodka in hand, she called me while I was in the middle of a sunset walk to fill me in on the evening's events.

I'm not sure how I expected Elizabeth to react. I braced myself for a chilly reprimand or worse, a stone-cold silence. Neither of those responses was Elizabeth's style. She had told me from the outset that she would be a professional wingwoman. She wasn't going to martyr herself on my behalf; still, she wouldn't abandon me in my time of need.

"I don't know what to say," I told her after she finished her account of that meeting in Alan's office.

"You don't have to say anything."

Minutes passed during which the only sounds on either end of the phone call were our anxious breathing and the pedestrians passing by me as I stood on the reservoir's crowded path. Elizabeth broke the wordlessness.

"You love her."

"No."

"It wasn't a question." I heard the tinkle of ice against glass. I could visualize Elizabeth taking a sip of her vodka on the rocks. "This is bad, Max. I will do everything I can to minimize the damage to you. But I need you to understand how bad this is."

"I get it."

"If it was just the sex thing or just the race thing, we could maybe spin it. The two combined . . ."

"Lethal."

"Yes." This time I heard the pop of a bottle stopper and the crystalline sound of liquid streaming over ice. "I know you didn't understand what you were doing wrong with Sly—"

"I didn't. I still don't."

"—but with Amanda?"

"It was fully consensual. She started things."

"You're sure?"

"I remember her starting things."

"You didn't stop things."

"No."

"We've never had a candid conversation about your personal life."

"There's no reason we need to now."

"You've sacrificed a lot to build Reveal. I see it and I feel how deeply unfair it is. It doesn't justify things. Still, I know hiding yourself has come with such a staggering cost."

"I don't see it that way."

"I know you don't. Maybe you should try to."

My voice trembled. "Once I see things in that light, I won't be able to unsee them. I don't know if I can live like that."

Now it was Elizabeth's voice that shook; it practically vibrated my phone. "Your version of living right now is not sustainable."

I think Elizabeth sniffled. I'm not sure. My eyes were cloudy at this point. The sunset was an orange-red blur.

"Whatever you decide, Max," she continued, "I'll always be here. I'm not going anywhere. We'll talk tomorrow."

Elizabeth ended our call, and my life caved in on me. The fence of the reservoir crept closer and closer. The path was so narrow, I felt suspended on a string of floss. I don't know how I made it back to my apartment without an accident. My doorman asked about my walk. I remember his perplexed expression at my terrified face. I could barely breathe by the time I got upstairs.

Hours earlier I was enveloped in the new success of Sly. I basked in that buzz of achievement. Now I sat on the precipice of destruction; I stared over the ledge. The land below looked hard and painful and deeply inhospitable.

I had no doubt about Amanda's motives in this betrayal. She was out to save herself. I had been too open when she was my assistant. I had shared concerns about my leadership of Reveal. That was my mistake. She had exploited my insecurity to team up with Alan. All those friendly chats with him in his office had laid the groundwork for this disclosure. She had handed Alan and by extension the Board exactly what they craved: an excuse to fire me. In return, they had promised her protection from whatever layoffs or restructuring might be in Reveal's future. So much for being my authentic self.

Okay, I admit that my ongoing relations with Amanda were not the best idea. She worked with me and for me and that complicated things. But she initiated all of it. She practically threw herself at me in London. I'm still not convinced that our run-in at the Victoria and Albert was a coincidence. For all I know, she tracked me there.

More crucially, Amanda wanted it. She clearly desired me. I could see it in her eyes, those damn gorgeous eyes. Still, I should never have been so careless as to mine our ongoing intimacy for my creativity. There's a reason my other muses were short-lived affairs. How can you draw a line in the sand between business and pleasure, though, when you care about your work as much as I do? Reveal is who I am. Desire is threaded through Reveal like my own DNA.

I can stomach the loss of Sly—but Reveal is not for the taking.

That night eight days ago after Elizabeth called, I went to bed determined to defend Reveal's honor, and thereby mine, to the bitter end. When I woke the next morning, the battlefield had shifted. On my phone was a deluge of headlines. *Reveal Founder Maxine Thomas Releases Racist Eyeliner Inspired by Former Assistant She Sexually Harassed. Reveal's Sly Takes "Bedroom Eyes" Way Too Literally. The Big Reveal Behind Sly—It Was Inspired by Sexual Predation. Racism AND Sexual Misconduct: Maxine Thomas Kills Two Birds with One Big Reveal.* And on and on. There were two voicemails from my assistant, another three from Ellen, Alan, and Elizabeth. My rousing battle cry was silenced before it could escape my throat.

EPILOGUE

The moment of truth has arrived. The Board meeting is scheduled for 9 a.m. at Reveal's offices. I shower and change into my favorite black pantsuit, all sinewy lines and sculpted shoulders. No more cashmere sweatpants for me. Dress for the day that you want. Sandrine will call me when the decision is in. We'll proceed from there. If they fire me, we'll be ready to push back and invalidate their so-called cause for termination. What I didn't tell Sandrine was I have no plans to be at home when her crucial call comes. I have built this company from scratch; whatever the outcome, I must be by its side in this decisive moment, like an army general. I am going to be at Reveal or as close as I can get.

The lone window in my office faces Broadway. There's a coffee shop directly across the avenue. I've never entered this establishment. Someone always fetches my coffee for me, and I don't partake of diner food. On occasion, I've observed this coffee shop from my elevated perch and marveled at its longevity. Neon signage claims it's been around since 1922. Imagine that: a ninety-three-year-old business that has survived multiple wars, countless social movements, gentrification. Reveal is seventeen, on the cusp of human adulthood, a teenager by comparison. My plan is to sit in a booth of this sturdy diner and channel its endurance in the direction of my corner office.

When I exit my building, it is my first time outside in four days. I squint in the sun. The air on my skin is like a daub of face cream from a freshly opened jar. New York isn't exactly known for its cleanliness, yet I could kneel on the sidewalk and lick the ground. This must be how released prisoners feel.

In the Uber downtown, we take the West Side Highway. To my right, the Hudson River is placid on this calm fall day. The New Jersey skyline stands stalwart over the unruffled water, its tall, silvery buildings as anonymous to me as a foreign land. I can't see the New Jersey of my past. It is too far removed, in miles and years. I am old enough that I have spent more of my time in New York City than I have in my home state. I have the life I had always dreamed of, and I couldn't manage half a century before I screwed things up.

The coffee shop is partially full when I enter thirty minutes before the start of the Board meeting. The place reeks of browned butter and bacon fat and fried eggs. A server gestures to one of the swivel stools that flank the bar, but I head straight to a booth that faces my office. She glares at me. Her eye shadow is turquoise, and her blush is a streaky coral. Her hair is the color of a lobster. A cartoon villainess comes to mind. I remember Ellen's criticism that all I do is judge other women and resist the urge to dole out some complimentary makeup advice. Not every woman is a Reveal customer; maybe not every woman wants to be.

I order the biggest fruit plate the diner has, large enough that I can pick at it convincingly for the duration of the meeting, however long it goes. Ms. Cartoon Villainess pours me a cup of coffee. It smells like poison. I drink it anyway.

My phone rests face up on that crappy yellow table. Every few minutes, between reluctant bites of unripe cantaloupe, I tap its screen to make sure it is working. The window of my office is opaque. The blue sky and wispy clouds flicker on its surface. No matter how hard I stare, I can't see in. I sit up straighter in my booth. Strength, I remind myself, project strength.

At 9:28 a.m., Sandrine's name flashes across my screen. I press accept with a shaky hand and hold the phone to my ear.

"That was quick," I say.

"Yes," says Sandrine. Her voice is even. Too even.

"They fired me."

"Yes," she says again.

Everything is as expected. Amanda is the victim, the innocent whom I have corrupted. I am the morally bankrupt transgressor. Reveal, a company devoted to transparency, cannot tolerate leadership whose behavior is at odds with this philosophy. I am out.

"This isn't the end. We can fight this," Sandrine continues. "That's why you hired me. We'll attack their claims of cause. This isn't over if you don't want it to be."

That poisonous coffee burns a hole in my chest.

"I want to fight this."

"I should warn you, it's going to take months," says Sandrine, ever practical. "This isn't going to happen overnight."

"I'm well aware," I say as I spear a sallow strawberry and drag it around my plate.

"Send me any bullet points you can on what might work in your defense, things that happened to you or at Reveal that could soften your image. Let's put a meeting on the calendar for the beginning of next week."

"Will do."

Ms. Cartoon Villainess brushes past me with a stack of dirty plates. "If you're not eating, you leave," she snaps, and slams a check down on my table. "Pay at the register."

"Who was that?" asks Sandrine. "You're not at home?"

"I went out to get some air and some coffee."

"Got it. Well, send me everything when you're home. Max, we always knew termination was a possibility. We're going to fight as hard as we can, I promise."

"Thanks, Sandrine."

I end the call. Sandrine is right, I always knew this outcome was possible. Possibility and reality are not the same, however. Nothing has prepared me for the sensation of losing my company, even temporarily. Reveal is no longer mine. I wait for the sharp slices of pain and the agony of defeat to overwhelm my body. There is nothing. I feel nothing.

My dismissal has been written in the sky since before the Board existed, as far back as Reveal's very birth. There is no pleasure in watching a woman succeed unless she is eventually punished. Stories of female achievement are never truly inspirational; they are, at their heart, cautionary. In that respect, my professional narrative has managed something that my personal life never will: it has adhered to convention.

The check is for twenty-five dollars. I guess that's how this diner survived into 2015; it charges a fortune for limp fruit and coffee that could double as euthanasia. I pick at my fruit plate for another forty minutes, to piss off my server, before I stand to leave. I've already been kicked out of my office. No one is kicking me out of a diner. As I turn in the direction of the cashier to pay my king's ransom, a flash of navy ribbon catches my eye. It is wrapped around a dark glossy ponytail that belongs to a young woman who sits on one of the swivel stools, her back to the diner. She wears a long-sleeved polka-dot dress. Black patent-leather ballet flats are on her feet, daintily crossed over each other like she is at afternoon tea. There is no uncertainty about it: Amanda sits at the bar.

My first instinct is to flee. Sneak out the door before you turn and see me. The register is directly next to your seat, though, and I can't have an accusation of theft on top of the other charges I already face. Besides, that emptiness from seconds ago has been replaced by an inferno of rage. Before common sense can stop me, I stride over to the register, check in hand.

"You should be the one to pay this, not me. Since you're the reason I'm here."

Your shoulders jolt at the sound of my voice and you hop off your seat in alarm. On the bar before you is an omelet with hash browns smothered in Tabasco sauce. I guess you're no longer dieting for me.

"What are you doing here?" you snarl. "Are you following me?"

"Get over yourself," I say. "I didn't think anyone I knew would come to a place like this. What are you doing here?"

"It's my comfort spot," you say. "Not that I owe you any answers. I shouldn't even be talking to you without a lawyer." You turn to the server behind the bar. "Could I have my check please?"

"I'm sure you heard," I continue. Your perfect face stares at me and that inferno in my chest morphs into something unidentifiable, some emotion I can't place. "The Board fired me."

"Yeah, my lawyer called me. That's why I'm here. Like I said, this is my comfort spot."

The server slaps a check on the counter and you pick it up.

"Comfort? What comfort could you possibly need? You got what you wanted. I'm done. Though make no mistake, I'm going to fight it."

Your dark eyes moisten.

"You think I wanted this? I didn't want any of this. You were my boss, Max. How do you not understand that? You had power over me this whole time."

"Oh, please. You initiated things. We're here because of you. All I did was go along with what you started. Look at yourself: Can you blame me?"

The moisture is gone from your eyes. I wonder if I should be afraid. If you want to hurt me more than you already have.

"That first time in London, I felt sorry for you. You were so upset. When you reached for me, I didn't want to deny you what you desired. I thought it would be a one-off incident, but it wasn't." You are steely now in a way I have never seen before. "I was powerless and not just because you were my boss. It was also about race. For my whole life I've been stalked and harassed and demeaned because I'm 'so exotic' and 'so sexy.' It was clear that I was nothing but a sexual object to you after London. You only paid attention to me because I was sleeping with you."

That unidentifiable emotion spreads across my chest and I try to ignore it. "You millennials make everything about race. You're an adult, Amanda. If you felt uncomfortable, you should have come to me. We could have ended things."

"I don't take pleasure in being the victim here. It makes me feel weak and pathetic. That's partly why I didn't say anything until now." You pull a wallet out of your bag and fumble with some bills. "I am an adult, yes, capable of giving consent. But you had a power over me that you never acknowledged. You still won't. I was your assistant for five years, five years before you promoted me. I felt like I would never be able to leave. I thought, I have to keep sleeping with her because it's the only way she'll promote me. But she also may never promote me because I'm sleeping with her. Then you promoted me and still expected me to sleep with you. Did you notice how much I drank before we had sex? How I stopped eating? Then the stuff with Sly. The whole thing makes me sick. I never really desired you. I used to respect you as a visionary, but now I wish I had never met you."

Your eyes are cold and unmoving. The fiery mischief that I saw in them so many times, a sparkle that set my insides aflame, is gone. Maybe it was never there. You never wanted me. None of your advances were genuine. My body turns to stone.

"What was your goal, then? To punish me?"

"To stop you from doing it to someone else. Women deserve to feel safe in their workplace."

A laugh breaks through the numbness.

"Safe? When is a woman ever safe in this world? What a crazy thing to expect."

"You need to dream bigger, Max, nothing will ever change until you do." Your gaze hardens. "Maybe you should spend more time looking at yourself in the mirror and less time telling other women how they should be." You crumple a twenty and toss it on the counter. Then you shove your wallet in your bag and storm out.

I give the cashier both checks and the twenty dollars, with an extra forty to cover my meal and a large tip. Outside, I stand on the sidewalk and stare across the street at Reveal's building. Around me, the bustle of SoHo is unrelenting. Tourists practically seep out of the asphalt, clogging the pedestrian arteries. The crispness in the air signals the coming of fall. I clutch my coat more tightly around me.

I turn right and head north on Broadway. Luxury retailers, their storefronts shiny and tidy, taunt me with their two-thousand-dollar handbags and three-hundred-dollar jeans. There will be none of that in the future to which I am headed. Challenging this termination will cost a fortune.

What about the rest of me? I have barely survived these nine days without the daily grind of Reveal. In the end, writing down my story has failed to achieve its intended goal: to convince me of my innocence. I was never innocent. I don't need a boardroom full of white men—and Ellen—to tell me that.

My attraction to women was the foundation of Reveal. I desired them in a way that other beauty entrepreneurs never could. Other female founders sought to make women in their own image, while male founders tried to control them through their patriarchal gaze. I imagined something different, giving them the greatest pleasure you can extend to a woman—the freedom to be herself. How has my desire, the superpower that set me apart and gifted me my vision, failed me so completely? I believed my sexual appetite was a form of resistance against a world that saw me as unnatural. And yet all I did was reduce myself and other women to a sexual definition that same world imposed. In the process, I became the very monster this ugly society insisted I already was.

I realize that my relationship with you was imperfect at best and inarguably wrong. You were beautiful. I lusted for you and I thought you lusted for me, too, though I was terribly mistaken. You never wanted me, only my approval. How did I misread the signs so completely? I held you in thrall not through magnetism, but through dominance.

I will never forget the expression in your eyes when you stared at me in that crummy diner. You hated me in that moment, it was plain. I was accustomed to inspiring hatred in other women, jealous hatred for being beautiful and successful, disgusted hatred for being different. Never have I experienced such venom from a former lover.

Elizabeth thinks that I love you. Maybe I do, though not in the sense that she means. I love your ambition, your ferocity, your refusal to settle. I love your beauty. Perhaps most of all, I love your admiration of me. More than anyone, you have seen me at my worst. You have seen my weakness and you have protected it—until now. I love the version of myself that was reflected in your eyes.

I look at you, Amanda, and I see a different reality. A world that is soft. It is a place in which women make aesthetic choices based on personal whims not expert dictates. I see a time when clear boundaries around sexuality, race, and gender are dissolving. This world confounds me. It resents me. What does power look like in a land of pink clouds and hugs and warm sincerity? What does womanhood look like in a world that demands vulnerability instead of strength? Maybe those two things are not as unalike as they seem. Ellen's proxy power through men repulsed me. Yet I have become Ellen to you. When the pink clouds of your world eventually turn gray, will you play Ellen to a future someone?

SoHo is hard beneath my heels as I stride up Broadway, my hunger for your forgiveness burning a hole in my lungs.

And Reveal. Jesus, Reveal. My baby has been ripped from my arms. I birthed Reveal into being. I suckled it into childhood. I sent it to private school and paid for its college tuition. After all that, I have been deemed an unfit mother. Put out to pasture with all the other middle-aged matrons. What a joke it is to be a woman.

I reach the intersection of Broadway and Prince. On a whim, I swerve right onto Prince. Broadway feels too wide; I yearn for a narrower street to squeeze me into submission. Prince is less crowded than Broadway. Quaint cafés, a hip Italian eatery, a teeming magazine newsstand—they still exist, who knew—lull me into a sense of control. This is what I need: small spaces, kitsch, the rustle of nearly extinct media. The cold air nibbles at my cheeks as I walk east, in the opposite direction from home.

Later, I will call Sandrine and tell her that I am done. I don't want to fight this. She should negotiate the best settlement she can.

At the corner of Mulberry, a colorful blur catches my eye. I turn left and walk a few steps north until the blur comes into focus. It is a mural that runs across a brick wall of what appears to be a pizza joint that has gone out of business. The bricks, visible only in the faint indentations of their grout, have been coated in a dull, slate gray. Atop this dour background, someone has spray-painted a profusion of multicolored hearts. Their shapes are inconsistent. Some of the hearts are perfectly symmetrical, like the red drugstore doilies that proliferate ahead of Valentine's Day. Others are shorter and wider, akin to misshapen loaves of bread. A few are so elongated and slender, they look more like teardrops than arterial cavities. The colors are exuberant, fuchsia and aquamarine and canary yellow and pumpkin and spearmint and cherry red. I didn't know hearts could come in such an array. Their shapes are layered atop each other in overlapping waves, like a mob of butterflies or a cascade of dead leaves blowing in the breeze.

Unlike that Alexander's mural of my early childhood, this artwork is unapologetic in its obviousness. In case the message somehow eludes you, the artist has inscribed #LOVEONLY on their masterpiece.

As I stand here and stare at this creative schmaltz, my face dampens with tears. They stream down my cheeks, silently, determined in their mission. My brain winds back from you to Ellen to Caroline and farther back to my mother. These tears suggest that I am not quite an impenetrable fortress. There is life in me yet. Maxine Thomas has a heart.

Don't you understand, Amanda, I didn't write my story for myself. I wrote it for you. So you can forgive me. Please, please forgive me. As soon as I am home, I will write down these final thoughts. I will confess my sins. I will attach my story to an email and send it your way. It is to you I owe my most unfiltered truth.

I continue to stare at the mural. The skin of my face is soaked. My body trembles in release. There are so many hearts on this wall. They are set to fly off the bricks, land on my skin, and devour me down to the bone. All that sincere, open-faced love threatens to destroy me. Let it. *What are you waiting for?* I ask those hearts. *Take me. I am here. At last, I am ready. I am ready to reveal all.*

Acknowledgments

I am so grateful to and thankful for the many people who have supported *Sheer* and me over the course of this book's life.

To Pilar Garcia-Brown, who truly saw and embraced this book from the first read and who has made it better ever since with such deep intelligence and empathy. Working with you is a gift and *Sheer* and I are both stronger for your collaboration and care.

To Julia Phillips for your incredible generosity and longtime advocacy of and belief in this story—and in me. How lucky I am to learn from and know you.

To Julia Kardon for your passion and wisdom. And thank you to everyone else at HG.

To the wonderful team at Dutton who worked on *Sheer*, including Lauren Morrow, Nicole Jarvis, Leah Marsh, Laura Corless, Chandra Wohleber, Alicia Lea, and Ariana Tyler. Special thanks to Ella Kurki for your notes, Emi Ikkanda for your early backing of *Sheer*, and Dominique Jones for *Sheer*'s stunning cover.

To Nelly Reifler, Sarah Conde, Lauren R., and Aimee Cho for your thoughtful and sharp readings of *Sheer* as a work in progress.

To Tia Ikemoto and CAA for initial steerage.

To Stephanie Tran, Adam Milch, and Kemper Donovan for your advice, and to Frances F. Denny for your gracious expertise.

To the readers for spending your valuable time in these pages.

To Cricky for your sweetness.

To Jennifer Barton for a long and beautiful friendship.

To my parents and the rest of my family for your faith and support.

To Dana for your constant kindness, humor, and encouragement. I love you.

About the Author

Vanessa Lawrence is a writer, editor, and native New Yorker. Her debut novel, *Ellipses*, was named a best book of 2024 by *Vogue* and a most anticipated book of the year by *ELLE*, *Electric Literature*, and *Autostraddle*. For nearly two decades she covered the arts, fashion, beauty, design, and New York society as a staff writer for publications including *Women's Wear Daily* and *W Magazine*. She has a BA in history from Yale University and an MFA in creative writing from Sarah Lawrence College.